THE DARK EARTH

Volume 1 - Nightfall

by Mike Maykin

Published by Mike Maykin

The Dark Earth

Volume 1

Nightfall

Published by Mike Maykin, Brisbane, Australia
mikemaykin@outlook.com

Other books by Mike Maykin

The Dark Earth series –

Book 2 'The Rise of Sol'
Book 3 'Emissaries'
Book 4 'Almost Human' (coming soon)

Ophelia Series –
Book 1 'Lavender Cottage'
Book 2 'The Land of Frankincense'

'Deep Sahara'

TABLE OF CONTENTS

CHAPTER 1

Time to stretch and exorcise the demon caveman hunch; so unbecoming. He'd been too long on the computer tonight, today, all week, probably for years. One day he'd get a neural link, then lay down on a big soft bed and drift through a lucid world. The day when it became a real thing, rather than a tech-bro's dream. Technically almost anything was possible, however, reality has different plans and a talent for getting in the way, spoiling what would otherwise be digital Nirvana.

He was wearing blue-light glasses, yet his eyes were still dry and weary. He took off the glasses and tossed them onto the desk. Stretching forward, he ran his fingers through a mass of long black hair. Ollie then peeled himself from the gaming chair as he stood up. It glistened with sweat and reflected the room's pulsing neonic blue green glow.

He'd been playing an online first-person shooter game. He had been at it for hours, along with other night owls and mid-day gamers around the world. It wasn't a game that he usually played, but he thought he'd try something different tonight. Anyway, it was too hot to sleep, and he'd had had a coffee after lunch, which was never a good idea with the mechanics and machinations of his brain.

Often in the evenings he would go for a run, but not tonight, it was too hot, and too sticky. This summer was warmer and wetter than last year, and every year before that. Climate changed, but people didn't. He never got why people denied it; being what's plainly staring you in the face, plan, solve the problem, and then move on to something else. Problems aren't intractable, people are. Oh to be king for a day he thought.

The cell phone came to life and buzzed; he slowly shifted his gaze from the city beyond the window to the rude piece of technology. The city, with its millions of lights, the streets, and buildings slick, crisp, and clean from recent rain, and the lightening receding to the horizon. It was a far more enticing prospect.

The power had been intermittent, and when it was working, the ceiling fan churned the thick air, as if it were turning it into butter. His computer ran on an uninterrupted power supply, but not the rest of the apartment. The screenless old casement windows were open wide. Yet the night was so still that it only offered-up oxygen by osmosis, still it allowed the distant sounds of traffic and life to waft on through.

In that lucid dream, the one where he'd be plugged into the World Network, he would jump through the window and fly free, not to die, but to soar and to live; lately everything was so predictable and boring. Maybe it was the heat, or maybe it was just the sum of his life.

It was after midnight. Who calls at this hour? Normally he would let it go to voice mail, but an unlisted number at this late hour had him intrigued.

"Hello?" he said.

He could hear a busy room, and there was scuffing and scratching noises.

A muffled voice called out to someone, "I've got him." Then clearer, "Ah, hm, hello, hello, is that Mr Oliver Truss?"

The caller sounded young, breathless, and slightly panicked.

"Yes, this is he," Was his cautious, stoic reply.

"Can I please confirm, this is Mr Oliver Truss from the consultancy firm Strategic Solutions?" the voice enquired.

"Yes, it is. How can I help you?"

A business call at this hour was unexpected, but not all together unknown. He would play along and see where it led.

"Can you please stay on the line for General Bruce Paterson on behalf of the Office of Prime

Minister."

"Sure, I'll hold," he said in a matter-of-fact tone.

Was this a prank? It was rather elaborate and well-acted if it was. Then after a bit more scuffing and banging, the phone changed hands, and a man of senior years began to speak. He was articulate and authoritative.

"Mr Truss, this is General Paterson, I need you to listen very carefully, and then to follow my instructions. We are dispatching a helicopter to collect you; I am presuming that you are at your home address?"

"Yes I am. Actually I was about to go to sleep."

"We are sorry about the inconvenience, but there is a very urgent matter we need you to work on. The helicopter will arrive in about 30 minutes. It will land in the park at the Southern end of your street. We expect you to be there when it arrives. Please be alone and bring any personal items you may need for an extended absence. Do not worry about packing clothes, we will provide you with all you need."

After a brief silence General Paterson asked, "Mr Truss, are you there? Please acknowledge you understand, and that you intend to comply."

"General Paterson, how do I know this is not a prank, or a scam, or something? Surely you must realise you've got to give me something more to go on. How do I know you are who you say you are? And if you are from the military, then how do I know I'm not in some kind of trouble, or if there really is an emergency. I mean come on man; I'm completely in the dark here. You've gotta give me something more to go on than just meet me alone, in the park, after midnight."

Ollie's gut instinct was telling him it was genuine, yet he was still going through due diligence and self-preservation, no doubt just from force of habit.

General Paterson mellowed, slightly, and responded,

"Fair enough Mr Truss, or Ollie if I may. We need your unique strategic planning skills, and we need them immediately. We are aware that the military, and various government departments, have contracted you for strategizing assignments in the past, so your name came up for this job. Thus, this is how we identified and then located you."

The General continued, "Are you able to look up into the sky from where you are right now?"

Ollie walked over to the window and said, "Yeah, I'm looking out over Brisbane."

"Did you see the moon rise this evening; it was a full moon. Presently it would be at its zenith, directly above you. So, tell me Ollie, can you see it?"

Ollie had seen the moon rise a few hours earlier. It was always picture-perfect when full, and rising over the city at dusk, especially when it backlit thunderstorms. In fact, he had even taken a picture of the scene on his phone.

But what the hell! There was no moon in the sky. He poked his head further out the window and then went to another window facing the opposite direction, and then another, but there was no moon, not even the glow of the moon.

Apart from distant storm clouds to the North, flashing occasionally with lightening, the sky was clear, in fact remarkably dark and clear. There were countless stars in the sky but there was no moon. That celestial keeper of time, inspiration for myths and rituals for all of human history, the taken for granted lesser of gods was nowhere to be seen.

"This is very confusing General; I don't see the moon anywhere. I know it should be there because I saw it rise just a few hours ago. I even took a photo!"

"Actually Ollie, as far as we ascertain, the moon is still there." The General said. "The problem is that it is not reflecting any sunlight, and it's not reflecting any sunlight because there is no sunlight shining on it. To put it as simply as possible, the sun has disappeared. As we speak, scientists are trying to figure out what is going on, but whilst that is happening, we need a response, and that is where you come in. This isn't something we have planned and trained for. Pardon the pun, but we are completely in the dark."

Ollie immediately went into strategic-deep-thought and running scenarios and options in his fantastically unique mind. It was the type of work he had done for the past decade, and what he would need to do for the foreseeable future, at least until this 'Emergency' was over.

"General Paterson, what has been the international response?" Ollie asked, but this time in a very serious no-nonsense tone.

"Well that is part of the problem," the general began to explain. "We have lost communication with large parts of the globe. It's as if they simply disappeared along with the Sun. I'm not a religious man, but it's as if we have just experienced The Rapture. All communications beyond our local region are dead, including large parts of Australia."

Ollie then asked, "How far away is the chopper?"

The General's voice went muffled as he conversed with someone and then he said, "It's about 15 minutes away."

"I'll see you shortly," Ollie replied.

He ended the call before the General could

respond. He had a pretty good idea what the problem was, and what the consequences would be. There was not a minute to lose, which thus required the suspension of pleasantries, even if he was talking with a General, and he representing the Prime Minister. They were now entering Ollie's world, and they had to follow his rules if they wanted to survive. The world of make believe, scenarios, the 'what ifs', just became the 'what now!'

Ollie was a very organised person, perhaps verging on obsessive compulsive. He knew where everything was at any time. This allowed him to drop the phone, shower, and dress, in 5 minutes flat. Then, in a deliberate and methodical manner, he went through the apartment and packed his rucksack.

He was very strategic in his packing because he did not expect to be returning. He ignored things like toothbrush, cologne, or underwear. Those were the types of things the military would supply, even if the fragrance, flavour, or fit, wasn't the best. But he made sure to pack his jacket, laptop, a cache of memory cards, as well as some trinkets and mementoes from the life he was leaving behind.

Within 10 minutes he was running out the front door, leaving his apartment and knowing it was for the last time. He didn't even bother to close the windows or door. He glanced at the garden as he rushed past and knew that all of his efforts were now for naught. It would be dead within the week.

With the rucksack swinging on his back, he jogged down the quiet empty street. Not even the dogs were barking, perhaps they knew something the humans didn't. He could hear a helicopter in the distance, and figured he would probably get to the park just before it landed.

As it approached the helicopter turned on its spotlight. Ollie stood at the edge of the wide grassed area and watched the spot of light sweep the area. A man driving past slowed and looked up at the spectacle and then sped away. Perhaps they thought it was a police helicopter cornering a fugitive; maybe they were a fugitive.

When it landed, an armed soldier jumped down and ran over to Ollie. He shouted over the noise of the helicopter,

"Mr Oliver Truss?" the soldier enquired.

Ollie nodded his head and shouted, "Yes."

The solider took Ollie's bag and they both rushed over to the helicopter. He was hunched over and running gangly across the open field of perfect lawn. He thought to himself, 'why do people always do that when approaching helicopters. The rotors are probably 2 metres higher than their heads'. But he did it anyway.

The sliding door was open and the solider

pushed him somewhat sternly from behind. This almost made him fall into the cabin, and he only just avoided making a spectacle of his entrance. How embarrassing that would have been. The planet's most important human of the moment, turning up to save the world with a bloody nose and a fat lip. But then again stranger things have happened during emergencies.

The beat of the helicopter grew to an offensive level as the ground began to fall away. From this vantage the neighbourhood was dim and still, with patches of light beneath the streetlamps. But it was likely that most people were now awake due to the aerial commotion. Awake but unaware of the existential threat that they were about to face.

CHAPTER 2

Some people were dancing to a slow country song, others were just joking around, telling tall tales, and having fun. It was mid-week, but still it was busy. Probably because of the heat.

"Hey darl'n, is this seat taken?" enquired a gruff voice.

Without looking up from her plate, and still chewing the last mouthful, Jan replied, "Yeah nah, you're right mate, you can take it."

She continued to cut her steak, stuff her mouth, and scroll through messages on the phone beside her.

She had gotten off to a late start from Mount Isa, and then 7 hours in 47°C heat before making Longreach just after sunset. The heat was so intense that in places the bitumen on the road was going soft. She was lucky it didn't peel and wrap around the tires. That would have cost her hours of driving time and prying it off was dirty stinking work in the mid-day sun.

Driving that evening, in this big sky country, with the high wispy clouds, the dust in the air, and the shimmer that still radiated from the road, made for the most beautiful moonrise she had ever seen. It was a scene that inspired poets and painters. So, it was a shame to be looking at it alone. She wanted to share it with someone, anyone, but all she could do was mumble "God Damn!" as she drove kilometre after kilometre, until finally a few lights and the silhouette of Longreach appeared on the horizon.

She was hungry, thirsty and not really in the mood for conversation. However, given how busy the pub was, it would hardly be fair to take up two seats for dinner, so she cut him some slack. Anyway, she wasn't going to be hanging around long. Just enough time to finish the mixed grill, a pint of light beer, and then off to the truck's sleeper. She'd get a solid rest, and then back on the road before sunrise.

A trucker's life is more regimented and disciplined than most would imagine. It takes a certain type of person to do the long hauls, especially across the vast and lonely plains.

He sat down with his can of rum and said, "They call me Davo. I'm one of the locals. I don't think I've seen you in here before."

She looked across at him. Of course he was called Davo. Probably half of the guys in here were called Davo, or something similar. He was a big bristly man, sporting a tattered stockman's hat. It was complemented by a dusty blue singlet smudged by seeping sweat, footy shorts, and the obligatory tan, steel-capped work boots. He smiled a wicked grin that was short of a few teeth.

"Hi, I'm Jan." She forced a smile and then continued, "You'll have to excuse me, I've got to catch up on some messages, and then I'm turning in for an early night".

Without missing a beat, Davo responded, "Aw yeah, where ya head'n? The heat's a bit much, hey, you may wanna slow ya roll like the rest of us. Me and ma crew are getting on the piss. Figure we'll start the weekend a day early. There's supposed to be a change in the weather by Monday. Things should cool down a bit, so we'll catch up with work then, hey."

Jan wrinkled her nose slightly, pushed the finished meal away from her, and said, "Yeah, sounds like a plan Davo, but not for me. I've got to be in Sydney by Sunday arvo, so I've still got a couple of big days ahead of me."

They really were going to be long hard days, especially if she ran into any problems with the truck or the road. There had been talk of a wash-out further down the road, but a fellow trucker who had come up from the South had said she should be right to get through.

It was crazy how a summer storm could dump enough rain to wash out the road, and then another kilometre down the track, it would be as dry as a bone. Such was mid-summer in North West Queensland.

He kept grinning at her, a dumb and dishonest grin, as she gulped down the last of her beer. She banged the glass down on the table and said, "Well, that's me done, I'm outta here."

She stood up and then continued by saying, "Nice to meet you Davo, have a drink or two for me".

As she walked away, he tried to grab her arm, but she was too quick and glided by as if not noticing. She heard him say, "Yeah right" and maybe he added "bitch" under his breath. She wasn't sure, but didn't really care and so just let it slide. There was one in every pub, probably dozens in this pub, and she always attracted them like stray dogs. Just like at any watering hole, natural or man-made, there is a mix of species. Some are predators and some are prey.

After using the lady's room, and getting some bottled water, she weaved her way through the crowd and headed for the door. Since finishing her meal, it had been about 10 minutes before she stepped outside. The air was hot and dry, with a taste of dust. Bugs and people swarmed around the string of lights nailed to the bargeboard below the gutter and then draped over a nearby dead tree. Music and voices spilled from the porch, to be sucked up into the vacuum of the endless still night.

The dry gravel crunched under her boots as she headed around back. There was a dozen or more trucks and road trains parked in the paddock. Noisy refrigeration units kept the trucks' shipping containers cold. As she approached, their rattles and drones drowned out the sounds from the pub.

A figure was leaning against one of the trailers and, judging by the silhouette, she figured it was Davo. As she got closer a second man appeared from the shadows. He was taller, lean, and looked menacing.

"Typical idiots," she mumbled to herself.

Davo said in a salesman's voice, "Jan, Jan, Jan, the night is still young, howz about we have a drink and finish our little chat? You know, *Jan*," he said with a heavy emphasis on her name, "it was a bit rude of you to just up and leave like ya did."

She kept walking toward them as casually as a Sunday stroll, and with the confidence of an assassin.

"You boys might wanna be careful about what people will think, hanging out in the dark like you are, waiting for little girls and ladies to walk on by. Some people might get to thinking you're up to no good."

It was an unfortunate fact of life, and a hazard of her profession, that she had to deal with situations like this, and more regularly than one may imagine.

She kept walking toward them with the intention of just walking right on past, but then they made the fateful mistake of stepping out and blocking her path. Now, in the moonlight, she could see two stupid grins. The tall one had a hand behind his back, which she presumed was to conceal a knife.

Still, she didn't stop walking, as most people would do, but instead she sped up taking them by surprise. She lunged and felled the tall one first, dislocating his shoulder, and breaking his nose into the ground with a heavy fall. A large hunting knife skid across the dust and lay glinting in the moonlight.

Then, before Davo could react, he had been kicked in the chest, and then the throat, causing him to fall heavily backward against the truck. As he gasped for air another kick busted his knee sending him to the ground. They lay whimpering in the dust on this otherwise beautiful summer evening.

Jan had been out of the army for a couple of years, but had been doing some tough jobs since, so was still in peak physical form. From a young age her father encouraged her to do a range of martial arts. When you are a 'pretty-little-blonde-thing', as guys often called her, then these skills came in very handy.

She had worked in transport and logistics with the army, driving big trucks through the dust, mud, and snow. While in her last unit, she had represented it in Mauy Thai kick boxing championships. She was pretty good, and people had often suggested she become an MMA fighter. But that kind of life wasn't really for her, especially the injuries that came with the sport, so she continued trucking, and dreaming.

Davo and Slim, whether drunk or sober, never had a chance. Yet they could also count themselves lucky. If the world were different, a lawless post-apocalyptic Mad Max type world, then she would have run them over with the truck where they lay. She wasn't a hard-line conservative, some may have even called her a small 'l' liberal, but in her imagination at least, scum like that didn't deserve to breathe.

She climbed up into the Western Star B-double and drove for several kilometres down the road before pulling into a rest-stop for the night.

She didn't want to hang around for explanations and recriminations at the pub. She was sure the boys would claim she attacked them unprovoked. It wasn't worth dealing with that kind of static.

However, if she simply drove off, then there would be no way Davo and company, would tell their mates that a pretty little woman had just beaten them up in the carpark. Instead, they would spin a story about how they heroically fought off a gang of big bad gypsy bikers, or something like that.

The road-side truck stop was deserted, as

were the barren plains surrounding it. There was no streetlamp, there were no headlights on the road, and there were no buildings on the horizon. No one drove cars at night if they could help it. It was just too risky with kangaroos appearing from nowhere, or cattle the colour of bitumen standing perfectly still in the middle of the road. Anyway, she had to keep her logbook clean. Sleep was mandatory, so why drive through the night if you shouldn't and you couldn't.

She kicked off her boots, tied back her hair, and laid down in the sleeper with a small fan blowing over her. There was soft, chill music playing on the cab speakers. She gazed through the window at the moon and stars. It was familiar, peaceful, and beautiful, yet, it was a lonely way to make a living.

During the night, while she lay in deep sleep, the sky was filled with the most brilliant aurora Earth had experienced since creation. It was so bright that it was as if daylight were in eerie shades of green, blue, and purple. The mesmerizing celestial shimmer continued through till the early hours, concluding just before she awoke.

Billions upon billions of tonnes, and volts, of charged particles had streamed overhead, the flood of energy, twisting, distorting, and eroding the Earth's ozone layer and magnetosphere. She slept blissfully on the very delineation between life and death.

If she had stayed in Mount Isa, she would have been killed, and even in Longreach she may have received lethal radiation burns, just like all those people that had been at the pub. She would never know how close she came to death that night. Instead, she was fated to live, and to love, and destined to do great things.

CHAPTER 3

In the helicopter was a visored pilot, two hypervigilant soldiers, and one other person apart from Ollie. This other person was a crisp and dapper officer who wore medals with pride. As soon as Ollie secured his seat belt, he was handed a headset so he could communicate.

"Mr Truss, thank you for coming at such short notice, it is an honour to meet you." Ollie gave a brief humble smile and then waved it off.

"My name is Major Roy Sandalwood, but you can just call me Roy, I'm with Air Force Intelligence. We are on our way to Amberly Air Base, where we will transfer to a fast jet bound for Mascot in Sydney. We should arrive in Sydney at around 0300."

"Hello Roy, pleased to meet you," said Ollie.

They shook hands and then Ollie said, "Roy, I need you to tell me everything you know about what is going on, and everything you suspect, even if you are not sure, or don't have the evidence to back it up. Just give me a core dump of your wildest theories."

Roy nodded his head and said, "General

Paterson ordered me to follow your instructions without question, so I am at your disposal, and will do my best."

"Excellent and thank you."

Ollie then asked his first question. "What contact do we have with the rest of the world?"

Roy looked down at a tablet for a short while, consult a crumpled map, and then did some calculations in his head. Finally, he said, "For the past several hours there has been no contact from any locations beginning latitude 150° West, so anything East of Anchorage Alaska, through to around 140° East. So that is anything West of, and including, Tokyo. In Australia that is pretty much anything West of the New South Wales – South Australian border.

We have effectively lost contact with about $2/3^{rds}$ of the Earth, and with that, the bulk of its population, but, and here is the crazy thing, for the most part, the Pacific third seems unaffected, although communications are very patchy."

"Do you have any theories?" asked Ollie.

"My first thought was a solar flare, you know a CME, or perhaps some type of gamma ray burst from deep space that we didn't see coming. It would have had to be something unprecedented, and energetic enough, to knock out power and communications. Unconfirmed stories and rumors from people on the boundary with the effected side of the planet, tell stories of electronics being fried, and plants and animals, including humans, being irradiated as if they were in a microwave oven. It was described as an invisible killer. They didn't know what was happening until it was happening, and then it was too late. Those outside and exposed just dropped dead, and then those that ran outside to help them also died."

"And what about the possibility of nuclear war. Were any missile launches detected?"

"No, there was no evidence to suggest any military activity. And there is no radiation fallout in the winds coming from the 'dark side', as to put it."

"I see," said Ollie. "So, what about the sun, why isn't there any sunlight reflecting off the moon?"

Roy shrugged, "I have no idea. I suppose we'll find out when it rises, or if it rises, the sun that is."

Ollie thanked him and then retreated into silence as he looked out the window. They were now only minutes from Amberly. He could see the blinking lights of a private jet at the end of a runway ready for take-off.

The transfer was efficient, seamless, and in other circumstances would have been clandestine. They just stepped out of the helicopter and walked straight up the steps of the jet. By the time he had buckled his seatbelt the plane was already taxiing down the runway

A military steward was on the plane, the two guards from the helicopter, and Roy. After a rapid ascent he was given a meal, a drink, and a phone. Roy told him that the General was calling.

"Hello General Paterson."

"Hello Ollie. I have you on speaker. You are also networked to senior members of the armed forces and government."

A second voice spoke up.

"Hello Mr Truss, this is Deputy Prime Minister Vanessa Stirling. I have been required to step-up because we can't contact the Prime Minister. His last known location was London, England."

"Hello, acting Prime Minister, and others. I will give you a frank assessment of our situation. You are not going to like it, but we have no leeway for debate or denial. It is what it is, and I might even suggest that if you want to survive, then democracy is over. You will have to do what I tell you. But I'm getting ahead of myself.

For whatever reason, which I'm sure we will discover in time, we are facing an extinction level event. Most of the population, on what I will call the exposed side of the globe, is either dead or will be dead within a few days. We have no effective capacity to help them, meaning being able to help any survivors on the effected side of the planet.

Indeed, we will be hard pressed to even help ourselves and our local population, as in the Eastern Capital cities. We do not have time for rescue missions, only self-preservation. I do not mean individual self-preservation, but collective preservation. We must preserve as much of the population that is concentrated in the cities. We will not have time for anything else."

He continued his briefing, "It is likely that something massive interacted with the sun, resulting in a surge of energy that scorched the planet's surface. It is also possible, that during this Oumuamua type event, the Earth was thrown out of solar orbit. Perhaps it was a wandering black hole. I cannot say. The universe holds many mysteries, and extinction probably is the norm rather than the exception.

Regardless, we now find ourselves on a rapidly freezing planet, with only the resources immediately at our disposal to create life preserving, and self-sustaining, habitats. Within a day or two, everywhere will be experiencing Polar Winter conditions. In a few weeks to months the oxygen and nitrogen will freeze out of the atmosphere. The surface of the Earth will become as hostile to life as that of the moon or Mars, and colder than Pluto. There is no escaping this reality, so face up to it now so we can move on to strategies for preserving life."

The audience remained silent as Ollie

continued.

"Our immediate task, is to preserve a seed of humanity, including knowledge and civilization, that can endure and with the aid of a few miracles, flourish once again. We have just enough time, technology and resources, to do this, but we only get one shot, and it starts now. Wealth, rank or political power are not criteria for survival or for privilege in this new age. We must be ruthless and single minded with our objective. If we are not, then it is likely that no one will survive."

Acting Prime Minister Stirling replied with a muted, "I see…", then tapered off. Everyone else remained silent. It was not sure what was more shocking to the audience, the loss of the world, or the loss of political power, and perhaps the shift to authoritarianism.

Ollie proceeded to dictate instructions, and explain strategies, all to be put into immediate effect, even as the jet roared toward Sydney. The specifics on how to achieve them were left to others, however. He often emphasized this "must" or, "must" not, happen at any cost! Therefore, by whatever means necessary.

The master plan was to utilize the existing network of road and railway tunnels, as well as underground parking and basement structures beneath the cities, as an Ark or Luna base, if you will, for everything required for immediate, through to intergenerational, survival.

These tunnels had to be interconnected and sealed as if they were in space, and they only had days, through to weeks, to achieve this.

He also laid down plans for establishing similar, habitats in Melbourne and Brisbane. No other locations offered the extent of underground hides, the workforce and the resources necessary to achieve this in the short time that they had.

These habitats were not only for housing humans, and that being the widest genetic and diversity of humans, but they also had to accommodate the widest genetic diversity of plants and animals.

Furthermore, it was not just for housing people, plants, and animals, but also room for activities, such as agriculture, or ecological services, including waste processing and filtration. They would also need room for energy production and industries, light, heavy, clean, and dirty, and with a special focus on advanced technologies.

Both the natural world, and the human world, with all of their disconformity and conflicts, had to be shrunk down to a handful of tunnels and basements, and all within a few days to weeks.

It seemed an impossible task, but failure meant extinction, so there really was no alternative. Everyone in power now knew what they faced and listened to the only person who had the solution already mapped out.

A simple low-tech life, as if going back into a mystical and humble Golden Age, like Eden, Arcadia, or Elysium, as romantic as that may have sounded, would, in reality, be a deadly fantasy. Instead, they would need to research and discover their way out of the confinement, this apparent dead end.

In short, humanity's hope and future was dependent on breakthroughs into yet unimagined technologies required to stop the flame from being extinguished.

The historically unrecognized, and unappreciated, value of things must now be overturned. People, perhaps many people, would have to sacrifice their place in the Ark to save things like exotic plants and animals that most had never heard of.

Those annoying and gross forms of life, traditionally of little economic value, be they bacteria, insects, snakes, bats, fungus, invasive weeds, or pond slime, had to survive. All were crucial for maintaining the ecosystems upon which humanity depended. For they not only performed vital functions within the web of life but were also reservoirs of genetic diversity that would spawn evolution, something that was now so desperately needed.

It was going to get ugly as the survivors

clung to life. For the immediate and foreseeable future, humanity would be returning to the caves, like in pre-history, but this time with the benefit of 21st century tools and technology.

For the remainder of the trip Ollie sat in quiet contemplation. On a couple of occasions Roy tried to initiate conversation, but Ollie had too much on his mind. He was, however, impressed by Roy's unwavering optimism, even in the face of the direst of circumstances. It was a quality that Ollie wished that he had himself.

His mind worked in a different way from others. He constantly saw the risks and pitfalls, all the ways in which failure could occur, and then he worked back from that. Hence, in this current emergency, he assumed that humanity was on the brink of extinction and had the shortest of timelines to save itself. Therefore, every step taken represented a desperate last hope. He reasoned that this would be the only way to have a chance at survival. 'She'll be right, mate,' just wasn't going to cut it.

The jet roared through quiet skies. there were no international arrivals or departures. He saw the lights stretching out across the landscape and knew they would soon be extinguished. The world would soon go dark. Hopefully, he could keep a small flame burning deep underground, smoldering like a coal-seam fire, that can burn for thousands of years. As much as anyone else, he himself didn't want to die. Some hero he turned out to be. Was he doing this just for self-preservation, the most selfish of all human traits?

CHAPTER 4

The alarm went off at 4:30am. Jan lay there trying to recall the dream as it retreated into the mist of her subconscious. She had been somewhere cool and pleasant, maybe it was a beach on a rugged windswept coastline, a slither of sand, a cove between rocky headlands. Somewhere sheltered and safe. It would have been nice to sleep longer and return to that place, but reality and wages dictated otherwise.

She climbed down from the cab and, using her phone as a torch, headed to the small concrete toilet block. It was spartan, graffitied, and had no working light, but still it did the job. At least it didn't have any poisonous snakes, or as many spiders, as the last one she used.

The air was still warm, around 25°C, but with a hint of dew that sparkled on the truck and the single scrubby tree that grew near the amenities. It was unusual to get dew at this time of year, and at this temperature. She touched the leaves and found that it wasn't dew after all. It was like dust, but a bit grittier, almost like powdered glass, or volcanic ash, and it covered everything with a light reflecting sheen. It was puzzling but seemed inconsequential.

There was no phone signal, but given the vast distances, it was not uncommon. There was a satellite phone in the truck she could use later to check for messages.

The truck rumbled to life and with flick of the switch the headlights pierced the absolute back. She was surprised that the moon had already gone. On her early morning starts she would enjoy moon set as much as moon rise.

Soon the sun would brighten the horizon, with rippled clouds of scarlet and orange. A prelude to another scorching day in the Central West. The painted sky was always something to look forward to, but not the heat that followed.

There was a hiss and trumpet as the air brakes released. The truck rolled forward, mounting the bitumen for another day of highway labor.

It was just after 5:30am when Jan approached the town of Barcaldine. She had been driving due East for the past hour expecting the rising sun to be in her eyes as it had been so many times in the past when making this early morning run. But there was no sun, no light on the horizon, no scarlet and orange clouds. Just the black of night, and a spray of a million stars. It was as if the world had stopped turning. An eternal midnight sky.

She checked her watch again. Surely it must be wrong! She checked the clock on the dash, and then on her phone, They all told the same time. She didn't feel like she had short-changed her sleep, it felt like she had gotten 8 hours, yet how could it still be the middle of the night.

The town's streetlights blazed over wide empty streets. Nothing was open, and not a person was to be seen. She turned South on the Landsborough Highway and kept on trucking, deciding to continue through to Blackall, another hour or so down the road. By the time she got there, shops and service stations would surely be open, and she could find out what was happening with the time. She shook her head and slapped her face just to be sure she wasn't still asleep and dreaming.

All her clocks now read 7:15am, but it was still midnight.

She pulled off onto the side of the road at the edge of the town of Blackall. It was the same as before. Streetlights swarmed by insects shone in the darkness. Otherwise all was quiet. Well, at least there was one bar of phone reception. Perhaps it would get better as she passed through the town center.

She had never known cell reception to be this bad. Usually, you pick up a couple of bars as you crest any rise in the landscape and then get full coverage within a few kilometres of a town, any town, regardless of its size.

She had had the satellite phone turned on beside her as it searched for a signal, but it read the same as it did a half hour ago, 'No satellites detected.'

Then something caught her attention. It was the lights of a car reflecting in the rearview mirror. It approached and then passed her, continuing down the main street, until slowing and turning into what she believed was the roadhouse. She put the truck into gear and followed, hoping to get answers.

There the car sat, parked in the service station. As Jan climbed down from the truck, she could see two people talking through the diner window. The outside air was noticeably cooler than when she first woke up. Normally after sunrise it would begin its inexorable climb through to the mid-forties, however, now without any sun, it seemed to be dropping.

She pushed the door open and stepped into the fluorescent light. Both men turned and had serious looks on their faces. Yet, despite this, they said a friendly, "Hello."

In a cheerful voice, Jan said, "Hi. You wouldn't maybe have the correct time? My clock seems to have gone crazy."

The first man said, "By my reckoning its almost 7:30am."

"Same here," said the other.

Jan stood silent for a few seconds and then said, "So, what the hell is going on? I mean, shouldn't the sun be up, and everyone out and about on the streets?"

One of the men pointed to the television mounted on the wall behind the counter. A message was scrolling that read, 'Emergency Warning. Please shelter in place until further notice.'

"It's been like that for hours, and it's the same message on the radio. We can't get any more information because the phone and the internet are both on the blink."

Jan looked down at her mobile phone. Although it still had only one bar, there was now a message on the screen. It was from the company that had contracted her for this load. It read, 'Emergency situation. Get to Sydney ASAP.' That was all it said. There was no further information. She sent a reply text, 'What is happening?', but immediately got a 'No Service' response.

She decided to top-up the truck's fuel tanks and to also stock-up on snacks and drinks. She figured she should get through to Sydney as quickly as possible, regardless of what the television, or authorities, said about sheltering in place.

She had friends and family there, and the trucking company was a good bunch of people that had always looked out for her. If they said get to Sydney ASAP, then she was sure they had a good reason for telling her this.

She waved goodbye to the men and then pulled back onto the highway. They had helped carry her stuff out to the truck and had wished her a safe journey. As the lights from the town faded behind her, she kept saying to herself, "This is just too weird." Yet a sinking feeling took hold in her stomach. As weird as it was, it was something bigger than her, bigger than everyone. It was a realization that she may not make it this time. As if in free fall, she had no control over when or where she landed.

She had travelled about 10 kilometres from the town when she noticed a faint light blinking and bobbing ahead on the side of the road. It wasn't a car. It was more like a torch or a bicycle light.

As she approached, she could make out two figures standing in the gravel. They were near a rusty tin bus-shelter. It was positioned opposite a side road and accompanied a grouping of letterboxes.

As she blasted past, she saw two children in school uniforms shielding their eyes as they looked up at her. She continued down the road for a few hundred meters before saying out loud, "Aw damn!" and then hitting the brakes.

The sides of the road were wide and firm

enough to turn the truck around and head back to the intersection. She rounded again and stopped, facing her original direction, and jumped down from the cab. The headlights were shining on the children.

"Hello girls, off to school, are we?"

The taller one, maybe 14 years old, but small for her age, replied, "We're supposed to catch the bus at 7:30am, but it hasn't come."

The smaller one, maybe 8 years old, then questioned, "Why is it still dark and why is it getting cold?"

Jan avoided the questions and instead asked, "Where are your parents?"

The older one replied, "Mom is away in hospital in Darwin, and dad won't be back from working in the Northern Territory for another week."

With a puzzled look Jan asked, "So who looks after you?"

"Well normally it's mom, but for the past week it's been just the two of us till dad gets back."

The younger one looked at her sister and then at Jan, and with wide eyes said, "I'm scared."

Jan beckoned the girls to sit with her in the bus shelter.

"I'm in a bit of a dilemma. I'm not sure what to do about you girls. You see, I don't think the school bus is coming, and I just can't leave you standing here by yourselves. There has been some kind of emergency, and it probably has something to do with the sun. I'm thinking we may not see the sun, at least for today."

The girls stayed silent and looked at her as if for the answers. She continued, "Is there someone I can take you to, maybe back in town?"

They both shook their heads and the older one replied, "We haven't lived here long, so we don't really know anyone."

With innocent, youthful pragmatism the younger girl unabashedly asked, "Can we stay with you?"

Jan looked down at the ground and thought the question over for a long time. In her head she contemplated all the variables as best she could. If everyone was effectively in lockdown, then no one was coming down this road, at least in the short term. And if it was a truly massive emergency, then no one may ever come.

It was clear that the sun was not going to rise any time soon, so it was just going to get colder and colder. Maybe it would get below freezing. She couldn't leave the girls here by themselves to freeze.

She could take the girls with her; she had the room. She could leave a note in the mailbox and at their house explaining the situation with instructions on how they could be collected once the Emergency had passed.

Anyway, she was planning to drive back through in about one week, so she could always drop them back then. She somehow suppressed how stupid that logic was. If the sun was gone and the whole of reality had changed, then why would she be driving back through here in a week's time. Instead, she rationalised that if her intentions were good, and if she genuinely believed the girls were in danger, then it wouldn't be classed as kidnapping or anything else illegal. It would just be her doing the right thing given the unique circumstances.

Finally, she said, "I'm on my way to Sydney, I think we will all be safe down there. If I took you to your home and you each packed a bag for a short holiday, then would you like to come with me? And while we are traveling we can do our best to contact your parents and let them know you are safe."

The girls looked at each other. The younger one was nodding and implored her sister, "Can we please? I don't want to stay here."

They drove down the dirt road to the girl's house. The time was 8:30am and the outside temperature had dropped to 15°C. Jan calculated that at this rate it would be below zero by this same time tomorrow.

As she wrote a detailed note, she instructed the girls to grab anything that had special memories, any medications, fill a box with nonperishable food, and to be sure to pack some warm clothes.

Of course, living in the scorching Central West, they didn't have much in the way of warm clothes, but they made up for this with a stack of folded blankets.

After bundling everything into the truck, the younger girl, whose name was Sally, climbed up into the sleeper and snuggled under a blanket. She became just a pale face and a shock of red curly hair. Mazie, the elder sister, made herself comfortable in the passenger seat.

Then Sally exclaimed, "Oh no, what about Goggles and Speedy? We can't leave them behind. There will be no one to feed them."

"Who are Goggles and Speedy?" asked Jan.

"They are my two budgies. Goggles is Blue and Speedy is Green. I have them in a cage. They won't take up much room."

"OK quickly go and get them, and Mazie, could you maybe get some extra birdseed? If you can find a full box, that would be great."

As they pulled onto the highway, Mazie asked, "How long will it take to get to Sydney?"

Jan replied, "I expect it will be 2-3 days, that is, provided everything goes smoothly."

Then Jan looked over at Mazie, smiled, and said reassuringly, "I don't expect any problems," but deep inside she held grave concerns. What kind of a world would these girls grow up in?

And what kind of a world would they find further down the road?

CHAPTER 5

Upon arrival in Sydney, Ollie was taken by armoured vehicle through cordoned streets and then deep underground into the Metro rail network.

Along the route, both at the surface, and below, tens of thousands of people using all manner of heavy machinery and equipment were working frantically, but purposefully, by artificial light.

Some were military and emergency services, others construction laborers and trade professionals, but many were just everyday people of every age, gender, and capability. The numbers would soon swell into the hundreds of thousands as the hours passed.

During his inflight briefing, Ollie had directed Paterson and Stirling to issue a statement to the country, or what was left of the country, through any and every means possible. The message was simple and blunt, and although he was unaware of the final wording, it could be summed up as follows.

'We find ourselves in a dire emergency and

martial law has been declared. Most of the world's population is presumed dead, as is any person, or living thing, West of the New South Wales - South Australian border.

The Sun no longer shines. We are not sure why, but without its warmth, the Earth will rapidly freeze. Every person, and living thing, on the surface and unprotected will perish within days to weeks.

To save ourselves we must build a network of ecosystem habitats capable of maintaining a remnant of humanity and nature. It is unknown how many people we can save, but we will attempt to save as many as possible, beginning with those who help during this time of great need.

Therefore, to have the best chance of saving yourself and your family, you must pitch in and help immediately. Any resistance, rioting, or sabotage, will be dealt with using lethal force.'

The message continued with instructions on how to register and volunteer, and also listed skills, jobs, and resources, that were a priority.

Roy escorted Ollie to a reinforced metal door. It was guarded by armed soldiers. Above the entrance a hastily prepared sign read Command & Control (C&C) Central.

He said, "This is where I leave you. Your quarters are through a door on the far side of the center, which is effectively the joint command, communications, and control room. We figured it prudent to put you at the heart of the information and communications processing center."

"Yes, that works for me. Thank you for all your help. By the way, don't disappear. I will be needing you over the next few days, and maybe longer."

A guard entered a code into a keypad, the door opened, and a uniformed woman received them. She extended her hand and said, "Mr Truss, I am Colonel Bright. Welcome. Would you like me to take you straight through to your quarters?"

"Hello Colonel. Umm sure, maybe in a few minutes, but firstly, can you explain the setup you have here, and what is it that I am seeing on all these monitors?"

Large screens were plastered over the walls, while below were rows and rows of computers operated by people both in and out of uniform. It was not so dissimilar to a mission control center for a space launch, but in here all the cables were exposed and none of the chairs or desks matched.

It was only a mere few hours old, and yet what a miraculous achievement it was. Like ants building a bivouac. It was amazing that no one tripped over or unplugged anything, or that anyone could hear anyone else, given how much talking, and occasional shouting, filled the room.

The Colonel methodically went through

the process of explaining the data and movements being monitored and coordinated. She also grumbled about how difficult it was to coordinate all of this without access to satellites.

She said, "Analog and low-speed digital is so out of date, it is as if it needed to be re-invented and the operators re-educated."

Ollie replied, "Sadly, it is soon going to get much worse. You have already discovered that the satellites are lost, but soon the ionosphere will dissipate. Therefore, we will also lose over the horizon radio communication.

Then, not long after that, we may find that surface poles, wires, and switching gear in the land-line networks and power systems will begin to fail due to freezing and becoming brittle in the extreme cold.

From now on, anything that is intended to operate on the surface will need to be constructed as if it were being sent into interstellar space, which can be a cold as -270°C. Thus, we will need to use new materials and techniques in the future to operate on the surface of Earth."

He made a mental note to himself to get a team working on maglev superconducting transport systems.

As he scanned the monitors, he noticed that one was showing shipping in and out of East Coast ports.

"Colonel, are any of these vessels moving?"

"No, almost all of them are stationary. They can't navigate without GPS. Magnetic compasses have become unreliable and, regardless, they can't contact their destination ports. So effectively they remain in limbo."

"What do these red markers indicate?"

"I believe they are naval vessels. Some are Australian, and some are foreign."

"Do you know if any of the naval vessels are nuclear powered, or nuclear armed?"

"I'm not sure on the specifics, but I believe we have several submarines in our waters and at least two of them are nuclear. Intelligence says that one is the USS Nebraska, an Ohio-Class nuclear submarine, and the other is the French De Grasse Barracuda-Class nuclear submarine. Both are in port and were preparing to depart.

There is also an aircraft carrier, the USS Ronald Reagan, which is a Nimitz-Class nuclear super-carrier. It is stationary just offshore from Brisbane. It was enroute to US Joint Region Marianas, Guam, however, I do not know what their intentions are now. I can have all of this confirmed by naval attaché within a few minutes if you wish."

Ollie said in a stern voice, "Put out the order that we need ships and submarines to return to, or remain in, port, and for them to come under C&C control. Hopefully, this will occur peacefully, and if not peacefully, then by whatever means necessary.

We need the Ronald Regan down here in Sydney Harbour, and it must be underway within the hour. Make it clear to the captain that if they head for Guam, it will take them a minimum of 4 days under ideal conditions, but without GPS, it will probably take them twice as long and they would face the risk of running aground or suffering a collision.

They will not make it to Guam before the ship's crew starts to freeze and even if they did make it, they will freeze before finding a second port of refuge, including returning to Australia.

Furthermore, there may not be anyone left alive in Guam by the time they get there. There are effectively no underground facilities on the island in which people can take refuge and most above ground structures are built for tropical conditions.

However, tell the captain that we will make every attempt to communicate with Guam and Hawaii, and if there is reason, and potential, for a rescue mission, then we will dispatch submarines for that purpose."

Ollie continued, "For the immediate future, the only safe mode for long distance travel will be by submarine, and within a few months, that will be limited to only nuclear submarines.

It may take up to 6 months for the ocean surface to freeze over completely, but this will only be a thin covering, at least for the foreseeable future. Beneath, it will remain liquid for thousands, to perhaps millions of years, due to its ability to act as a thermal reservoir, and also because of the Earth's geothermal heat."

He began to walk away, then paused, and said to the Colonel, "If you are wondering why we need the Ronald Regan, it's for the nuclear reactor. It will become our power station. Also, it has all those aircraft that contain valuable metals we can salvage, such as titanium, which will be hard to secure elsewhere.

"We will be facing a future with no solar, no wind, or hydro power. We do not have any geothermal plants along the East Coast of Australia, and we will not have enough oxygen to be wasted on burning fossil fuels.

"I am no fan of nuclear power. I think it is expensive, and just as damaging to the environment as fossil fuels. But given our current situation, it is our best short-term option."

As he walked away, he mused and mumbled, "Bioluminescence! Hmm, we could really do with a scientific breakthrough in bioluminescence. I need to get someone working on that."

It was now around 11am old time. He'd been awake for some 30hrs and was starting to get foggy. He couldn't afford to get too tired and make mistakes. So far, everything was going to plan. The next phase couldn't begin until certain milestones had been met, so he decided to retire to his quarters and sleep.

There was a pang of guilt knowing of all the people working for their lives on the surface and also throughout the labyrinth of tunnels and basements. He knew that many people would not make it because they were too far away and could not get to a shelter in time. And neither could the city afford the resources to collect people from the regions. There were not going to be any rescues. For the most part, one's fate was sealed by where they happened to be when the Emergency occurred. It was as random and as decisive as that. Perhaps this was one of the greatest determinates in evolution, but one that never got considered.

He also held grave concerns about the proto-habitat's ability to manage the scared and desperate crowds, especially as it got colder. If work did not continue on schedule because the people started to flood in, then they may never get sealed in time, which would put the entire habitat, and the human population, at risk.

The way to his quarters was through a heavy sound-proof door and then down a corridor. His room was a small, repurposed, office. There was no bathroom. That was further down the corridor, and no doubt a shared facility. Neither was there a kitchenette. He would be eating gruel in a canteen along with everyone else.

A lone picture hung on the otherwise plain concrete walls. It was a view of a Mediterranean island, possibly Santorini, or some similar place. In the picture the sun blazed over rustic white and blue buildings, the calm sea stretched out under a perfectly clear sky. It was almost as if it was deliberately placed there to taunt him. On multiple levels.

It was depressing to look at the picture because of what it symbolized. It was also somewhere that he had always wanted to visit to climb the cliffs, to dive in the water, and to enjoy the restaurants and night life. Now it was all gone. A paradise enjoyed by people for thousands of years, then lost in an instant. He had missed his chance. But the location was ironic. It had happened there before, but for known reasons, being volcanic explosions. All he had was the picture, the concrete walls, and the mental facsimiles of an imperfect past.

He wondered if this was how a prisoner feels when sentenced for life. Yet he was alive and safe, and for that he should be thankful. Then again, maybe his position was only secure so long as he was useful. He reflected that his only useful attribute was his mind, not his hands, or technological prowess. All he could offer was strategic planning and advice, and thereafter, he had to leave it to others to implement. But in his fog and humility, he underestimated his ability to learn and adapt.

Who could know what kind of society the Emergency may spawn? He contemplated the brutality of absolute utilitarianism. Being at the whim of the greater good. Everyone was now at the mercy of the greater good. The luxuries of individualism and self-determination had to be revoked for the greater good and the mob that replaced it had to be guided with an iron fist.

With the loss of the sun, so also was the loss of the greatest parts of The Enlightenment. One could only hope the ensuing Dark Age would be as short as possible and that humanity could once again climb back up into the light.

CHAPTER 6

The night was relentless, in every direction, and for every moment of the nine hours they had travelled. Jan pulled the truck over in Bourke. It was around 7pm old time.

The air temperature continued to drop and now sat at 8°C. They were still ten hours, or more, from Sydney, and by her reckoning, it would be well below freezing by the time they arrived.

She still wasn't sure what she was going to do once they got there. It was a choice between going to the transport depot, her parents' house, or a friend's place who happened to be enroute. Unfortunately, she couldn't contact any of them so she would just have to play it by ear.

The girls got out to stretch their legs and went into the town's only roadhouse to use the restroom. Jan walked around the truck with a torch, banging the tires and probing underneath to ensure everything was in order. Then, when coming up on the passenger side, she noticed oil dripping down and forming a pool on the road.

"What the heck? Just what we need!" she said in frustration.

She crouched down for a closer look, and it became apparent that there was a major oil leak. She immediately turned off the engine to stop further loss, and to allow everything to cool down. She calculated that they would probably be delayed for a couple of hours while she made repairs.

Sure, she could ignore it and just keep topping up the oil. But, then again, if it got worse or failed completely, they could be stuck in the middle of nowhere with potentially fatal consequences. Surely it must have only started in the last few kilometres because there had been no warning light or drop in oil pressure.

Many people had gathered at the roadhouse and as she entered they turned and looked at her. However, she ignored them as her attention immediately went to the television screen. There was a scrolling message that provided information about marshalling areas, volunteering, and registrations. She pointed at the screen and turned to the crowd saying, "Excuse me, what's this all about?"

Various people explained what was being implemented in the Eastern capitals and how there was an urgent call for skilled and able-bodied people. They continued by telling her that those that wouldn't help or were not of value in the Emergency, therefore, those who would hinder efforts, would be best to shelter in place.

This effectively amounted to asking them to make a polar explorer's sacrifice: 'I am just going outside and may be some time.'

Jan recoiled in disgust.

"What the hell! What kind of monsters are these people?"

She continued, "Why on earth are all of you just standing around in here? Shouldn't you be heading to a volunteer center? Doing at least something to save yourselves?"

An elderly woman stepped forward. She was calm and resigned when she spoke.

"Some people have already left. Mostly the young and those with the desired skills. But just look at us! We are too old, unfit, or unskilled. It would be a waste of everyone's time. Best just to accept our fate."

"That's not true. Everyone has value, everyone has something to offer. Even if you can't swing a pickaxe or do electrical wiring, it doesn't mean you can't help in other ways. What about teaching, preparing meals, or watching the kids? Surely there must be a place for you. How could they just leave you out in the cold like this?"

It was a problem as old as humanity, what to do with the old and infirm. At what point does their usefulness expire? It was easy to avoid the question in the modern world, with medicine and aged care homes. Society just poured money on the problem until it became an industry, just like pharmaceuticals or the military industrial complex.

But the world had now changed. Pragmatism trumped obligation, compassion, and empathy. All of those taxes and investments in their futures that people had paid all of their lives, it was now wiped from the ledger. Nature had again reared its ugly head, and the tribe had asked, 'What can you do today, right now at this very moment to justify your existence. And not, "What do I owe you, or what can you offer in the future?" It was do or die, and the town-folk had made their own choice to die.

It was as if the tribe had to follow the migrating herds, regardless of the conditions and difficulties. The sick, old, and frail, those who could not keep up, would find themselves abandoned along the trail. Left to face the elements and the wolves alone.

This had been the reality of human existence for millions of years. We had just forgotten, or sidestepped it, in the modern world. But now the ancient ancestral reality had once again surfaced, and its unfamiliarity and bitter taste was difficult to swallow.

An elderly man said, "Well, that's the thing. There just aren't going to be enough places, not enough seats in the lifeboats, if you get my meaning. And neither is there going to be enough time. Most of us would freeze before we got there. I've lived a good life It's time for the next generation to either fix it or mess it up. I've had my turn."

Jan looked at them silently as a tear trickled down her cheek. Mazie and Sally came out from the restroom and stood next to her. They were wrapped in the blankets they had brought in from the truck. Jan wiped away the tear and tried to look upbeat for the girls' benefit.

From the back of the crowd an elderly woman spoke up, "Now you get yourself and the young'uns down to Sydney as quick as you can. It doesn't help anyone for you to be fussing and worrying over us. We'll be just fine. We'll keep each other warm and cheerful."

A retired schoolteacher quoted Homer, "The Gods envy us. They envy us because we're mortal, because any moment may be our last. Everything is more beautiful because we are doomed." The crowd cheered, high-fived, and hugged each other.

Finally, Jan pulled herself together and announced, "I've got a problem with the truck, there is an oil leak that needs to be fixed. I'm pretty sure I can get the job done, but I may need to borrow some tools and parts."

At hearing this, the motley crew of veterans and invalids sprang to life with renewed vigour and purpose, the last honour and act of their lives.

Several were former mechanics of varied backgrounds and experience, and a selection of parts were sourced from the adjoining mechanics' workshop. The crowd swarmed the truck with torches, advice, and cups of tea.

Mazie and Sally were offered any and everything from the roadhouse to eat and drink, and what they couldn't, was stuffed into their hands and pockets for latter. It was as if they had a dozen grannies and pops to spoil them.

It was past midnight, old time, before the truck was repaired, fuelled, and ready to pull away. People stood along the roadside, huddled together as the mercury retreated to zero. One old trucker had the foresight to cover the truck's radiator with a tarpaulin to keep the engine warm and the heater working.

It was a sad farewell for those in the truck, being in stark contrast to the cheers and wishes coming from the crowd. In the rear-view mirror Jan could see them shrinking back into the night. Forever night.

Suddenly Mazie called out, "Watch out!"

A woman was standing in the middle of the road with two small children. She was frantically waving her hands for the truck to stop. Jan pulled to a sudden halt and wound down the window. The lady ran over and pleaded.

"Please take my boys with you. They are only small. They won't be any trouble, I promise.

Please, you must take them."

Jan looked down at them from the cab, and although the children had heavy coats, they wore shorts, and their feet were bare. She knew that in this condition they would not last the night. She looked around the cab and then asked Maize to open her door.

She called back down to the lady, "OK get in. All of you get in. The children need their mother."

After she said that, she realised how that must have sounded to Mazie and Sally. They had not said a word about their parents during the trip. Surely, they must be missing them and worried about their well-being. She supposed, that with everything they were dealing with, they probably hadn't had time for that part of their lives, and trauma, to surface in their conscious minds.

No doubt it would hit them hard as soon as the drama settled down. The first opportunity, when they thought they were safe and secure, it would hit them with all the ferocity of PTSD. She would have to step it up if she was going to fulfill the role of being a substitute parent. She had always been Aunty Jan. Now she was going to be both mom and dad.

The lady began to thank her, over and over, while sobbed uncontrollably. The three of them climbed up and made a nest in the back of the sleeper cab. The two small boys were shivering from the cold. Sally took them under the warm blanket with her, their wide-eyed dark faces peering out next to hers.

Jan knew she would not be able to take every person that they came across, and that difficult life and death decisions would need to be made. She didn't want that responsibility and dreaded the thought of abandoning helpless people to protect herself and her passengers. Damn this situation. She never realized how easy life used to be.

How could the world have been turned upside down like this? How did she become an instant hero, and potential villain, without warning or consent? She could only imagine what lay ahead as they got closer to Sydney, and closer to so many more people.

CHAPTER 7

When Ollie awoke, it took a while for his mind to adjust to the bleak world being forced upon him. He looked at the time. He had slept a solid 6 hours. Today, tonight, whatever they were now going to call it, was going to be full of difficult and consequential decisions, and all of them would be based on imperfect knowledge, assumption, and gut feeling.

He knew why they had been chosen him for this role, but just like everyone else on the planet, he had not seen the Emergency coming. This was the part of the Fermi Paradox that most people don't consider. It seems that the universe can be so chaotic, and hostile, that even though life may be able to spring up anywhere where the ingredients are right, but perhaps it is also extinguished at the same rate. Life bursting forth like sparks in the night sky, only to be snuffed out as soon as it gets interesting.

From an early age Ollie had been a computer gamer. He had grown up in the 'Fortnite', 'Apex Legends', 'Frostpunk' generation. With mostly absent parents, it became his home life, social life, and comfort. He self-medicated with the adrenaline, endorphins, and oxytocin of virtual reality. It was said at the time that he was wasting his life, stunting his development, and would never amount to anything.

He was fortunate that he didn't stuff himself with junk food and become a slovenly, bloated, teen. Instead, his genetics, and penchant toward exercise, allowed him to mature into a tall, fit, and lithely man.

Regardless, he never did develop much in the way of practical or sporting skills. That is, unless it related to a computer. He may have been a champion in the FIFA World Cup computer game, but he couldn't kick a ball in real life to save himself.

By the time he was in his late teens he had achieved global success in gaming competitions. This afforded him a modest income through tournament winnings and sponsorship deals. Yes, you could say he was famous, but only within the gaming community. And even then, it was not by his real name, but via an avatar.

To anyone else he was just a pale, goth looking, and socially awkward, introvert. Perhaps that is what was meant by stunted development, but he was happy with himself. Probably more so than most people are with their inner child and demons.

He had little desire or need for expensive

clothes and fancy cars. He was perfectly satisfied with practical, efficient and, well, elegant solutions to everything in his life and with what he applied himself to.

With the development of Artificial Intelligence (A.I.), the new frontier in gaming became human versus A.I. strategy battles. One particular game from South Korea dominated, being globally popular, enormous in scope, and infamously difficult. It was called "No Kan Win," or NKW for short.

For several years, after its launch, no one could beat the A.I. programming. It just kept throwing up too many obstacles and outmanoeuvring any and all players. Humans were just rats in its maze. Within the gaming community, the A.I. program became known as 'God', with all the indifference and malevolence of yore.

Ollie was late to the challenge, but within weeks he had defeated the first generation of A.I. foe. But the A.I. learned from this, and fought back, initially out-witting Ollie, but its dominance didn't last.

As the A.I. learned, adapted, and became more powerful, so did Ollie. Eventually he cracked the 'God Code'. He could see behind the veil, and for that feat he became known as the 'God Slayer', and as famous as the Grand Masters of chess in decades past.

It had been 5 years, and he remained undefeated. Not one person had even got close to defeating the first generation of A.I., let alone the higher levels where Ollie operated. Basically, he was a freak of nature that came along maybe once in every few billion people.

Because of his abilities, various militaries, and governments, contracted him to do gaming, planning, and strategizing. He gained a reputation for problem solving and responding to all manner of rapidly evolving situations, be that with conflict, natural disasters, or social and economic trends.

Most of his work was done online, so there was little need for travel and face to face interactions. This suited him and his personality. He was comfortable in his tech-heavy apartment, and having his avatar speak on his behalf.

It's not that he didn't like people. It's just that he had kind of moved on, if that made any sense. If robots or cyborgs existed, then he'd probably be hanging with them, but for the present, he enjoyed his screen friends and his own company.

A large part of his success was due to his ability to assess a situation, or challenge, rapidly, and then mentally model its consequences, well before it was apparent to others. This must have been a product of how his brain was wired, and it effectively put him many steps ahead of his adversaries and gave him an unassailable advantage.

In his apartment the previous evening when General Paterson called and said that the sun had disappeared, Ollie was already planning the intricacies of ecosystem habitats before that call had ended. It was as if his brain was capable of multi-thread processing.

This talent was excellent for gaming and scenario modelling, but it also proved to be a drawback when interacting with people. It was not something that he could turn off in a social setting, and it had proven a significant hinderance to having intimate relationships.

Presently he was single, and without social interaction, there was little prospect of that changing. Yet now, with the remnants of humanity to be crammed into a network of tunnels and totally reliant upon each other to stay alive, who knew what opportunities, or disasters, this could present? Even his imagination had limits, and there was no 'Seldon Psychohistory' to draw upon. In this new world he may die, or he may find love.

People often asked him why he wasn't a 'Prepper'. Why wasn't he building a bunker and hording supplies for some imminent apocalypse? Surely, of all people, he could see the writing on the wall. To this he would say, "We cannot know the nature of the disaster until it occurs, and with so many disasters to choose from, which one should you prepare for?"

Each disaster requires a different strategy. Therefore, one could either prepare a catch-all, yet poor facsimile, of all the world's diversity, and stuff that into a bunker, or they could respond to whatever apocalypse unfolds in real time. He would suggest the later because it gives one the ability to adapt and evolve.

The resources you need are already around you, and the greatest of these is people and an appeal to their skills and humanity. A case in point, no amount of preparation for the broad range of crisis that people expected could have ever prepared them for what eventuated, being where they found themselves today. It was also a convenient strategy for him, given he couldn't shoot an arrow or build a log cabin. He would need to rely on others for the very basics of life.

He left his room and made his way up the corridor to C&C. His hair was long, black, and coiffed, falling across to one side of his pale, youngish face. He wore a black trench coat over a black stencilled T shirt, and black canvas trousers. The look was finished with high-laced, heavy black boots.

He could have passed as Dracula in some b-grade movie. The incarnate of evil itself. Yet there was no intention of theatrics, although, the irony was not lost on him. It was just how he normally dressed even though the clothes did not match his introverted personality, and benevolent intentions, which may, or may not, end up paving the road to Hell.

Perhaps this was part of the reason he preferred to work remotely. When people couldn't see you, they formed their opinions based on work results, or literacy and prose, rather than your hair style and dress sense. Yet, when they finally meet you, they may do a second take, and you must waste time soothing their prejudices and allaying their fears.

It's funny how people can form a monster in their mind based on hair style and clothes. It just goes to show the power of symbolism, of flags and badges, and the triggers that they can pull.

A bold desk with a large leather chair had been placed on a low platform at the back of the cavernous control room. It would be the kind of place you would put the drummer in a rock band. He was escorted to his station where he could see all the wall monitors and all the desks of each of the operators. The scene was both medieval and science fiction, all at once.

For the foreseeable future this would be humanity's limbic system. It would be his responsibility to keep the heart pumping, the lungs breathing, and to also keep hope alive. Life was more than just the ability to live, it was also the will to live. It would, therefore, also be his job to find a future and then to orientate the complex organism toward it.

He leaned back in the oversized chair, the throne, and contemplated how long it would be before the first attempted coup. The job would be thankless and prematurely aging, and yet people would fight over the chance at some imagined, yet elusory and fleeting, power, and prestige. As men have always done, they will blindly reach for that golden chalice full of poison, but not fully understanding why. The thankless tasks of the thoughtless man.

CHAPTER 8

The journey seemed to have no end, and as they passed through towns, with the memory of normality still blazing in the streetlights, there was barely a sign of life. Everyone was inside keeping warm and spending time with friends and family. Unless you were traveling toward the coast to find salvation in capital city, there was no reason to be on the road anymore.

Jan and her passengers headed South and then East, starting to climb the Western Slopes of the Great Dividing Range. With elevation the temperature dropped faster. Outside the cab it now read -15°C. Crystals of frost had formed on the road and blanketed the landscape. It was beautiful to look at, yet horrific to experience when unprepared. If the truck broke down now, they would not survive for very long.

The cold could be felt on the inside of the windows as the truck struggled to maintain temperature. It had not been prepared for extreme cold like those that operated during the Alaskan, Canadian, or Russian winter.

She wasn't sure what may go wrong, or

what could fail. Most of her experience was in hot weather driving, so she just kept the motor running and limited the times that they stopped for rest breaks.

Ahead of them lay the mountain passes that needed to be negotiated before descending into Sydney. It was important to get back down to the lowlands nearer the coast if they were going to win the race against the cold.

She had faith they would make it. It was true faith because she had no logical reason to believe they would succeed. And she believed that when they arrived, they would be accepted and welcomed as refugees, as people of value and worthy to live, and as such they would find community and safety. Sheer faith kept her awake and drove her forward, and pure horsepower and inertia, the truck.

As they approached the highest sections of the journey, the outside temperature dropped to -25°C. Without the sun, atmospheric dynamics had simply shut down. There was no discernible weather. No clouds, wind, nor sleet or snow. But this was deceptive. Treacherous black ice had formed everywhere, especially on damp sections of road that had been flash frozen. Each time they hit an invisible patch of ice, the truck would begin to slide, or the driving wheels would lose traction. Given that it was the middle of summer, of course, she did not carry snow chains, which would have proven very handy under these conditions.

It took all her concentration and skill to stay on the road, maintaining a slow, but respectable speed. Fast enough to have a chance. But they needed to be especially careful going downhill. Just the slightest loss of control could prove disastrous, hence, they were often forced to a crawl, lingering longer and longer in the growing cold. At times she was afraid that they were losing the race.

It had taken about five hours to travel a distance that would normally be covered in one hour. Ahead, they could see bright spotlights that they hoped illuminated a huge construction site or marshalling area.

They were on the WestConnex M4, on the outskirts of Sydney, and according to the official reports, this was one of the designated areas. The temperature had partially recovered and was now sitting at -15°C, yet was still frigid for what would have otherwise been a pleasant summer's day.

A barrier had been erected across the road and several policemen waved them down. Jan wound the window down and the cold almost took her breath away. The policeman was wearing a large puffer jacket, and his face was wrapped in a scarf, meaning all she could see of him was his eyes.

"Hello. Papers please. I need to see your

papers."

"Umm, I'm so sorry, we haven't registered yet, so we don't have any papers. We just drove nonstop from Queensland, but we will register as soon as we can, that is, as soon as we pass a registration area."

He referred to some notes and then asked, "What load are you carrying in the back of the truck?"

"There are metal barrels. They are barrels of high-grade cadmium and zinc oxide concentrate. They come directly from the processing plant in Mount Isa."

"I will need to see a shipping manifest, and then I'll have to get you to open the trailer so I can verify it."

She found the paperwork and then grabbed one of the blankets before stepping out onto the icy road. She handed over the papers and wrapped herself tightly in the blanket before proceeding to the back of the trailer and opening the doors. The policeman climbed inside, shone his light over the load, and checked it against the manifest. He climbed back down and gestured to her to close the trailer door Then he said, "Please wait here."

"Is it OK if I wait in the truck? It's just that I'm really, really, cold."

He paused as he looked at her, and then up at the young faces peering through the cab windows.

"Are those your children?"

"I suppose they are now. I picked them up along the way. There is also another mother inside the sleeper cab."

"Sure, wait in the truck. It's not like you have anywhere else to go."

The policeman went back to his car and spent a long time on the radio, then he returned with the shipping documents.

"It seems that you are carrying what has now been designated a priority cargo, Class 3. That means that you will have to go to the South-West Motorway marshalling area near the airport. There is a special area for receiving industrial goods. You'd be best to go via the M7."

He then took out a large document pad and wrote something down before tearing it off and handing it to her.

"Here, take this ticket. It confirms that you have been inspected and approved to enter a secure area. If you get stopped at any barrier, show this ticket, and they should wave you straight through.

"Also, be sure to register as soon as possible, or you will be designated as Overflow, and then you will get pushed back out into the cold."

Finally, he said, "It is going to take you at least 30 minutes to get there, so you better get moving as the temperature is dropping fast. Oh, and just a warning, there has been some trouble on the roads with rioters. All I can tell you is that, as of 1 hour ago, the road you will be taking was clear, but I cannot give any guarantees to how it is now. The situation is constantly changing."

He finished with an ominous valediction by simply saying, "Good luck."

She turned the truck around and headed back the way they had come. After a few minutes they turned South onto the appropriate motorway. It was surprisingly busy with trucks, heavy machinery, and military vehicles.

It made her feel safe knowing that there were other people around who could come to their aid if needed. However, as she approached the next site, one that was bigger and brighter than the previous, she began to see people standing around fires lit along the side of the road. The fires were burning any and everything, including furniture, construction materials, and even cars. It looked like a post-apocalyptic scene straight out of a movie.

Those huddled around the fires did not look like military personnel, construction workers, or organized work crews, but instead they were a ragged mix of desperate people. She guessed that these were the Overflow. Those that were yet to be put to work, assigned a value, or were refugees waiting to be processed. They looked cold, desperate, and angry.

Some of them tried to wave her down. Others started shouting at her with contorted faces, but with the windows closed she couldn't make out what they were saying.

As she drew closer to the site there was a loud bang on the side of the cab. It caused Mazie and Sally to scream. Someone had thrown a brick, or large rock, at the truck. They were lucky it hadn't come through the window and injured one of them.

Just then a half-frozen blob of slush and stones splattered across the windscreen. It completely blocked Jan's view. She put on the wipers, but already the mix had started to freeze.

She instinctively used the window washer, but that liquid also started to freeze as soon as it hit the glass. Still, she kept trying, driving without knowing where she was going. Not knowing where the edge of the road was, or if there were any bollards or people in her way.

Gritting her teeth behind the screen smeared with mud, and the disorientating blurred lights, she kept up the truck's momentum. The wipers were making a horrible scratching sound as they bumped across the glass, ice, and gravel.

Finally, they managed to clear a small patch of glass in front of her, allowing her to see the road again. She had veered dangerously close to the crowd on the passenger side of the road.

As they progressed, the situation deteriorated. She had to slow down, even though she knew it would make them more vulnerable. There were more people, and they were spilling out onto the road. They were also more militant, with some wielding timbers or pipes as weapons.

After nearly running some people over, and swerving around others, she eventually saw the flashing lights of police and military vehicles, but they were on the other side of the crowd. Clouds of smoke, perhaps from tear gas canisters, were illuminated red and blue as the lights flashed.

It seemed there was a riot between the authorities and the Overflow crowd. It was taking place near the barricade; the same one she had to drive through. She had no choice but to slow down even more, and her only way forward was to push directly through the people.

However, because she had slowed down to almost walking speed, this allowed people to climb up onto the outside of the truck. She locked her door and told Mazie to do the same.

People were banging on the windows and pressing their faces up to the glass. They were shouting all manner of things, some pleading, some cursing.

"Let us in!"

"Save me!"

"Save my baby!"

"We're going to kill you!"

"You are going the rot in Hell!"

Everyone in the truck was scared. Very scared. Jan had instructed Mazie to climbed back into the sleeper, and all the passengers buried themselves under the blankets.

Jan thought to herself that these Overflowers were no longer rational people. But then again, what would she do in their circumstance, if she thought she was going to die. Surely dead people don't feel guilt. Therefore, does one survive by any means? Would she survive by any means, or would she just give up? No, she would survive. So maybe they are as human and as rational as her, or she is as savage as them.

Eventually she passed through the front line of rioters and was now in no-man's land between the opposing forces. A line of soldiers spanned the road in front of her, their guns raised and pointed at the truck.

As she crawled forward, covered in the people of the Overflow, all she could think to do was frantically wave the ticket the policeman had given her. This was in the faint hope that they could see it through the mud smeared windscreen.

The soldiers opened fire, she could see the flashes from their muzzles, and whiffs of smoke in the cold dry air. The bullets hit the people who had clambered over the truck, even those that were straddling the bonnet. It was precision shooting, because as far as she could tell, the truck didn't get hit.

The screams and cries from the people, the barnacles, were haunting. Most fell off and she could see them tumbling and rolling on the road behind her. Others had wrapped their limbs around parts of the truck, like the bullbar and door mirrors. Those people just hung there, lifeless, like Christmas decorations, trophies, and roadkill.

The soldiers parted, allowing the truck to crawl through the cordon. Uniformed men pulled the remaining bodies down from the truck. They threw them to the side of the road, as if they were council workers cutting up the limbs off a fallen tree and then tossing them onto the verge.

When it was safe, she wound down the window and again waved the ticket. Eventually, she stopped at the formal barricade and handed the ticket to the military police. This was something she had done many times while driving in the army. They reviewed the ticket, then shone a torch into the cab, into the eyes of each occupant, and asked if they had registration papers. She repeated that they had just arrived from Mt. Isa. The officers then proceeded to inspect the cargo.

In short time, she was waved through and told to take the road to the left. There she would pass another check point before reaching the receiving station. With great relief, she continued down the road and was through the second checkpoint within 10 minutes.

The receiving station was now only a few hundred meters in front of them. It was an enormous industrial building that had a ramp on the side that led underground.

It looked peculiar to her, but in the cold, snow blowers were now coating the outside of the building with snow. It was as if they were turning it into an igloo. In fact, as she looked around, she could see that this was being done to all the buildings in the industrial zone.

As she descended the ramp, large doors opened, allowing her to drive into the bright, warm, underground complex. It was a hive of activity. On their way down the ramp, they noticed a second set of doors being constructed. 'Why would you want two sets of entry doors,' she thought? 'Surely it wasn't for keeping the Overflow people out!'

Workers swarmed the truck and promptly unloaded it. As their little group stood watching, another driver jumped in, took the truck back up the ramp, and disappeared into the night. Jan was agast and approached someone who looked like a supervisor.

"Where the hell did he just go with my truck?"

"I don't know. He would have gotten a pick-up order from C&C. No one is allowed on the roads without the proper authority now. You should know that."

"I think you misunderstood my question. Why did he just take *my* truck?"

"Oh, I see. That's simple. It is no longer your truck, the boxes of food you are carrying are no longer yours, and any money in your pockets is completely worthless. Welcome to the brave new world."

Jan though it sounded like the army all over again! She knew that martial law had been declared, and that was reasonable given the circumstances. But how long would it last, and what kind of state or administrative structure would it evolve into?

She had left the army because she got sick of all the rules and regulations. Now she wondered if she was slipping back into that, or might it even be worse? Well at least the girls and her were safe and warm, and while they, the authorities, were giving her instructions, then she didn't have to think anymore. At least that was one burden taken from her shoulders.

CHAPTER 9

Ollie sat beside Major Roy Sandalwood in a C&C conference room. Roy had been assigned as secretary and military attaché to Ollie. Attendees included General Paterson and several other of the Defence Force's top brass. There was as also a bevy of politicians and senior civil servants.

One after the other, people delivered briefings and updates on the progress of habitat construction, supplies, logistics, and population management.

It was reported that almost all existing tunnels, and underground structures, had been insulated from the cold, and that they were on track to be fully sealed within a couple of months, before the Earth's atmosphere failed.

Unlike in *normal* Polar conditions, the temporary barriers against the cold did not have to contend with gale-force winds and snow drifts. Only the ferocious cold. By the time the barriers had to be airtight, they would need to withstand at least 1 standard atmosphere of pressure, or 1.01325 bar.

There would be so many holes that needed

to be plugged. Leaking air would be analogous to the leaking of life. To replace any lost air, they would have to go onto the surface and collect it like blocks of ice, bring it underground, and then melt and evaporate it. So theoretically, there wouldn't be a shortage of air, at least on the surface, it's just that it wouldn't be in the form of a gas.

Between road and rail, over 500 kms of tunnels had been identified, and at an average width of 10 meters, and if split into two levels, they would provide around 10km^2 of habitats. Another 10km^2 was expected to be gained from underground structures such as car parking, basements, and above ground buildings, such as shopping malls and sports stadiums. If sewerage and other incidental underground facilities were included, these may yield another 5km^2.

Three tunnel boring machines were currently in operation. If they avoided difficult geology, and they did not break down, then they were forecast to collectively excavate 150 linear meters of new tunnel per day. Thus, they could expand the underground habitats by around 1km^2 per year. Furthermore, it was suggested that the deeper they could bore, the better it would be for exploiting Earth's natural heat, thus allowing the habitats to be geothermally heated from below.

It was also identified that many small

branch tunnels and grottos could be sunk through the walls of the major tunnels, useful for creating living quarters and storage spaces leading off from the primary tunnels.

In this manner people and goods could be domiciled close to places of work, such as agricultural or industrial precincts, eliminating the inefficiency of commuting and the movement of goods.

These smaller tunnels would not require large-scale boring equipment, so were less likely to cause disruption during this crucial development phase. They could be constructed using low-skilled manual labor, principally the people from the Overflow.

The most vexing question related to how many people could be kept alive before all habitats became fully operational. There were over a million people scattered around the perimeter, and they were destined to freeze to death unless they could be brought into the shelters.

Rudimentary structures were being erected, but they were flimsy and temporary, and even then, they may not be able to accommodate everyone. Some of those temporary structures were also needed for saving plants and animals. That is, until their final place in the 'Ark' could receive them.

And then there was the rioting. It was

already getting ugly. If people found out that cows and chickens were being preserved in temporary shelters while people were left to freeze outside, then both would be at risk. Everything would be at risk.

Yet, as pragmatic and inhumane as it was, someone noted that the problem may only continue for a couple of days before the people, those of the Overflow, simply froze in place.

Ollie addressed the table, "We must adapt and respond. We are now more than 24 hours into the Emergency, and based on the miraculous rate of progress, I believe we can update our plans.

"We must get every Overflow person into the habitats, even those that are rioting, for we must not only preserve human life, but also our humanity. Also, we cannot yet gauge the true value of these people to our future. We have reached a point where we can *technically* house them, in a pinch, and we can certainly put them to work." By this he meant working like ants or moles digging to justify their existence.

He continued, "It is horrendous that we have already lost so many people, but such is the scale of the Emergency. There was little we could do to save everyone, so let us now save those that we can."

There was applause from the crowd. It seemed that one problem was solved, however there was the risk that this may open the door to many others. But at least the burden of guilt was lifted ever so slightly.

"Our challenge will now be feeding them all. Hungry people become desperate people. But we cannot fall victim to short-term solutions, like using the livestock, or seeds, destined for long-term production in the habitats. Therefore, we must re-double our scavenging program, as well as fast-tracking preparation and distribution.

"We will need to collect as many frozen farm animals and crops from the countryside as quickly we can. We can leave what we gather in stockpiles just outside the tunnels now that the surface has become our deep freeze. After that is done, we will resume our scavenging of the city's supermarkets and warehouses."

Thus, it was decided to gather in all the people who had made it to the Overflow, volunteer, and marshalling areas, and to pack them in wherever space could be found.

The population would be stratified into 3 divisions, although it was also acknowledged, and furiously argued, about how antiquated and dangerous the concept of stratification was. It was agreed that every effort must be made to ensure it does not become a permanent structure of the society.

The first strata, Level 1, included managers and professionals in C&C, Knowledge, Health, and Essential Industries, with the latter including food, power, construction, and waste.

Level 2 would comprise skilled laborers, (oh how Marxist it all sounded), the ones tied to specific jobs in specific locations.

And then there was Level 3, the great un-skilled, the unwashed pool of everyone else, the 'Proletariat'. These people would be assigned jobs and locations as required, like itinerant day laborers. It would be these people that scavenged the frozen world above, stripping it of its resources and modern trinkets. And it would be they who dug the millions of micro tunnels, by hand if necessary, shovelling the dirt from where the machines could not reach.

No system is perfect, and there is always an exception, but for now, it was all that they could imagine, and agree too, to stay alive.

There was, however, one caveat placed over the whole society. Everyone was in this together. Everyone was to get the same ration of food, and to eat in the same places, as well as to bathe and defecate in the same facilities.

Equality would be codified through the total elimination of money and wealth. With no currency, then none could be horded, stolen, or leveraged for advantage. Everyone was equal, differentiated only by the value of their innate abilities, knowledge, and the sum of their contribution worth to the habitats and society.

Humans innately gravitate toward elitism.

Yet even though democracy, and it could be argued law, had been suspended, and it was hoped that this would only be temporary, every effort would be put in place to stop a class or caste system from forming.

Perhaps this had been the original, and well-meaning, intention behind some of history's most brutal, regressive, and repressive regimes. Faced with an emergency, perhaps a revolution, or war, a small group of self-proclaimed 'righteous' people, consolidated power, and so began the downward spiral.

Yet Ollie was an accidental leader. He was not someone that history would have chosen, so perhaps this could work. At least for a while. He did not seek power for power's sake, and neither did he seek wealth, glory, or fame. As was always his motivation, he just wanted to win this game. The ultimate game between humans and the elements.

Unfortunately, history also attests that it is not always the first ruler that is the tyrant. Often, they are the hero, the liberator, and the one who unites the country, as with Pericles in ancient Greece, or Bolivar in South America. Instead, it is the heirs, underlings, and enemies, in the following generations that devour the fruits of freedom.

In this time of crisis, they could not afford the luxury of democracy, but in the long-term they could not survive without it. Systems had to be established that would lead the survivors toward enlightenment, liberty, and equality, regardless of who was at the reigns.

It was reasoned that this could only happen if money was eliminated. That didn't just mean a cashless society, it meant a different way to value effort and contribution. Something other than the accrual and exchange of credit and wealth.

The academic Fisher had said, "It's easier to imagine the end of the world than the end of capitalism".

They now had the end of the world, they didn't need to imagine it, for it was happening before their eyes. Now it was time for capitalism to also end. It could not outlive the end of the world itself. It was not a god, but merely a system, like so many other systems, and systems can get improved, dissolved or replaced, and no one needs to die.

CHAPTER 10

Jan and her small band of refugees presented themselves to a registration desk. The process was officious, invasive, and streamlined, culminating with each of them sporting a code on an identification tag.

She was assigned to Transport & Logistics, with an appended M classification, meaning military, and a 2A person classification, denoting that she was a mother, due to Mazie and Sally being made her wards. Thus, with the check of a box on some innocuous form, Jan became a mother of two.

A special designation was given to Sally because of her bright red hair. She was deemed to be of genetic interest.

It was explained to them that her differences made her important to the long-term genetic strength of the human species. Having gone through the bottleneck of losing 99% of humans, it was important that repopulation afforded the species the best resistance to genetic uniformity, therefore, weakness.

It was eugenics plain and simple, but in

the opposite direction to many of history's evil projects. Instead of white supremacy, or the House of Hapsburg, this was 'tan', or Le Guin's 'grey', supremacy.

The mother and her two small boys, the ones they had picked up in Bourke, received the highest classifications for genetic difference, which therefore equated to societal value. This was due to their First Nations heritage.

They were immediately taken to a separate area for further processing, and thereafter assigned lower risk jobs, and more secure accommodation. Their survival was to be assured at all costs. If it came down to it, their lives would take precedence over the average, common garden variety, European or Asian.

It was ironic that only a few days before, they had lived in relative poverty on the fringes of society. In times past, their people had been referred to as a genetic dead end and destined to die out. And now, in this new world, it was they who were the genetic elites, by virtue of being so far removed from the European and Asian stock that dominated the survivor population pool.

Jan and the girls were housed together in an open-plan Class 2 domicile, designation number I-17, "I" denoting igloo. This meant that they were not formally in the tunnel system, but neither were they in the temporary shelters used for the Overflow.

On balance, given Jan's job, and Mazie's soon to be assigned job, which was also likely to be in Transport & Logistics, their housing, and the advantage afforded by Sally's red hair, placed them squarely, and securely, in the mid-range of Strata 2 classification.

Jan's faith had not let her down. This outcome was more welcome and secure than she had dared imagine only several hours earlier. She was confident that she could have made the best of wherever she ended up, but now she had to think about her 'children'. It was a new and frightening responsibility.

Their new home, which was a giant repurposed warehouse, contained row after row of triple bunk beds. The outside of the building had been sprayed with a thick layer of artificial snow in the fashion of making a giant igloo, and then haphazardly, the inside was lined with a patchwork of insulating materials. It was cold and cavernous but still it remained above freezing.

Each of the beds had a single pillow and a heavy blanket. They were required to give up all but personal items when they left the truck. People in the Overflow needed them more than they did.

There was a busy 24-hour food hall with trestle tables and benches that adjoined the sleeping area. Meals were modest, rationed, and flavored as best the catering corps could manage. It was clear that no one was going to get fat, and those that were, were going to lose it.

There was also a very 'public' amenities block. Fortunately, one for each gender. Showers were limited to 2 minutes of hot water, and 3 minutes if you included tepid. For Jan, this was not so different from her time in the army, but for many, including Mazie and Sally, this new way of life was a shock.

On the first day in their new home, Jan and the girls were given a generous, one-off allocation of 8 hours sleep. This was due to how many consecutive hours they had spent traveling over the previous days. However, most people were already doing 4 hours on, 4 hours off rotations. Every hour of work was crucial in the effort to create the habitats, and collect resources, before it got too cold, and the atmosphere collapsed.

Transport & Logistics was on a war footing. There was a limit to how much time people, and equipment, could operate on the surface. And as each day passed, and the temperature dropped, surface time would shrink effectively to nothing. Then, not even combustion engines would run, so no trucks. And anyone leaving the habitats would have to wear a spacesuit.

Presently every truck, train, and boat were being used to retrieve resources. They would bring them closer to the habitats, dump them, and then head back out to scavenge for more. They worked like a colony of ants, stripping the city and surrounding countryside, and then transporting the cuttings and bounty back to the nest.

After their sleep, Jan and Mazie were assigned to a specially prepared scavenger truck. Jan was the designated driver, and Mazie was part of the four-person crew.

Each truck was assigned a resource and a location where they were likely to find it. They would dash out to the site, load all that they could, and then rush back and dump it in the designated areas. If the location was close, then they may get several runs done in a shift. However, there were times when the resources were further afield. In those instances, they may have to access a staging post, as a refuge from the cold, thus breaking the journey and exposure into more manageable durations.

Sally was assigned to processing and distribution; it was assessed that she was old enough to contribute to the workforce. She worked within the distribution precinct, just a short tunnel-walk from where they called home. She was part of the team that dispatched products requested by other parts of the growing habitat complex.

She had been reluctant to get separated

from Jan and Mazie, but the lady who came to get her was kind and sympathetic. Fortunately, because she was being put in what was designated a low-risk area, she would be with other people of genetic difference, and many that were closer to her age group. Also, due to her age, Sally's sleep schedule would be on a 12-hour rotation, which meant she would only see Jan and Mazie when their rotations aligned. Gone were the carefree days of childhood, of lazing in bed, or wasting hours on social media. Every able-bodied person had to carry their own weight, plus some.

On their third day in the habitat, Jan and Mazie received an assignment to travel to Goulburn, a journey that would normally take around 2 hours along the Hume Highway. When they arrived there, they would liaise with people at the staging post, located next to a railway line, and get directions for scavenging frozen farm animals. They were to collect them and then dump them at the staging post ready for loading onto a train that would transport them back to the habitats.

Jan drove the truck through two sets of doors, then up onto the surface. As they passed through the second door and looked out into the dark, ice crystals began to form on the truck's windows. The needle on the thermometer could be seen dropping rapidly, bottoming out at -30°C. The truck was ex-military, a heavy tank transporter that Jan was familiar with. It had been fitted with a small crane, and they had chains and slings for manipulating and securing their load. It had been winterized so that it could operate in the cold, however, it was getting near the limits of its serviceability.

The location of the habitat, being from where they started out from, was only about a kilometre from the coast, and only a couple of meters above sea level. It was likely, given where they were traveling, that it would be at least 10°C colder, and of course there was the black ice, and the perpetual night.

It was scary to leave the safety of civilization, even if civilization was only their igloo, an annex to the greater habitat. This was especially so, now that many of the city lights had failed, thus causing the darkness to creep closer.

They had been traveling for nearly 3 hours before the lights of the Goulburn staging post came into view. They drove past produce and material stacked into piles along the side of railway tracks. The temperature outside was now down to -40°C. It was not known for how much longer the trains and trucks could continue running.

The staging post was also an igloo structure, complete with double sets of doors. Its warmth, light, and human faces were a relief.

A man with a clipboard immediately

attended to them, giving instructions on how to find an extensive pig farm. He said that they had tried to save the facility, but their attempts were overwhelmed when the heating failed. All the animals were lost to the cold. He was going to send a second crew with them to help retrieve the frozen animals.

The second team had a forklift on board, so between them, they should be able to load the two trucks, and if they could complete several runs over a few hours, then they would hopefully empty the pig farm.

The plan worked well. It was only for short durations that anyone needed to leave the warmth of a truck, such as opening barn doors, finding animals, or coupling chains. Anyone who did leave a truck needed polar clothing. The forklift operator had the worst of the jobs.

Over several hours they managed to do enough runs to empty the facility, and thereafter, relaxed with hot soup and bread inside the staging post.

After eating, the floor supervisor came over and said, "Time to get moving people. The temperature has dropped to -45°C, and you've got some colder elevations to negotiate before you get back to Sydney."

Jan could feel the truck's drive wheels slipping on the ice as they climbed the gentle gradient away from the staging post. She wasn't sure how much weight they had on the trailer, but it wouldn't have exceeded what the vehicle was designed to carry.

Every now and then the wheels would slip, then grip, and the truck would lurch and hop. This required her to feather the throttle so as not to get bogged or break something in the increasingly brittle drive line.

They were about 4 kilometres from the staging post. It was slow going due to the road being so slick with ice. There were snow chains on the drive wheels, but they did not seem to have much effect. She slowed down to negotiate a corner, but when she turned the wheel, the truck continued straight ahead. Neither braking, nor accelerating, helped. They had simply lost all traction and were sliding toward a ditch on the far side of the road.

With a slow gentle slip and bump they went off the road and down a small embankment. It was neither abrupt nor jarring, but it put them into an unrecoverable position. She knew the reality of the situation without needing to look or trying to extricate themselves. To make matters worse, they were just beyond the range of the low-powered radios, so they could not call for help.

There was nothing else they could do but climb down from the truck wearing all their Polar clothes and begin the long walk back to the staging post.

It was biting cold as they walked in the gravel at the edge of the road. The bitumen was just too slippery to walk upon.

They could feel their fingers and toes getting cold. All they dared expose to the outside, was a small slit for their eyes. Other than that, their heads and faces were wrapped in wool and polyester.

With a torch at the front, they walked silently in single file. It was unknown how long the torch battery would last in these conditions, so they maintained a brisk pace. It took nearly 2 hours to get back to the safety of the depot.

When they arrived, all the remaining stock was being loaded onto a train.

The foreman said, "Just as well you came back because you may not have gotten through. Just after you left, we were ordered to shut everything down and return to Sydney.

The railway tracks, and bridges, have reached their safety threshold. In the higher passes the temperature has dropped to -50°C and the steel is becoming brittle. So, it looks like you'll be coming with us. We've got some specially prepared insulated carriages. Ironically, they are repurposed refrigerated shipping containers. They will hopefully keep us warm and comfortable, but it's going to be a very slow trip."

The train moved at a crawling pace. The wheels would slip and screech, and the rails would crack and spit out splinters. It took them nearly 7 hours to get back to the Sydney habitat.

Both Jan and Mazie drifted in and out of sleep, cushioned in their puffy clothing, but regularly woken by violent jolts and screeching, as if the train was navigating deformed and twisted tracks. When the train finally stopped there was a loud banging on the door. After a minute or so it swung open. The latching had frozen shut and needed some persuasion to get it open.

They stepped out to find themselves in a warm and bright railway tunnel somewhere under the city. It was buzzing with activity. Workers descended upon the wagons and flat-tops to unload them.

They went up to a person who looked like a conductor and asked how they could get to I-17. He pulled out a map and showed them the shortest combination of tunnels required to get there.

In a couple of places, they would have to take surface walkways that only had minimal thermal protection, thus requiring them to wear their outside clothes. He gave them the map and advised them that it would probably take an hour, or more, to get home.

The journey through the tunnels was loud, busy, and exhausting. Their senses were overwhelmed as people labored on any and everything. Everywhere one looked, someone was digging a tunnel, or running out a cable, or carrying something between work sites. It wasn't only Transport & Logistics that were working in double shifts, it was everyone, everywhere, in every way.

It amazed Jan just how coordinated everything was, despite the superficial appearance of chaos. She wondered if there was a single brain behind it all. There must have been structure, and authority, because everyone had their orders, and everything operated like clockwork.

Yet, from her experience, it didn't quite seem the way the military would have planned and executed such a project. There was something different about it that she couldn't quite grasp. It really did seem like it was one person's vision, but how could that be possible in such an emergency? Could someone have planned all of this? And maybe years before it happened? That would be ridiculous. But how could have someone come up with all of this on the spot? Such a plan in the midst, mist, and confusion of the Emergency? That would be equally ridiculous.

Finally, after nearly 24 hours away from home, they returned to I-17. Sally screamed with joy and ran over to hug them. She had been extremely worried and was so overwhelmed to see them that she started crying. She said that no one could give her any information. All anyone knew was that they had headed to Goulburn in a truck, and they were only supposed to be gone for 6 hours.

Due to their ordeal, Jan and Mazie were given leave for another 8-hour sleep. They pulled the curtains around their triple bunk and went to sleep feeling warm and relieved. That was the last time anyone attempted long-distance scavenging using conventional vehicles, including trains. There was no point in further winterizing conventional vehicles. Within a few weeks there would not be enough air to run them.

CHAPTER 11

It had been more than 12 months since the Earth lost the Sun. The average land surface temperature had dropped to -215°C. Chemical elements in the atmosphere had started liquifying at around -180°C and fell like rain. It flowed in the old river channels and then formed lakes on the lowlands.

With time, those lakes froze over to form solid sheets of oxygen and nitrogen. A mist of remnant atmosphere spread out across the oceans as a low roiling cloud, boiling near the surface and re-freezing with height, constantly, and hypnotically, overturning.

In the ensuing years, as the sheet of sea ice would thicken, this mist would also freeze, capping all sea ice, and eventually equalizing the planet's surface temperature to that approaching the cold of space.

Ironically, the Earth would remain tectonically active for billions more years. It would still have volcanoes spewing lava and gas, with the latter falling as carbon dioxide, methane, and sulphur snow around the vents. There would still be earthquakes and continental drift, thus presenting the strangest of contradictions, a planet with a dead surface and a still beating heart.

The habitats were successful at keeping alive the specimen of what was once Earth's complex life. With great effort and sacrifice an 'Ark' had been burrowed into the earth. The humans lived like termites, constantly boring and constructing, gnawing at the earth, all the time regulating temperature, and air flow, throughout the tunnels and igloos.

During the days and weeks after the Emergency, there had been patchy communication with nations across the Pacific. There had been a scramble of emergency flights in the first few days, evacuating people from various islands and cities, including Auckland and Wellington in New Zealand.

An attempt was made to establish habitats in each of those cities, however, their underground networks were not extensive enough for sustainable populations. After considerable hardship and loss of life, most of the survivors were evacuated by submarine, leaving behind a small contingent to staff what would become a network of outposts.

Similarly, various US Pacific Island territories were partially evacuated, but there was also considerable loss of life. In Hawaii there remained two outposts, one being the US naval base, and the other being a loose affiliation of bunkers occupied by the ultra-rich.

Regarding the latter, there was little interaction with those groups because they were not willing to take in survivors. Isolation and self-preservation were the whole reason they built their bunkers and fortifications. Ironically, though, these structures were built to deal with nuclear war, pandemic and civil decay. Not the extreme cold and zero atmosphere. Therefore, without assistance they would fail. Their principal design flaw was reliance on diesel, solar, or wind generators, for power. Of course, none of these worked anymore.

Large-scale military bunkers around the world, such as the Cheyenne Mountain Complex in Colorado, would face the same fate as the ultra-rich in Hawaii. Also, given that the Emergency happened without warning, and the radioactive flaring occurred over less than a day, the only people that would have been in these bunkers during that crucial time, were the staff on duty, primarily being the maintenance crews and cleaners. The Emergency was indiscriminate. It was the great leveller.

There would not have been time, or ability, to get the U.S. President, or other dignitaries, to such bunkers. During the flaring, there was no communication, there were no flights, and there was no safe way to travel outdoors. And moreover, in the 12 months since the Emergency, there had been no way to communicate with, or travel to, Colorado or other sites, to check for, or assist, survivors.

Fortunately, a submarine communication cable did link Australia's East Coast habitats, and this extended to New Zealand, Hawaii, and Guam. Nuclear submarines regularly visited these outposts with supplies and technology.

The frantic pace of the early days had subsided, and people were now back to standard diurnal work cycles. The habitats resembled and acted like a mycorrhizal fungus network that luminesced and hummed. High intensity hydroponic horticulture, grown under artificial light, and fertilized by a cocktail of wastes, offset the inexorable draw-down of scavenged food.

Heating and ventilation were, for the most part, passive, by virtue of the thermal difference between the lower tunnels and the frigid surface. In some instances, through innovative use of convection and differential engines, electrical power was generated as a by-product of thermal transfer. Effectively, steam turbines could be run from any element or compound that phase changed from liquid to gas between -200°C and +20°C.

There was a heavy emphasis on scientific research and engineering, with a gusto exceeding that of the Manhattan Project. Any idea that may yield some improvement, regardless of how outlandish or unconventional, was pursued. Without the limitations imposed by money, competing interests, or any of the distractions in the former world, boffins toiled away in labs, on high rotation, by simulated day and night.

It would be technological breakthroughs that would allow humans to once again visit and utilize the surface. It would be breakthroughs in microbiology and toxicology that would lower the risks posed by viruses and bacteria, being a constant threat in the warm, confined, and crowded habitats. A food blight, or a severe respiratory infection, could prove fatal to the whole population.

There was, however, one field that was of particular interest to Ollie. Astrophysics. For him, it was not enough that they had survived. He wanted humanity to have a future beyond the tunnels. Given what he knew of the human spirit, it was so much bigger and adventurous than the trajectory they were currently on.

Humans had evolved to live under, and worship, the Sun. To walk through green fields tossed by summer breezes, to sail oceans, and to experience reckless adventure and freedom. Instead, in the habitats, all they had to look forward to was an existence on life support, as if they were comatose yet conscious, victims of locked in syndrome.

It was his mission to break free from the Earth, to find a new planet with a new Sun. Yes, he knew these were crazy notions. Maybe the dreams of the doomed. Yet, he believed deep down that it had to be the next stage in human evolution. Just as an asteroid strike had wiped out the dinosaurs and changed the course of all life, so too would be the loss of the Sun.

The day-to-day administration of the habitats had been returned to the politicians. Ollie recognized that it was not optimal, and it certainly wasn't merit based, but the struggle, and the politics, to remove them may not have been worth the trouble it could have caused.

Provided the 'politicians' could be kept in check, and the removal of money certainly helped with that, then at least they presented a familiar face. A power structure that the population had already been conditioned to accept.

His own role was now akin to a Head of State in a constitutional monarchy. Insidious ideas of leadership and hierarchy have long half-lives. But, being no longer bothered by the day-to-day issues of administration, he could focus on distant and greater dreams, and thereafter the strategies and proclivities to achieve them.

While taking one of his walks through the tunnels, Ollie overheard a conversation between two people. They were a couple of tunnels over from the Department of Knowledge, it being a collection of facilities that in the past would have been called a university.

As people are known to do, they were gossiping and complaining about one of their colleagues.

"He just won't let it go. It's a waste of everyone's time."

"I hear what you are saying. For me, the biggest problem is that he can't prove any of it. Perhaps in the past, if he had access to The Large Hadron Collider, then maybe, just maybe, he could test the first stage of his theory."

"Yes, well that's Danny Wilson for you, brilliant and yet half mad all in one."

Ollie mumbled to himself, "Danny Wilson, Danny Wilson" as he made an abrupt turn into the cross-connector-tunnel leading to Knowledge. He had a gut feeling that he had to find out who this Danny Wilson was and, more so, what were his crazy ideas? Ollie liked crazy ideas, the thinking outside of the box kind of ideas. They were the type that allowed for technological and cultural leaps.

Apart from some scavenged artwork and statues, the Knowledge looked the same as everywhere else in the tunnels. It comprised a series of long parallel tunnels with grottos dug into the sides every 10 meters or so. In each was a workstation, and if necessary, enough room for equipment. Above each ingress was a number and name plate. Many of the workstations doubled as living quarters, thus allowing the occupants to fully immerse themselves in their work.

Ollie wandered down the first tunnel, noticing the different disciplines. They ranged from structural engineering to entomology within just a few hundred meters. It wasn't that they were all mixed up, but rather that they all existed in such close quarters. And also, after the Emergency, there just weren't too many scientists left. One or two entomologists could be the whole department of entomology, or seismology etc.

Halfway down the tunnel he found a modest communal area with a directory board on the wall. People were gathered, drinking scavenged coffee, eating food from cans, socializing, and talking about their work. He ran his finger down the directory until he came across the name 'Danny Wilson'.

Danny was located two tunnels across and one level down. If one drew a straight line, it wasn't very far away. However, due to the tunnel network and the placement of interconnectors, it was a zigzagging 1km walk.

Mobile phones worked throughout the tunnel system, although their use was limited mainly to text messaging. With everyone living and working in such close quarters, talking on the phone was considered a social faux pas, just like on a Tokyo commuter train. Also, due to network limitations and radiation, data intensive uses like streaming was discouraged.

Instead, ethernet and fiber optics were used to connect monitors and keyboards to central servers. Most communal areas had public monitors, but only a few were found in sleeping quarters. Ollie could have texted Danny to check if he was at his workstation, but he decided to walk there instead, exploring Knowledge, and arriving unannounced.

He eventually found the workstation. The sign read 'Danny Wilson, Knowledge 484, Astrophysics & Propulsion Engineering'. To the layperson, Danny was a rocket scientist.

There was a slim ratty looking man pacing back and forth behind the plastic film window. Ollie tapped on the door frame. Danny rushed over, dragged him in, and then practically forced him into a chair. Then he quickly closed the door as if they were meeting in secret.

Without even looking at Ollie, he raised a finger to compel silence and patience. Danny resumed pacing while mumbling to himself, and then finally rushed over to his desk and typed something on his keyboard.

When finished, he turned to Ollie and smiled, saying, "Hi, I'm Danny. I'm sorry about that, I was just wrestling with an idea."

He talked at a fast pace, and it seemed

like he was half talking to himself, or to a third unseen person in the room. He continued with no noticeable pause for breath.

"Sometimes you just can't let the opportunity slip. You know, ahh, you know how when you are desperately trying to recall something, even as it is fading and slipping through your fingers, so you try harder and harder?

I've got this big, big, idea, but I keep only seeing slithers of it, so each time I get a glimpse, a glint, a fraction, a reflection, I write it down. Maybe, maybe one day, I will put together the whole puzzle and see the full picture."

He continued, "Coffee? I've got coffee, it's the good stuff. Beans that I grind myself, and I've got some sugar and whitener. Or maybe tea, is tea what you like? I've got a couple of different types, but sorry no biscuits, we've been short of biscuits for a while now."

Ollie smiled and said, "Coffee is fine."

He liked this man, this strange crazy wiry ratty man. He could relate to chasing an elusive idea, and the frustration of not quite catching it.

As Danny was fussing over the coffee, he continued to talk.

"You know we don't see many people down here, but I don't mind. A couple of times a week they make us socialize, go out and talk to people. I suppose that is OK. I get it. I know why they do it.

"Mostly I stay in touch with people via text and email, so I still know what my colleagues are doing. They say we are going a bit stir crazy, you know cabin fever, but it's OK, we are doing our part, we are getting work done. Like they say, we need to 'tech ourselves' out of this hole, so yeah that's what I'm doing, that's me, working away at things and all that."

He paused for a breath as he handed over the coffee. Ollie thanked him, and then introduced himself as just someone from C&C. Then Ollie said that he would be interested to hear what Danny had been working on, to tell him about this theory that he had just mentioned.

Danny, wide-eyed, looked to an imagined horizon and theatrically slow-waved his hand in the air, and started with a proposition.

"What if we could get out of here? Yes. Yes, but not just out of the tunnels, and not just onto the surface, but back into space. Like we used to do before the Emergency, when we went to the Moon and Mars. When we sent probes that travelled beyond Pluto, and launched telescopes that could see to the very beginning of time.

"And what if we could travel further than before? Yes faster, so much faster. And what if we did not have to worry about radiation, micro meteors, time dilations, and whatever other obstacles and dangers are lurking in deep space? That is, when you travel at, or beyond, the speed of light."

Ollie really liked the picture Danny was painting, but he was also wary that he may be going insane from being alone with his thoughts for too long.

"Well that all sounds fantastic, it's a lovely dream, but how does that dream become reality?"

"Ah yes, reality. That brutal mistress. But what if I suggested that we could get around reality, figuratively speaking?

"In the past, science fiction would create alternate realities, like warp drive, faster than light, worm holes, or the bending of space and time in some fanciful way. These allowed spaceships to travel to distant places within the scale of a human lifetime.

"Or otherwise, they would put people into suspended animation to sleep for hundreds, or thousands, of years, until they reached those distant places."

"Yes, it made for good movies, but it was always hypothetical and would probably prove impossible in real life."

"Exactly, exactly, it was just fantasy."

Danny became more animated and excited.

"Now, let me present a different way of thinking. Imagine that reality, as we know it, is constrained within 4 dimensions, including time.

"In this reality is the full electromagnetic spectrum, therefore light and heat and such, as well as all matter such as atoms and electrons and stuff, and all of this exists in a medium, let's call it a gravity soup. Think of gravity like a watery soup, and everything that we experience as reality is surrounded by, and part of, this soup. We are part of this soup. Even your thoughts are part of this soup. This very idea I discuss at the moment is in the soup.

"Now this soup is constantly in motion. Swirling around, and within that soup, are blobs of denser or more energetic soup. You and I and the planets and stars are all blobs of that denser soup, in a vast ocean of soup. And it all moves like currents and waves in that soup. Some people postulate that the soup particles are strings and think of the cosmic background radiation of the known universe as being an energy map of that ocean of soup."

"OK Danny, I am with you so far," said Ollie.

"Now, imagine you can repel the soup, like you can repel water. You are hydrophobic, you can split the soup in front and behind you, creating a hole in that soup through which you could travel.

"In that hole, that void you have created, you are no longer affected by gravity, or light, or mater, or time. You are outside of the known universe. You have, in fact, entered a different reality, or you could call it a different dimension."

"Hmm, that is an interesting idea. So are you suggesting that you can generate some kind of field, or beam, or frequency, that can repel, umm, let's call it reality, or the gravity soup analogy you used?"

"I have a theory, or at least part of a theory, but I need some very sophisticated equipment to test it."

"And what about your colleagues, what do they think?"

Danny laughed and casually said, "Oh, they think I'm a raving lunatic."

"Well lunatic or not, what you have told me is the best news, or idea, I have heard in months. This kind of thinking can give us hope and something to strive for. Let's see what we can do about testing this theory of yours. So, what do you need?"

Danny became coy and lowered his voice.

"Well, um, I need to get access to a particle accelerator and some other high-tech equipment. Oh, and I need to create a fusion reaction. Umm, and a supercomputer would be pretty handy also."

Ollie's jaw dropped before he said in a friendly but sarcastic tone, "Oh, is that all?"

"Well, it would be a good start," Danny said, completely unphased by Ollie's sarcasm and attempt at humour. Often the uber-focussed and savants don't pick up on these interpersonal subtleties; they are below their plain of thought.

In a more serious tone, Ollie continued,

"So, let me get this straight. You want to go to somewhere like the Large Hadron Collider in Switzerland, somehow power it up, and then do some high energy particle experiments?

"Then you want to find a nuclear fusion reactor, which doesn't really exist, and somehow power that up, all in the hope that you can get enough data to feed into a supercomputer to test a theory?"

"Yeah, that about sums it up," said Danny, as if it was a perfectly normal and rational request, as if he was applying for a research grant or something.

There was a long pause before Ollie stood up and started pacing the floor. Danny also resumed his pacing until the two were at equidistance orbiting a chair in the middle of the room. Ollie suddenly stopped and said, "I love it, leave it with me."

As he started for the door he said, "We don't have a minute to waste. I'll be in touch. Just keep working on the theory." And then he disappeared into the tunnels as mysteriously as he had arrived. The ideas, strategies, and connections beginning to storm in his brain. He could visualize the chain of events required to get from the present to a new future. This, now project, only minutes old, now consumed him. He walked back through the tunnels as if on autopilot, stepping over pipes and going up and down stairs without really looking, such was how clear and bright the visions were in his head.

CHAPTER 12

The habitats were constantly pushing out feeders, like tendrils or roots, just below the permafrost, probing the dead cities for resources. Many of these micro-tunnels were cold, poorly lit, being just large enough for a person to stand upright. They resembled the mines of hundreds of years ago. Each of them terminated with a mobile airlock that could be repositioned as the tunnel grew.

Like miners chasing veins of gold, scavenger teams used old maps of the city to guide their tunnelling and to emerge as close as possible to resources. The mother-loads were supermarkets, shopping malls and warehouses.

After a year in Transport & Logistics, Jan and Mazie, like most in the Department, were assigned to scavenge detail. Resources would be retrieved from the surface by scavengers wearing rudimentary space suits and then fed down through the airlocks into the tunnels. Other people, receivers, would load the pickings onto carts and pull them through the micro-tunnel network to distribution hubs. A couple of times a week, Jan and Mazie were rostered to do above ground scavenging.

Most people did not enjoy the above ground shifts. Apart from the obvious danger of running out of oxygen or freezing, which was typically caused by snagging one's spacesuit, the greatest bugbear was that the suits were bulky and uncomfortable, especially in Earth's gravity.

But Jan did not mind. She could manage the weight of the suit, and because the helmet did not have to deal with radiation like space suits of the past, it afforded an unobscured view of the stars.

When she ignored the dangers, suppressing her fears, then being away from the tunnels, with their noise, smells, and crowds of people, was invigorating. She loved to gaze upon the stars, and to enjoy that long lost feeling of solitude and freedom.

After Jan and Mazie finished their shift, they found themselves a considerable distance from home. They had recently been assigned a three-person grotto apartment in a tunnel, which they treasured, even though it meant a longer walk to work. Sally was now splitting her time between online school and working in logistics. Every child was expected to work and to also complete school.

Fortunately, Jan and Mazie were able to hitch a ride on one of the many electric service trollies that plied the tunnels. It was headed close to where they lived, so they climbed atop some crates, and the trolly proceeded at a brisk walking pace.

The route took them through one of the high vaulted terrariums. This one was made from a repurposed underground railway station. It contained large, coppiced trees, tropical vines, and a rich tapestry of exotic plants, animals, and insects. Lilies floated over the surface of a small lake which was fed by a waterfall tumbling into a meandering rivulet. In places, if one ignored the rendered concrete ceiling, you could almost believe you were in a rainforest.

A walking trail wandered through the ecosystem so anyone could enjoy the serenity and indulge their memories. It was a popular spot for artists, poets, and lovers. As the trolly brushed past overhanging palm fronds, butterflies took flight and circled up toward the artificially lit ceiling.

But the experience was all too short. Within minutes they had passed through another door, and again the trolly was rolling through a noisy crowded residential precinct.

Their apartment was one of the few that had a computer monitor. It had been provided for Sally's school work, and when they arrived home, Jan logged in to check for messages. She was surprised to see a message from C&C informing her that she had been reassigned to a new project.

She was to report to a division of Knowledge the following day.

"Ooh, I wonder what it could be?" Sally said.

"I have absolutely no idea," replied Jan.

Mazie immediately became upset.

"Oh no, they are going to split us up. I don't want to go to the surface without you."

Jan calmed her down by saying, "It's almost time for you to start higher education. How about, if I *am* permanently reassigned, then we make an early application to Knowledge for you to start full-time study. I'm sure they will agree, especially given it will allow you to look after Sally."

The following morning Jan reported to the nominated division within Knowledge. The layout was very different from other areas of the habitat. It was a combination of tunnels and igloos, with some housing very large machines.

Part of the complex included an electric arc foundry for smelting and casting metals. There were cranes and gantries for manipulating heavy equipment, industrial chemical vats and retorts, and lots and lots of signs saying, "Danger Keep Out" or "Authorised Personnel Only."

As she walked through the facility, she was guided down paths delineated by yellow lines and arrows. Finally, she arrived at what she presumed to be the administration center, and there she explained that she had been asked to report for work.

The woman at the desk looked up her details and said, "Ah, yes, Jan, excellent. I believe they are all gathered in building 44, that's KI-44, it's an igloo."

Any building on the surface was now called and igloo, regardless of its shape size or purpose.

"I suppose you wouldn't know what they are working on would you?" Jan enquired.

"Sorry dear, they have been a bit hush, hush, on that project. All I can tell you is that it is some kind of vehicle."

The precinct was noisy with clanging, and banging, and grinding. The air was filled with sparks and fumes. There was a pervasive hum from large extractor fans as she made her way up a series of ramps to reach KI-44.

Pushing through a heavy door, she entered a large industrial shed. It reminded her of a mechanical workshop, with all the necessary tools and equipment. There was a group of people standing in front of what looked like a very strange buggy, or truck, or bus. It was just weird. Huge, and weird.

"Hello, you must be Jan. My name is Roy Sandalwood. I'm from C&C."

Roy was no longer a Major in the Air Force because the military had officially been disbanded. Although unofficially, a chain of command and loyalties persisted. Most officers had been merged into C&C, while lower ranks were distributed across the general workforce.

Roy spun around and directed Jan's attention toward the vehicle. Then sounding like a used car salesman said, "So, what do you think?"

Jan took a long look at the futuristic, retropunk, contraption and said, "Um, that depends. What am I looking at?"

"This is the MHEV, short for Mobile Habitat Exploration Vehicle. Isn't she a beauty! It's designed to travel across the surface and can provide weeks of life support for a crew of up to 15 people. We are currently developing a towable module that will double its crew to 30 people."

Jan took a closer look at the vehicle. It was long, had eight large alloy-composite wheels, triple glazed windows circling the whole body, and there were bulbus overhanging windows at the front. Without thinking she blurted out, "It looks like an insect."

The small crowd laughed at her description. She continued, but this time trying to sound more technical and professional, "So, what powers this thing?"

Roy invited one of the other people to answer. He was the stereotypical engineering boffin, compete with hard hat, white lab coat, and clipboard. He proudly said, "It's nuclear powered. We disassembled one of the Trident II D5LE

100 kiloton nuclear missiles from an Ohio-Class submarine we acquired during the Emergency. Then we used some of the lithium-6 deuteride fissile material as fuel. That is, we made up fuel rods."

He was rather cocky and paused for effect, perhaps expecting applause, then continued, "But without getting too technical," which he already had, he said, "we created a thermal exchange engine. It exploits the heat difference been the fuel rods and the -250°C outside temperature. This powerplant will operate for centuries, generating electricity that drives the vehicle's wheels and ancillary systems. It also powers the life support systems including CO_2 scrubbing, and water recycling. The only thing the crew needs to carry is food."

Jan said with a cautious tone, "So, effectively, you have created a nuclear submarine to go on land."

Roy said, "Yes, that about sums it up. And here it is, the MHEV," still sounding like a car salesman. At least it was *new* car salesman.

As Jan walked around the vehicle, her hand gliding over the grey ceramic-feeling metal, she said, "I can see the obvious benefits, especially for scavenging, but do you have a particular purpose in mind, and more to the point, why are you showing it to me?"

After looking at the others, and exchanging

expressions and gestures, Roy said, "Well Jan it's like this, we want you to take it out for a spin."

"Me!?"

"Sure, why not. You have extensive military and civilian heavy transport experience. You also have plenty of surface scavenging experience. And anyway, we want someone who is not familiar with the vehicle to give it a shakedown, just to see what you can break."

Again, the crowd laughed. It seemed like they were easily amused, or perhaps they were nervous, and just perhaps she was going to be used as a guinea pig.

"Don't worry, you won't be going out alone. There will be several technicians and engineers, the people who designed and built the vehicle, going out onto the surface with you," said Roy reassuringly.

He continued, "What we have in mind, is that you do a few laps of the city over the coming week. Just to make sure everything is running as it should, and then we will do some longer trips.

"The last long-distance scavenging trip done by anyone was by yourself when you went to Goulburn. Let's see if we can do that trip again, but hopefully with better success."

Jan thought about if for a while. She walked around the outside of the vehicle and then climbed the steps and inspected the interior. She sat in the driver's seat and gripped the controls.

All the time Roy was explaining what this and that did, pointing out features, and basically doing the car salesman thing.

"OK, I'm in," said Jan. "Anyway, it sounds a bit more exciting than the scavenging duties I've been doing of late."

She had also considered that saying 'no' may not have been an option, at least when she reflected on her army days.

Roy smiled and said, "Excellent, welcome to the team, the Oak Ridge Team. We will spend today doing briefings and preparation, and tomorrow we'll take it outside for its maiden voyage."

Jan wasn't sure what she was getting herself into, or if Roy was being completely honest with her. However, it would be good to get out of the tunnels, and if this was the future of truck driving, then so be it, she'd give it a try.

They gave her a bundle of schematics to take home with her and review before tomorrow. She balanced binders and rolls of blueprints in her arms, all the while opening doors and negotiating stairs. Retracing her steps, she followed the designated paths past the worker bees. They were just as busy and sulphurous as when she had arrived. This meant that the night crew had taken over from the day shift.

As she was about to grab a door handle, it opened toward her, knocking the study material from her grip, and spilling it all over the ground. There was a tall man, dressed in black, coming through the door. He had an air of urgency about himself.

"I am so sorry I startled you. Are you hurt?" he said as he bent down and started picking up the materials.

Jan was a bit annoyed and though to herself, 'Who goes barging through doors when they don't know what's on the other side?' Still, she thought it best to keep her thoughts and comments to herself.

However, the man did seem genuinely sorry, and he was going to lengths to collect and clean every piece of paper, putting them in order before handing them back to her.

He said, "It was completely my fault. I was in a hurry, as usual. I wanted to meet someone before they finished their shift, but I fear I'm going to be too late."

Jan replied, "Well I wouldn't be worrying about that. It's not like they can go anywhere. I'm sure you'll run into them again in this circular micro-world we are all trapped in. The only escape is in your dreams or in death."

He stood back and looked at her, as if she had either said something very offensive, or very profound. He had kind eyes that seemed to look right inside her. For some reason she looked away. That was odd. Involuntary, and odd! And why was she talking all philosophical? Perhaps because she was annoyed, and the incident had let some of her underlying frustration bubble to the surface.

Then she forgot to be annoyed as he replied, "I hope everyone doesn't feel like that. Given the circumstances, we've come a long way from where we started. Regardless, take comfort in the knowledge that I'm working on creating a better future for you, and everyone else. Goodbye."

He turned and walked away as quickly as he had entered. She watched him and thought, what an attractive, but very strange man. As he reached a flight of stairs, he turned back and looked at her, smiled and waved. Then he said the strangest thing, "I'll see you soon."

Jan waved back the best she could, and then puzzled over what on Earth he meant by 'I'll see you soon'?

She arrived home with all of the study materials and spread them out across the floor of the apartment. Mazie and Sally helped her to try and make sense of it all.

They found it very exciting. It was something completely novel and removed from the otherwise drudgery of existence in the tunnels. Yet every now and then her mind would wander to the face of the stranger she had bumped into. That was also a separate and unexpected spark of excitement in her otherwise grey and predictable social life. It felt like change was afoot.

CHAPTER 13

The formal announcement was taking place in the Knowledge lecture hall. The panel, which included Ollie, Roy, and Danny, among others, fronted a crowd of 100 or so scientists, engineers, and eminent persons from various departments. After some administrative announcements, Roy took the microphone and addressed the crowd.

"Distinguished members and guests, you may have heard rumours that we at C&C are proposing a mission, called the Oak Ridge Mission. These rumours are true. However, before getting into the fine details and taking questions and comments from the audience, let me lay out the broad objectives of this mission, as researched and formulated by our Head of State, the great strategist, Mr Oliver Truss."

There was standing applause, but not for Roy. Rather it was for Ollie, whom, since the Emergency was held in high regard by the survivors.

Roy continued, "Now please hear me out before passing judgement. In a nutshell what we intend to do is take two nuclear submarines, each towing a cargo pod, through the Southern Ocean, around Cape Horn, then North through the Atlantic Ocean to Charleston, South Carolina, in the former United States."

There was a murmur in the crowd. After a brief pause, he continued, "This, my friends is, actually, the easy part. We believe the oceans are still navigable, and that we will be able to use historic seafloor bathymetric maps to guide us. It is presumed that we will only encounter a thin covering of sea ice, perhaps less than 1 meter, when we arrive at Charleston. Thus, we should be able to break through to the surface when we arrive.

"When we get there, we will unload our cargo of two Mobile Habitat Exploration Vehicles, or MHEVs, and their accompanying trailer modules. These are surface vehicles that we have recently developed, and they are undergoing trials as we speak.

"This proposed land convoy will be able to carry, and sustain, up to 60 people indefinitely, provided we can scavenge supplies of food enroute. These vehicles will then travel overland 640 kilometres to Oak Ridge, Tennessee, where upon they will establish a temporary, and if possible permanent, habitat.

"The next challenge will be for the mission's crew to reactivate a nuclear power station and thereafter supply power to sections of the Oak Ridge National Laboratory. In this facility are two particle accelerators that we want to bring online, being the Oak Ridge Isochronous Cyclotron, and the 25 MV Tandem Electrostatic Accelerator. And, and…," he paused for a moment and then continued, "and if that were not enough, at the same facility we need to power up equipment in the Fusion Energy Division. This is so we can continue experimental work on magnetic constrained plasma fusion reactions.

"Finally, while we are there, we would like to activate the 200 petaflop Frontier supercomputer. I am also sure we will find many other resources that will be of great value to us. So, if we can salvage them, then that would be a great win."

The director of Knowledge, who also sat on the panel, spoke up, "Essentially my friends, we want to set up a new division of Knowledge at Oak Ridge, to take advantage of the wide range of facilities and resources that are located there."

He then invited questions from the audience. The first question asked was, "Why Oak Ridge was chosen to be the first site for expansion?"

Roy responded, "It has the highest concentration of advanced technologies, and research equipment, in the world, and those capabilities aligned with C&C objectives. It also has the right design of nuclear power station nearby. Meaning, that it was not likely to have gone critical during, or after, the Emergency. And finally, there is a good interstate highway system that should allow the MHEV's to get access to Oak Ridge."

Someone also asked why they didn't just drive the MHEVs across the frozen oceans, especially given that they could reach 80kmh while the submarines only averaged 50kmh. Roy acknowledged that it was a good point, and that in the future, over-land and over-ocean driving may become common place.

However, for now the sea ice was of unknown quantity and quality. Whereas the submarines had been designed for long-distance endurance and had proven life support capabilities. Thus, for now, although the submarines were slower, they were the lower risk option.

He also added that while the MHEVs were on their land mission, one of the submarines would search for other nuclear submarines that may be docked at ports along the east coast of North America, specifically Kings Bay Naval Submarine Base, Georgia.

And finally, for such a long trip, the MHEV's would be less comfortable and could not carry enough food for a crew of 60, along with their equipment as opposed to the submarines.

There were questions about other sites,

but Roy listed the difficulties for each including access, the distance from a power source, the type of power available, or the limited diversity of resources at each site. However, he did acknowledge that if they were successful at Oak Ridge, then there would be no reason why they couldn't investigate other sites as candidates for habitats in the future.

Someone joked that they may need to instigate a breeding program, just so they had enough people to run all the potential sites, to which everyone laughed.

After some more light-hearted banter, Ollie took the microphone and addressed the crowd.

"I'm sure you have many questions, and I am also sure you will have much advice to offer. Valuable and welcome advice. We will establish a directorate to manage all of the correspondence, and to organize further conferences on the matter.

"Now, as you may have guessed, we will be looking for crew members. In some cases, and you know who you are, you are the only person who can practically do the job. If that is you, then I hope that you volunteer, and if you don't, then we may need to have a little chat."

He paused and smiled, some people laughed, and some just squirmed in their seats.

Then he continued, "Given everything we have gone through in the past year, I assure you that this is a lower risk mission compared to what has been asked of you in the past."

He then changed his tone.

"You must be wondering why we are engaging in such an ambitious mission, especially so soon after the Emergency. Why don't we just sit back and relax now that the habitats have stabilized? Why don't we start to enjoy our lives down here in the tunnels, perhaps spend a decade or more making it more pleasant, and let a new form of termite society grow and flourish?

"Well to this I say, I am not convinced that the Emergency is over. I do not believe that the current habitat model is a long-term prospect. Sure, we can exist, but there are still risks of failure, and more so, in time I believe it will crush our spirit. We are a species of dreamers and explorers. It is in our DNA to venture over the horizon.

"Thus, our long-term goal must be to colonize, not only other parts of the Earth, this doomed and dying Earth, but to find other worlds and colonize them. We need to find suitable planets, and presently we are so far from that goal that it is almost ridiculous to contemplate.

"To break free from the Earth, and to explore new worlds, we need, by today's standards, incredibly advanced technology. If we remain here in the habitats as we currently are, it may take decades, through to centuries, to develop the kind of technology needed to chase our dreams."

He then gestured toward Danny and continued, "My friend, Danny, has an idea. An idea that is so outlandish, that under normal circumstances it would simply be dismissed out of hand. However, nothing is normal anymore, and by my reckoning, it is our best chance at a new and brighter future. It is acknowledged that it may not work out as Danny hopes, but what we learn along the way, both in the sciences, and about ourselves, will still be worth the effort.

"We need a dream, a goal. We could even call it a religion. And it must be big. Really big. And it must be long term, and by that I mean intergenerational. I put it to you that finding another planet, another Earth, is that dream.

"Now for that to happen, we must develop the ability, once again, to launch ourselves into space. But to not only do that, but to be able to travel faster and farther than we ever thought possible. We must create a new reality for ourselves and for all humanity."

Following his speech there was enthusiastic applause, and also much discussion between the attendees. He did his best to talk to everyone who was there, but it was a difficult for him to maintain the public persona. He did not like crowds or all the attention. Yes, he could give a rousing speech, but only when he thought of it as a performance. Something he could walk away from once it was delivered and return to his own skin.

Later that night, when he was alone in his room, he reflected upon his speech and the mission. It was such a long-shot, and there would be many dangers. So many things could go wrong.

This was not a game where one could re-spawn if they died. Yet he had to have faith in himself and his judgement. It *was* he who had kept this fragment of humanity alive, and against insurmountable odds. Now as their leader, which was a term he wasn't very comfortable with, he had to now sell this new dream. The belief in a science fiction, planet hopping, future. Even he found it a bit outlandish.

It was almost as if he had to start a cult and have them follow blindly. And should something happen to him, which was a real possibility, the dream, and the momentum, must continue. He had to make it bigger than himself, and any personality cult that may, or may not, develop around him.

Part of the reason why he had, for the most part, remained in the shadows, and let the politicians be the face of stability and authority, was to cultivate a mystique of administrative knowledge and superiority in the eyes of the general population. And, with regard to himself, it was better that they did not see him as a mere mortal.

This was a subtle, but insidious, control strategy older than pharaonic Egypt. He just had to be sure he didn't start believing his own press or 'Drink the Kool-Aid'. It was arrogant, and under other circumstances, would be considered morally corrupt, but still it had gotten them through the difficult times. Society wasn't ready for full secularism and democracy. But crucially, he must also recognize when it was ready.

CHAPTER 14

Jan climbed the ladder and stood on the vehicle's mesh platform. It was about 2 meters above the ground. Directly in front of her was the MHEV's side airlock. There was another airlock on the other side, and one at the rear which doubled as the connector tube when towing a trailer module.

The doors were like those found on, now obsolete, jetliners. They had big hand levers and airtight seals, except in this case, they were using a two-door system with a decompression chamber between them.

Inside, the vehicle was spacious and well appointed. It reminded her of the passenger saloon on a sea going ferry, like the one she had taken when island hopping in Greece.

The cabin was four seats wide, and each seat reclined to form a bed. At the back of the vehicle was a kitchenette, washroom, and toilet. Up front there were three seats, with the outer two for pilot and co-pilot respectively. The center seat was for a navigator or commander, it was the shotgun seat. Otherwise, it simply folded down to make a map table. There was an almost $360°$ view

from the cabin, as well as windows in the roof.
Jan sat in the driver's seat, and like in a glass-bubble-helicopter, she could see the ground below her feet.

She could feel a slight humming coming up through the cabin floor. It was the nuclear thermal generator that kept the batteries charged and provided heat for the cabin and other components. Another five technicians joined her in the MHEV, the last one closing both the outer and inner airlock doors.

Roy came through on the intercom, "Come in, MHEV. Can you hear me? Over."

The person in the copilot chair replied, "KI-44. Affirmative. Loud and Clear. Over"

"MHEV, we are opening the KI-44 inner airlock door. Proceed to airlock chamber and then hold position. Over."

This time Jan responded, "Roger. Wilco. Proceeding to airlock chamber now. Over"

As she activated the accelerator, the large heavy vehicle started to move forward. It was silent, smooth, and effortless, as the eight large metal wheels, shod with some exotic mesh, rolled over the polished concrete floor.

The vehicle stopped in the airlock, and the inner door closed behind them with a solid thump. They were then blasted from every angle with hot dry air to remove as much moisture as possible from the MHEV's surface. This was to minimize icing when the temperature dropped.

A warning siren sounded, and lights began to flash red as the air began to be evacuated. They held their position at zero atmosphere while technicians checked for any leaks or problems. After a few minutes the technicians gave the all-clear.

"Come in, KI-44. All systems optimal. MHEV is ready to commence surface operation. Over," reported Jan.

"MHEV. Copy. Commencing opening the outer airlock door. Over.

There was no sound as the outer airlock seal cracked open despite splinters of ice and powder falling to the floor. With no atmosphere there was no medium for sound waves to propagate. The only noticeable force acting upon the world now was gravity. The planet was as silent as deep space. Hence, if the proverbial tree fell in the forest, then no, no one would hear it.

The cold was creeping into the airlock, but with zero atmosphere, it was slow and invisible. There was no swoosh or billowing clouds of snow and ice. Like sound, the cold had no medium upon which to travel. It was simply the absence of heat. Therefore, it could only draw-out the energy from surfaces at the rate at which those surfaces could radiate their heat and slow the vibration of their atoms.

And now, with the total absence of any

atmospheric particles, surfaces like the MHEV's outer skin could be at -260°C, yet have no coating of ice to indicate their frozen state. A damp spacesuit glove grabbing a door handle could immediately freeze to the surface, effectively cementing the wearer to the surface. For this reason, special materials, and strict safety protocols, were required. Those traveling to the surface, and especially those that would be engaging in extra-vehicular activities, were effectively, astronauts.

The co-pilot dimmed the cabin lights and then turned on the external lights. Bright beams shone out front, while running lights illuminated the sides and the ground beneath.

Jan drove the MHEV carefully out of the airlock and into the night, the big wheels biting into, and gripping, the hard icy road. Through the rear camera she could see the outer airlock door of KI-44 closing behind them. There was no reason to leave it open and pointlessly draw down the temperature in the airlock, only to have to restore it later.

She looked across at the co-pilot and asked, "How is it looking?"

He gave her the thumbs up, and through his space suit intercom replied, "All systems good."

All the crew were wearing their space suits just in case there was a catastrophic failure.

Jan partially turned and ask the same of those sitting behind her, to which they replied, "All systems good."

Jan then called Roy.

"Come in KI-44. This is MHEV. Reporting all systems nominal. It's a beautiful night for a drive. Requesting permission to commence trials. Over"

"MHEV. Copy, all systems nominal. Proceed with trials. Repeat, proceed with trials. Over."

"KI-44. Roger that. Proceeding with trials. MHEV is just going to nip down the shops for a carton of milk. See you soon. Over."

"MHEV. Affirmative, enjoy the drive. Over and out."

They drove slowly along the abandoned motorways that ringed the city. Road signs, power poles, trees, grass, and buildings, all snap frozen and covered in crystals. Some comprised of water, others of oxygen or nitrogen, each reflecting at different wavelengths.

The bright light beams from the MHEV splintered when striking the crystals, refracting a rainbow of colours. It was beautiful, mesmerising, and yet haunting at the same time. Everything looked so fragile and otherworldly. So cold, brittle, motionless and untouched. There was nothing to break a single crystal or to dislodge a sheet of ice. Was this what death looked like? Is this what hell would look like if it froze over?

They spent a few hours negotiating the city before returning through KI-44's outer airlock door. The vehicle sat in the airlock while slowly being brought up to temperature. Warm air flooded in, and the pressure increased.

It looked as if the MHEV had been on fire. A smoky fog poured off the vehicle's surface and spread out across the floor. The process was akin to a deep-water diver staging their ascent to avoid the bends.

Finally, after 15 minutes, the internal airlock door was opened, and they drove back into the bright, warm, habitat. The first trial was a success.

They repeated this process, each simulated day, for a week, traveling further and further from the habitat, and negotiating different terrains with each mission. They also tested the MHEV's airlocks, having technicians in spacesuits leave and re-enter the vehicle. All systems worked as designed.

The air in the cabin remained sweet and fresh. Perhaps, it was even better than the habitat's tunnels. And importantly, it maintained a comfortable cabin temperature. By the end of testing, they no longer wore their full space suits, although they kept them close in case of an unexpected depressurization.

Finally, the day came when they were going

to make the 185km journey to Goulburn and back. They had done trials towing the trailer module, or the TM as it became known, so it was decided to take it with them.

The TM was basically a people, or cargo, carrier that received its power and heating via an umbilical from the MHEV. A flexible connector joined the two, and people could transfer between them without having to go outside of the vehicles.

A second MHEV had also been completed, but it would remain on standby at KI-44 in case they got into any trouble, and it had to come out and rescue them.

Technicians had developed small portable telecommunication relays, effectively mini cell towers, which were stacked in the TM. It was intended to place these at high points along the route, so that they could maintain contact with KI-44 throughout their journey.

Jan liked to start work early. This afforded her the time to give the MHEV a thorough inspection, and to run diagnostics, just for her own peace of mind. It was a hangover from her days as an outback trucker, and it had saved her on more than one occasion.

She wore the Oak Ridge Team uniform. It was a bright orange jumpsuit, not unlike what prisoners used to wear. It was double layered, with a quickly inflatable thermal gap between fabrics. It wasn't the normal or proper spacesuit. However, in an emergency, argon gas would be pumped between the layers to put pressure against the wearers body, and to provide a thermal barrier against the cold.

The helmet and gloves could be snapped rapidly into place and were stowed close by. There was about 5 minutes' worth of oxygen in a tank attached to the back of the helmet. This would give you enough time to put on the proper spacesuit, with its extended oxygen supply and CO_2 scrubber. She was familiar with these latter suits because they were the same design she had used when working on scavenger detail.

She sat in the pilot's seat reviewing technical specifications. You never know when you may need to jump-start a nuclear reactor. The crew began to file in, and she was surprised to see that Roy was joining them.

"Hello, Captain", he said in a cheerful voice. "Permission to come aboard?"

She laughed, "You don't have to ask permission. It's your MHEV isn't it? I'm just the chauffeur."

Roy sat in the seat behind her and said, "Well, it's not actually mine." Then he pointed out the window at a man walking toward the vehicle and said, "If it belongs to anyone, then it would be him, that guy in the black."

Jan looked up and said, "OK, so who is

he supposed to be when he's not cosplaying Dracula?"

"That, my dear Jan, is the boss. And I do mean, *The* Boss. The great and venerable Mr Oliver Truss."

"What him! Nooo, you're kidding me, right? Isn't Truss some elderly professor, or eminent statesman or something? Not a kid. Not a Goth looking kid. I mean, I've only heard about him, I've never seen his picture, or heard his voice, or anything, but surely that's not him."

"Well, I grant you that he does look young, but he's actually the same age as you. And don't let appearances fool you, he is more eminent and professorial than any one, or any combination, of people within the habitat.

"That man there is the reason you are alive, and the reason that humanity has a second chance. In my book, he is a freak of nature, and yet I'm glad to say that I work for him, and that I can call him a friend."

She felt a bit embarrassed by her previous comments and said, "You won't tell him what I said, will you?"

Roy laughed, "Your secret is safe with me. Oh, and when you meet him, just treat him like you would treat me, or anyone else. On the outside, and when dealing with you and me, he is just a normal person. He is only different on the inside, in his mind, and how he interacts with himself, if you get what I mean.

"So, there you are, talking about something with him. Everything is normal, and then 'Bam', out of the blue, he will say something so profound and inexplicable that you think, 'Where in the heck did that just come from?' And before you know it, a problem is solved, a plan is made, or a strategy is being devised. It's like he is dropping pearls as he walks and talks, and we mere mortals are just following him and trying to scoop them up."

Roy laughed again and said, "I hope I haven't scared you."

"No, I'm fine, he's still human like the rest of us. OK, maybe only *just* human, but he still bleeds red like the rest of us. I just hope he has a good sense of humour. He's going to need it after spending the next 5 hours cramped in here with the rest of us."

"I don't think he's going to complain. He actually designed the MHEV. Sure, he left the technical details and construction to others, with their specialist skills and qualifications, but essentially this is his baby, so you had better treat it well. No fender benders."

"Ha, if you haven't noticed, this MHEV is also my baby, so he's going to have to learn to share his toys."

Jan had seamlessly transitioned from her former truck to the MHEV. She was always proud of her rig and kept it clean and polished. If there had been chrome on the MHEV, then she would have been sure to polish it after every trip. Even now she had placed bins in the cabin and instructed crew to use them and keep the kitchenette tidy.

When she was on the road, therefore on a mission, it was her home away from home and an extension of her personality. And those rules would apply to Ollie, whether he liked it or not.

CHAPTER 15

Ollie stood before the MHEV and admired its elegant simplicity. It was built to fulfill a specific purpose, and he hoped that it would do that flawlessly. It was a tool and a step toward a greater goal.

When he came up with the design, unlike engineers of the past, he didn't have to worry about so many things. These included aesthetics, speed, handling, aerodynamics, sunshine and heat, fuel efficiency, or construction costs. None of the things that were typically associated with vehicle design. Instead, all he needed to create was a habitat that could move over land, or the frozen ocean, with both surfaces being as solid as concrete and as slippery as a skating rink.

However, many of the obstacles that they would encounter, such as trees, or even metal structures, would be so brittle they would disintegrate with the slightest push.

The design brief was to ensure the crew were safe and comfortable, and that they could survive in the MHEV long enough to get to Oak Ridge, establish a habitat there, and then return to the submarines.

Of course, in the future there would be additional, and improved, MHEVs. Ones that were purpose built for a range of tasks, but he would leave that for others to design and build.

His primary goal was still to get off the planet. He needed Danny to succeed and develop the 'alternate reality drive', or whatever crazy name they were going to call it. Then, depending on what form that drive took, he and others would come up with spaceships capable of exploring the galaxy and colonizing other planets. Unlike Earth, planets that actually had a sun, an atmosphere, water, and hopefully friendly life.

But as usual, he was so many steps ahead of himself and his situation, that his head was spinning. For now, he was just going to accompany Roy and the crew on the MHEV's first extended trial. By gaining firsthand experience, he could make any adjustments for the success of the Oak Ridge Mission before it embarked.

Ollie climbed the ladder and entered the cabin. Roy was there to greet him with a hearty handshake.

"Hello boss, welcome aboard. We have a suit for you. You can either slip it on over your clothes, or you can change in the washroom down back."

"I'll just quickly change, otherwise it may

get a bit hot and uncomfortable with the spacesuit over my clothes."

By the time he returned in his orange jump suit, all the crew had settled into their seats, and the airlock had been sealed. Roy invited Ollie to sit in the center seat up front, between himself and Jan.

Roy said, "Here you go, sir, you can ride shotgun," then he continued, "Please allow me to introduce our driver, pilot, captain. This is Jan. Jan; this is Mr Ollie Truss."

Jan then realised where she had seen him before. It was that guy that knocked the papers out of her arms a few weeks back. He looked at her with those same eyes. So, this is what he meant by, "I'll see you soon." So, he knew who she was all along, that sneaky so and so.

They both said, "It's a pl..." at the same time while reaching to shake hands.

Jan laughed and said, "Oh, sorry. I was just going to say it's a pleasure to meet you."

"Haha, same," said Ollie, "So, let me also say, it is a pleasure to meet you, Jan." Then he said, "Umm, I think I may be needing my hand back now, or at least before the end of the journey."

Jan giggled and clumsily pulled away. She did not realize that she had continued holding his hand even as he tried to pull away. She felt she may have blushed on the inside, and maybe just a little on the outside also. Quickly she returned to her seat and began pushing buttons and shifting levers in a desperate attempt to appear composed and professional. Ollie sat next to her and watched how she negotiate the MHEV into the decompression chamber. She did indeed come across as professional and accomplished.

They went through the slow routine in preparation for surfacing, then exited the outer airlock door. The MHEV with its TM in tow, now truly looked like an insect with 16 legs and a segmented body. Even the forward communication antennae that protruded at an angle above the front bubble windows added to the look of a giant centipede scuttling across the landscape.

They headed onto the motorway, and within about 15 minutes they had reached an elevation suitable to deploy the first transmitter. One of the technicians went aft into the TM and prepared the apparatus. Another technician suited up ready to leave the vehicle via the TM airlock and emplace the unit.

Like with the MHEV, surface astronauts had to be dehydrated before the air was evacuated from the chamber. After 5 minutes, the technician opened the outer airlock door and stepped onto the mesh platform. They lowered the transmitter to the ground and climbed down the ladder. The rest of the crew watched through the side windows.

The whole outside scene was illuminated by the side lights. Jan, however, stayed in her seat. She could see everything happening outside via remote cameras. She also wanted to monitor vital systems and be able to respond quickly at the controls should the need arise.

The transmitter was placed a short distance from the vehicle, and a bright green beacon flashed on the top of its telescopic mast. The transmitter was powered using a nuclear battery, like satellites and space probes in the past. The transmitters were intended to be temporary until a more permanent overland solution could be put into place. The technician returned to the airlock without incident, and for expediency went through re-pressurisation while the MHEV drove to the next site.

Ollie immediately recognized that a systems change was necessary, given how much time was wasted in handling and using the airlock. In the future they would store the transmitter on the outside of the vehicle and deploy them remotely. 'Oh, well,' he thought, 'just a teething issue exposed by personal observation'. That was now the second reason he was glad he came on this particular mission.

It took them about four and a half hours to do the 185 kms to Goulburn, including the regular stops to place transmitters. The communication network allowed them to stay in contact with KI-44 and, in time, they would do a line of them all the way to Canberra, and then probably though to Melbourne, thus opening an overland route. It was almost as if the pilgrims, or colonists, were heading West over virgin country. Manifest destiny and all that stuff.

As they headed toward the now abandoned staging post on the railway siding, they passed the truck that Jan had been driving when it slid off the road. It was exactly how she remembered it, perhaps with an additional coating of ice from atmospheric deposition.

Perhaps one day it would be recovered, or scavenged, or something. It wasn't like it was going to rust or deteriorate in any way. So, unless someone, or something, interfered with it, it would just stay on display forever. A permanent reminder of her stupid cockup.

They passed the staging post, with its doors left open and remnants of resources stacked by the railroad. It was obvious it had been abandoned in a hurry.

Roy then suggested they do a proper lap of the town while they were there.

In the recent past there wouldn't have been time for the luxury of sightseeing, or for that matter, returning to the habitat without of full load of scavenged resources. It was hard to believe how far they had come, and how secure they were after only 12 months. Secure enough to go sightseeing.

Jan thought to herself, this Ollie Truss guy really did come through for all of us. Sure, it was hard, and everyone worked and lived like slaves, at first, but it was a necessary evil. But just look at where they, and she, are now. Joyriding nearly 200km away from the habitat.

They drove down the main street of Goulburn with its grand Victorian-era buildings. The cut sandstone blocks glistening in the beams of light. They passed the Big Merino, the giant ram tourist attraction, now looking like an attraction in a long abandoned fair ground. It was comical to see, as if they were looking at some fictional life. One that had never really existed, which was crazy, because it was their own past they were looking at.

So much had happened since then, so much had changed that it was now difficult to even relate to it anymore. Then again, just when Jan was thinking that, Roy spotted a wine shop and said, "You know, they did very good wine in this region. How about we scavenge that store there," and he pointed to the store. "I'm sure when we get back, we can find a reason to celebrate."

"Do you think the glass bottles, or the wine, would have survived freezing," asked Jan.

"Well, Jan," replied Ollie, "In the name of science I think we should find out. And I agree with Roy. We should pick up a few cases to celebrate the success of this mission."

"You're the boss," said Jan. "I'll just pull alongside and shine the side lights into the shop."

Two technicians suited up and scavenged the liquor store. They managed to retrieve several cases of different varietals, all perfectly preserved in their glass bottles.

It was decided not to take the risk of bringing the bottles up to temperature inside the MHEV, so they stowed them on the mesh platforms that ran down each side of the vehicle. Only when they were back at the habitat would they attempt to re-heat the bottles, doing it very slowly though a small airlock adjacent to KI-44.

The return journey along the Hume Highway only took two and a half hours because they no longer needed to stop and place transmitters. The green flashing beacons were heart-lifting each time one came into view. As cold and inanimate as they were, they still represented a sign of life, each a comfort on the soulless surface.

Then, as each beacon was passed, they counted down, one after the other, getting closer to home. When they finally reached KI-44, Jan stopped the MHEV by a side entry, and the cases of wine were unloaded. Technicians in space suits placed them in an airlock and closed its outer door. They would manage the slow re-heating from inside the building. Those technicians then walked to KI-44's main airlock where the MHEV was waiting. The outer door was closed, and pressurisation began.

When they finally entered the building proper, they were greeted by a crowd, and congratulated on their success. Ollie had disappeared into the back of the MHEV to change out of his suit. Jan walked around the outside of the vehicle, personally inspecting it to make sure there was no damage to the wheels or external surfaces. She thought to herself, *No one else has changed their clothes. Doesn't Ollie think orange suits him or something? Surely, he couldn't be that vain, or that insecure?*

Ollie finally emerged through the airlock and climbed down the stairs. He walked over to Jan and personally congratulated her on her driving and all-around professionalism. She felt a little humbled and wasn't sure what to say. Then she just blurted something awkward, again!

"Aww, its nothing compared to what you have done. We are all so grateful, sir."

"Ollie, please, call me Ollie," he said.

"Ok, Ollie, hi I'm Jan." *Oh my god, did I just say that?*, thought Jan.

"Um yes I know, we met in MHEV earlier." He laughed and she giggled.

"Thank you for your kind words. I actually don't do much. I just think things up. It's other people that then make them or make things happen. I just pride myself in finding the right person for the right job."

"Well, then you do that well," and this time she managed to say all of that while maintaining eye contact.

"Well Jan, I'll see you soon, goodbye."

The Ollie turned and briskly walked away. Jan thought to herself, *There, he's done it again! When will he see me, and why will he be seeing me. Who is this funny man?*

Ollie looked back at her as he opened the door to exit the workshop, smiled, waved, and repeated, "Soon."

He was starting to grow on her. It had been a long time since she had felt anything remotely like the tingle of romance. Could that be what just happened? Could that be possible? Her a single mom truck driver, and him, the saviour of humanity and venerated as a demigod.

She spent some time with her work colleagues before heading home. It felt good to be accepted into their ranks, even though they had qualifications she couldn't begin to understand. And yet, as their pilot they actually looked up to her. They relied upon her for safety and for guidance. How strange her world had become.

CHAPTER 16

It had been several days since the expedition to Goulburn. Jan was in the apartment helping Sally with her schoolwork. It was her rostered day off, so she bummed around in her pyjamas, her hair in a clown-like spiky tangle.

All students were required to learn modern history as part of the curriculum. Some of that could be taught through formal texts, but some, including the subtleties of human society pre-Emergency, could not. It required discussions with someone who had lived through those decadent carefree years of the early 21st century.

To complete one assignment, students had to interview an older person, and Sally had chosen Jan. She had joked if this now meant she was a senior citizen? Ironically, given the habitat's demographics, it actually did. The baby boom had already begun and soon the demographic pyramid would be inverted.

Already Sally, and other children, were beginning to forget things. Like how money had worked, or what it was like to go shopping for food at a supermarket, drive home, and then to prepare a meal in one's own kitchen. It now seemed such a strange concept, and so time-consuming and wasteful. It was difficult for Jan to convey to Sally that this was not only how people lived, but it was how they wanted to live.

For Sally, and her generation, life, society, work, and nature were all one. All bundled together in an area you could survey in a single day. Everything was interconnected and any impact upon one, had consequences on another, be that people, or anything else in the habitat.

Jan tried to explain, although quite unsuccessfully, that that is how it had always been. It's just that in the past it was on a so much larger scale, and that sometimes the consequences did not become obvious for years. Sometimes not even until generations later.

She tried to explain global warming to Sally, but the idiocy of it was just lost on her. Sally couldn't understand. In her world every breath was precious, and every morsel of food so hard won and valuable. It was inconceivable that people in the past could just pump poison and gas into the atmosphere, and this was despite knowing that it would eventually destroy their crops, their climate, or more to the point, their very global habitat. Sally repeatedly questioned whether people of the past were sane, and couldn't understand how democracy and the laws could have failed the Earth and the poor so badly.

For Sally, and all the other children, habitat was the world, it was everything. The relationship was symbiotic. They were part of it, and it was part of them. And humanity was also a single organism. If one person is hurt or disadvantaged, then this reflects upon, and hurts, everyone.

There was a knock at the door, and through the opaque plastic film they could see the blurry outline of a person. Sally jumped up and ran to the door, opening it with no fear of strangers, no shyness, or embarrassment. This is how one becomes when surrounded by a family of tens of thousands.

She looked up at a tall man dressed in black. He had a kind and young-looking face, which seemed at odds with the formal, and somewhat sinister look of his attire. She had not seen many people who looked like him. Most people wore plain work overalls, light cloth shoes, and their hair was short, or shaved. They dressed for life in the tunnels, with its steady temperature and paved walkways. Clothing fashion had not re-emerged since the Emergency, but it surely would in time, along with unique hair styles and makeup. It's just what people did when they were secure enough for those types of individual expression.

"Hello, you must be Sally. My name is Ollie. I'm please to make your acquaintance."

Sally giggled at the man's formality and extended her had.

"Hello, Mr Ollie. Yes, I am Sally. How may I help you?"

"I have come to see if Jan is at home, and I am wondering if you would let me speak to her."

Sally turned around and called out, "Jaaann, there's a man here to see you."

Jan was still in her pyjamas and knew her hair was a mess.

"Who is it, Sally?"

"It's Mr Ollie. He wants to talk to you."

Jan gasped. "Arrr! Tell him I'll be out in a minute. Close the door, close the door."

"Mr Ollie, Jan says she will be out in a minute. I must close the door now, she needs to get dressed, but don't go anywhere."

Jan ran around the apartment looking for clothes, getting dressed, and trying to stop her hair from sticking out in all directions.

Sally and Mazie watched her, whispering to each other and then giggling.

"What are you two gossiping about?" she asked.

"Oh, it's just that we've never seen you fuss over a man so much," said Mazie.

Then Sally enquired, "Is he your boyfriend?" and they both giggled again.

Jan looked indignant and flustered.

"No, no, of course not. He is just a very

important man."

"Who is this very important man?" enquired Sally.

"It is only Mr Oliver Truss, the designer of the habitat and, some may say, the saviour of humanity."

"Really!" squealed Sally, and she ran back over to the door and opened it just slightly so she could peek out. Ollie was still standing there and saw her.

Sally said through the crack, "She is almost ready. She is putting on some nice clothes and brushing her hair."

Jan screamed and threw some clothing at Sally, yelling, "Stop it you little horror! Get back in here."

"Oh, my God," said Mazie, "and you're going out on a date with him? Wait 'till I tell my friends."

"Maaazie, I'm not going out on a date, and don't you dare tell anyone. I'm sure it's just something to do with work. Remember how I drove the MHEV a few days back? Well Ollie, I mean, Mr. Truss, was part of the crew. I'm sure he just wants to talk about that."

Finally, Jan opened the door, the beaming faces of the two girls peering past her.

"Hello, Mr Truss. What a surprise to see you."

But, she thought to herself, *what kind of guy*

just turns up at a girl's house without an invitation. Surely it must be work related, of course its work related, bummer!

"Hello Jan."

He then pulled a bottle out from a bag, winked at Mazie, and said, "I'm here for our date."

Mazie jumped up and down excitedly saying, "I knew it, I knew it, I knew it."

"Oh my God, you could hear us, you could hear everything, how embarrassing," said a flustered Jan

Sally smiled and said, "I like him," and both girls proceeded to push Jan out the door.

Mazie said in a cheeky voice, "Have fuuunnn", as they went back inside and quickly closed the door.

"I'm so sorry about that, they're just kids having fun."

"Oh, that's perfectly fine. We need more fun. Everyone, and everything, is too serious. I'm too serious. Sometimes I think that we forget why we are living. It certainly can't be just to toil and worry, surely. That's one of the great things about having Roy Sandalwood around, he always jokes and lifts the mood. He reminds me to have fun."

"Yes, you are right. I like Roy. He's good to have around."

"Anyway, Jan, I suppose this is a date. Sorry I didn't call you in advance."

"Oh, dear. I mean, um, that's OK."

"You see, I've got one of the bottles from the Goulburn trip, fresh out of the decompression chamber. It hasn't been opened yet, so I hope it's still OK. I have some things I want to talk to you about, and I thought we could go somewhere pleasant and discuss them over this bottle of wine."

"Well, aren't you a surprise, and a gentleman. That sounds wonderful, where would you like to go?"

"I know a very special and secret place."

"OK, I'm intrigued, lead the way." How strange, she trusted his judgement, and she trusted him. She supposed that if he was the saviour of humanity, then who was she to judge his character or intentions.

They walked through Jan's residential tunnel, and then caught a trolly to the far side of the habitat, a place she had never seen before. The trolley stopped in the middle of a horticultural precinct. There were planters with trellises running from the floor to the ceiling. LED lights covered the firmament like a million tiny suns, and the plants wound around their supports stretching for the light. The vines were heavy with bounty, including cucumbers and melons. It was a Cornucopia of fruits and vegetables providing the population with some traditional fresh food. This added balance to the scavenged tins of dehydrated stocks, and the vats of yeast and bacteria that had been the staple.

The sealed precinct was also alive with insects to pollinate the plants, and to keep a biological balance. Bees and butterflies took to the air as Ollie and Jan pushed their way through the thickets until they reached a concealed doorway.

Ollie unlocked the door, which was unusual because there were very few locks in the habitats. They stepped into a long dim connector tunnel and the door automatically closed and locked behind them. Their footsteps echoed as they walked. It was unusually long for a connector tunnel, and it took about 5 minutes before they reached the door at the other end. Ollie then said, "This is an area that has remained off-limits. Information of its existence has been on a need-to-know basis, so you'll have to keep it secret for now."

Jan was a bit excited by the intrigue, and felt privileged that he would bring her here, wherever or whatever here was going to be.

When Ollie opened the door, the light was bright in their eyes and made them squint until they could adjust. Jan stepped out onto the grass of what she thought to be a vast mountain meadow. At one end it was high and rocky, extending beyond her line of sight. Then there was a long sloping plain that reached all the way to a distant lake.

The panorama must have been one to two

kilometres in length. However, due to the clever use of graphics and design, it gave the illusion of being completely un-restrained in width and length.

One could believe that mountains rose on three sides surrounding a valley, and then a vast plain stretched out beyond the distant lake. The ground was covered in meadow grasses, sedges, and herbs. A cloud of vibrant blooms floated above the green carpet, of red, yellow, purple, and white flowers. There was a gentle breeze blowing from the lake and up the valley to the mountains, making the grass and flowers sway.

Insects and birds busied themselves among the flowers and bushes, while various grazing animals were scattered across the landscape. It was the perfect recreation of springtime in the mountains. It made her want to run through the meadow like a child, to pick flowers, chase butterflies, and to swim and frolic in the lake. All that was missing was a cow with a bell, Heidi, and a Swiss chalet.

Jan just stood there, wide eyed and speechless. Her long blonde hair being tossed in the breeze.

"Not too shabby, hey," said Ollie with a beaming smile.

Jan though to herself, *"Not too shabby?"*. *Well, that's the understatement of the year.* It was absolutely glorious, like something out of a travel brochure or a daydream.

Ollie continued, "This is one of the environments we created as part of our genetic preservation program. It includes the genetic ancestors, and cousins, of many domesticated plants and animals. It is also used to cycle through our stocks of breeding animals, and therefore, have a particular species in for a week and then back into the stables, replaced by a different mix of animals. We don't want some of the animals to become too domesticated.

"Many of these plants also need to be grazed, or grown under certain conditions, that could only be replicated in a semi-natural environment. There are even fish and aquatic animals in the creeks, ponds, and lakes, which includes both fresh and salt water. In those we are hoping to stimulate fish migration and spawning.

"We also simulate the seasons, presently it's spring, and those animals you see in various small herds, including deer, sheep, goats, and there is even bison, are starting to breed.

"We also have other locations that simulate different ecosystems, including ones for the African savanna, American prairie, Russian Steppes, and the Australian outback."

Jan said, "I am speechless. Truly speechless. It is just so beautiful. The scale is immense. I feel like we are really there, like maybe somewhere in Switzerland or Colorado. Those mountains look so real, I feel like I could climb them. I want to climb them."

"It is a mix of clever design and optical illusions. However, you are correct. Compared to the scale of habitats you are used to; it is truly immense. And in fact, you have not seen all of it yet. If you look down there to the left, you will notice a small glade of trees. What you don't see though, is that those trees are at the entrance to an adjoining tunnel. That tunnel simulates a dense temperate forest, complete with all the plants and animals you would expect to find in a natural forest.

"We simulate day, night, the phases of the moon, and even the weather. When we want it to rain, we dim the lights and sprinkle water from the sky, well, the ceiling, but let's pretend it's the sky. In fact, if you look up toward the mountains you will see a light shower of rain. It is those regular showers that keep the springs fed and the creeks running," said Ollie.

Jan said with disbelief, "Why is this hidden? Shouldn't everyone get to experience this? I mean, it would just be so soothing and nostalgic for people."

"Yes, you are right. Everyone should be able to experience this, and the other natural ecosystems. Trust me when I say they will in time. But, you must remember that these are only recently established, they are very fragile, and we are still ironing out some of the bugs in the system.

"Also, you will recall that immediately after the Emergency, we were extremely pressed for safe spaces, and we had people stuffed in wherever we could put them. It was very difficult for everyone. What do you think would have happened if people found out that we were allocating prime igloo, or tunnel space, for rare or predatory animals, or plant species? There would have been riots.

"Most people from our generation don't understand what is required to survive. They only think of packaged food and bottles of filtered water. Yet, the web of life is so much more complex than that. What we are trying to do here is the preserve that complexity, and even allow it to evolve.

"We will not repeat the same mistakes with the following generations. They are taught, and live, the experience of being connected with nature, and to understand the value in all the intricate pieces that go into making it up."

"But what about things like seed vaults? Can't we just preserve things as seeds and then plant them when we have the space for it?"

"Yes, seed vaults, and the like, are very important, and soon we will mount a mission to the Svalbard Global Seed Vault in Norway to see what we can revive. That is, when we create additional habitat space to plant them in.

"Unfortunately, at present, our technology isn't advanced enough to preserve animals in suspended-animation vaults. We must have live animals, and we need to feed those animals, and the insects, and the soil, and the water organisms. Thus, we needed to preserve living ecosystems. Life comes as a package deal. You can't *just* have the bits you want, or the parts that are convenient. You take it all or nothing. So sure, seeds are fine, but they are only a small part of the total package."

As they talked, they walked uphill toward a rocky outcrop below a cliff. A flock of long horn sheep bleated and moved further up the rocky slope, before disappearing into a side tunnel partially obscured by rocks and bushes. They sat down on some flat rocks that formed perfect seats, and beside another rock that formed a perfect table.

"Did you design this?" asked Jan. "I mean look at it. This is almost the perfect outdoor dining setting."

As Ollie took the bottle, and two glasses, out of the bag, he said, "Well, actually, now that you mention it, yes, I did. Or more to the point, I suggested it to the construction crew. I said to them, 'Do you think you could give me somewhere to sit, where I can think and plan, and survey and enjoy the surroundings?' So, this is what they came up with.

"I really like coming here, especially in the evenings. Every day there is a simulated sunset where the ceiling turns orange and dims, and at the correct date, an image of the moon rises over the lake. In reality, it is just historical footage on video screens, but from most angles it looks authentic."

"Thus, the heavens and the earth were completed in all their vast array. And on the seventh day God finished the work. So, he rested and sat on a rock, surveyed it, and said, 'aren't I a clever chap?'"

"Haha, yes, sometimes it does feel like I'm acting like the God of creation and believe me when I say it's extremely satisfying when it all works out."

"How often do you come here?" asked Jan.

"Oh, let me think. Maybe once a week? On other days I may go to similar ecosystems, like a desert or a coastline, just to check on how they are progressing, and to think, and sometimes just to spend time alone. I'm a bit of an introvert, so I don't do so well in the crowded tunnels. I need my space and my peace."

"Say, what? We have a coastline?"

"Yes, it is not very large, but it simulates a rocky headland and a beach, complete with waves and tides. We pump in water from the real ocean, which unfortunately is slowly dying. We warm and aerate it, and then mix it with our living water.

"So, yeah, you can have a day at the beach. You can even swim. It's relatively safe because we keep the sharks and other things that bite, or sting, in separate aquariums."

"So, how many people have you brought to this exact spot?"

"No one. I have brought people from C&C and from Knowledge to the meadow, standing just inside the doorway, and also to the lake via another door, but you are the only person I have brought to my... What did you call it? Outdoor dining setting?"

For the first time in a long time, Jan felt special, in a special way. The scent of grass and flowers drifted on the breeze, and a hint of orange began to appear in the fading sky. The simulated sky doing a simulated evening.

It was uplifting to think that despite all the death and misery, all the hardship and sacrifice, that something so beautiful, and peaceful, could be re-created among the rubble and ice. It gave her hope that all was not lost, and that if somehow, they could re-plant the world, then all could be right again.

But then she reminded herself that this was all an illusion. A very clever and sophisticated illusion, propped up with electrical cables and water pipes. She hoped, however, that what she was feeling was real, and not an illusion as well, for how sad would that be.

CHAPTER 17

She wondered what Ollie was going to do or say to burst the bubble and ruin the moment, purely based on her experience with men. The better things felt, the more she immersed herself in the moment, the harder she would fall.

As they sat at the stone picnic setting on the edge of the meadow, she took the glass of wine from him and had a sip, neither of them knowing what to expect. It was sublime. The snap freeze and the slow thaw had taken an already good wine to the pinnacle of alchemy.

Or maybe it was the location? Or the company? She wasn't sure, but it felt warm, fuzzy, and far, far, removed from everyday life. Alcohol was not something that was regularly consumed in the habitats, in fact it was quite rare. It had not been a priority for scavenging. Food was more important, and lots of the surface stocks had been destroyed by the freeze.

Ollie said, "Jan, I wanted to talk to you about a mission we have planned. Perhaps you have already heard the rumours about the Oak Ridge National Laboratory, in the former United

States?"

"I have heard some talk. It was something about Knowledge setting up a satellite habitat in the United States. And I am presuming that the MHEV crew was named the Oak Ridge Team because we are in some way part of that mission."

"Yes, that is all correct. What we plan to do is use two submarines, the Nebraska and the De Grasse, to travel 22,000km from Sydney to Charleston in South Carolina.

"These submarines will be towing underwater containers housing two MHEVs and two TMs. We expect that the journey will take 20 – 30 days. The MHEV's combined crew of 60 will travel in the submarines and disembark with the vehicles. Then, the De Grasse will remain on station while the Nebraska scouts for additional submarines, or other assets and resources, along the East Coast of North America."

Jan listened while enjoying her wine, and thought to herself, *Is there anything this guy doesn't know, or can't dream up?*

Then her thoughts started to drift, *He has a nice voice, I wonder if he's any good with his hands? Perhaps he is hopeless at doing anything mechanical, musical, or artistic. I wonder if he can cook? I wonder if he brought anything to eat in that bag? I could kill for cheese and crackers right now.*

Then she snapped back to the moment when Ollie asked, "Are you with me so far?"

"Oh, yes, yes, right with you, yep, submarine searches for other submarines."

"Right. So, after unloading we need to take the MHEVs around 600km to Oak Ridge. The problem, however, is that we don't know how difficult that journey is going to be. We plan to take the highways, but that is based on the presumption that they can be navigated. They may have been damage during the Emergency, or they may be blocked by abandoned cars and trucks. This could make sections impassable, and in places we may need to go overland, which may, or may not, slow us down, or present unknown dangers.

"The trials you have been conducting with the MHEV, over the past few weeks, were to simulate a range of conditions that we may encounter."

"So, the journey out to Oak Ridge could take anything from twelve to twenty-four hours. Do you know what we are going to find when we get there?" enquired Jan.

"We have looked at maps, and where possible, building schematics, but most of the latter were lost during the Emergency. Regardless, we have identified several sites suitable for below ground habitats, as well as above ground sites for iglooing.

"We will carry primary habitat building equipment on the overland journey. Given all our experience, we have gotten very good at putting up temporary habitats, and also permanent ones for that matter."

"How long do you think it would be before there is a stable habitat and the MHEVs can return, or even if they are returning?" she asked.

"I expect we are looking at one month for semi-permanent accommodation habitats. Any food supplies and other items will need to be scavenged. Probably from Knoxville, being the nearest city at about 45km away.

"Once we are there we will need to assess if it is viable to set up a self-sustaining habitat, with food production, that can support a larger population. Hence, it may just remain an outpost, or it may become a full-fledged habitat city. I just can't say based on current data."

"And what about the timeline, and logistics, for crews to return to Australia? What is the plan there?" asked Jan.

"I'm figuring, we leave one MHEV and TM at Oak Ridge for the foreseeable future. The other will return to the Nebraska and then make its way back to Sydney. The De Grasse would stay at Charleston for the time being to evacuate the Oak Ridge Team if necessary. We can't afford to lose our top scientist to a simple planning error.

"I expect the total mission time, for those crew members returning to Sydney, to be two to three months if all goes according to plan.

However, we are likely to leave most of the crew at Oak Ridge, to get the facility up and running. So, it will only be four or five people that return to Australia."

"OK, well that all sounds pretty clear, but where do I come into all of this?" asked Jan.

Ollie took a sip of his wine and looked out across the vista. He said, "It's going to be sunset soon, you are going to love this, the illusion is almost perfect. And if we are lucky, some geese will fly across the meadow and land in the lake. Soon the crickets will begin to chirp, and the frogs will croak. If we go down to the forest, for the half hour after sunset, there is the most amazing display of fireflies."

"I would really like to see that. Can we walk down there now?" said Jan.

"Sure. I'll take everything with us because we'll exit via the door near the lake."

As they walked down the hill and across the meadow, in places the grass was up to their knees. Jan brushed her hand across the top of the stems, with their heads starting to swell with seeds, and she bent over to smell flowers.

She said, "It would be lovely to stay in here. To pitch a tent and camp. Oh, what an adventure that would be. My girls would absolutely love it. That is, provided you don't have any wolves or bears in here," she said as she looked around her.

"No, there are no predators in here, you'll

be safe," he said with a laugh, then continued, "Yes, it would be good to stay in here, and to fish in the lake, and to have a campfire. Maybe one day we, or should I say, everyone will be able to enjoy life's little luxuries. That is once the ecosystem stabilizes and matures."

"So, Ollie, you were about to tell me how I fit into your Oak Ridge plan."

"Yes, so I was," he paused and then said, "Jan, I'd like you to lead the MHEV part of the mission. Therefore, you would be responsible for getting everyone safely from the submarines to Oak Ridge, as well as coordinating the transfer of resources and materiel. I don't think there is anyone with more experience, or as level-headed, and as resourceful as yourself for this task.

"Basically, once the MHEVs leave the submarines, they are completely on their own in uncharted territory. The crew will be totally reliant on the MHEVs for survival, therefore, reliant upon you, until they establish a viable habitat at Oak Ridge. So, there will be a lot of responsibility resting on your shoulders."

Jan said, "Wow, that *is* a big ask. Are you sure you want me to take the lead? I'm sure there are other people that are equally, or better qualified, than me."

"I have reviewed many personnel files and given it a lot of thought. Without a doubt, you are the person for the job."

"Can you give me some time to think about this? I must also consider Sally and Mazie. I could be away for up to 3 months, and if something were to go seriously wrong, then I may never come back."

"Let me tell you how confident I am in you, and in your abilities. I will also be coming on the mission. So, I will be putting my life completely in your hands."

Jan laughed nervously and said, "So, no pressure, hey?"

"No, there is no pressure," then he said cheekily, "as long as I have your answer before we get to the lake."

They reached the bottom of the hill, which in reality was just the bottom of a sloping tunnel. There were some ducks and geese paddling on the long narrow lake. Reeds, draped with spiderwebs, lined the bank, while dragonflies hovered and skimmed the water, which now reflected the orange of sunset. Some red deer grazing nearby took flight toward the forest as they approached.

"Oh, my God, would you look at that?" Jan said as she pointed back up the hill toward the faux mountains.

She said, "You even have the last rays of light on the mountain tops as the sun dips below the horizon. How clever is that!"

"Yes, it is a nice touch. It is created with a bit of clever computer programming and some strategically placed spotlights. Oh, sorry. I shouldn't be spoiling the illusion with technical explanations. I really need to stop over-thinking things and just enjoy the moment.

"There, look to the other side, you can see a faint rainbow as the sunlight shines through the rain shower."

Jan took Ollie's hand and tugged him toward the forest.

"Will you *please* show me these fireflies? I don't think I've seen fireflies since I was a child staying at my grandparents. Oh, they were such happy memories. I would go out into the forest, in the evening, with my cousins and their dog. We used to pretend we were in Enid Blyton's Enchanted Woods, and look for pixies and fairies and the Magic Faraway Tree. Ah, the imagination of a child."

Ollie found what she said very cute and endearing. He could imagine himself also being there, instead of being in front of a computer, as he would have been at the same stage in his life.

They walked toward the small glade, and now that they faced it straight on, she could see that it turned into a forest that stretched back down a long tunnel. It progressively got thicker and darker until it was just a tangle of dark green and black.

There was a noticeable rise in humidity as they entered. The air was still and musty. On the ground were fallen rotting logs that supported many species of lichen, fungus, and mushrooms. In the distance she could hear an owl, and maybe the sound of a woodpecker.

The woods muffled the normal, and ubiquitous, echo of the tunnels. Echoes were something that everyone had to learn to live with. Some people never noticed them, and for others, it was a constant annoyance and a reminder of their confinement.

But here in the forest, it sounded like, well, like a forest. Everything was closed in, and nothing echoed. She liked how it was both silent and yet each noise could be heard as a distinct entity. A chirp and then silence, another chirp and then silence, instead of chirps that kept swirling around and running over each other as the sound bounced its way down a tunnel.

There was no faux moon that evening, so darkness came on quickly. It was not long before the woods were filled with the flashes of fireflies, and the very faint glow of luminescent fungi peeking out from under the fallen timber.

In the fading light of dusk, all the illusions blended seamlessly with real nature. It was almost impossible to separate this ecosystem from a forest that had existed on the surface. Places that she had visited as a child, read about in story books, or pictures she had seen. Perhaps a forest that was many thousands of years old and full of life unique only to it.

It was so mesmerizing and enticing that she wanted desperately to believe it was real. It was like she had taken a mind-altering drug and was on a high that she didn't want to come down from. She didn't want to go back to reality, but instead, remain in this fairytale fantasy forever.

She would have forsaken reason and taken the winding path to find the house made of gingerbread, or the Magic Faraway Tree. Anything to lose herself in here. She could understand why people took drugs if this is where they thought they were while they were tripping.

Ollie interrupted her high. That thoughtless and oh so pragmatic man. He was probably used to this, but for her it was the first gasp of air after being underwater for so long.

He said softly, "I think it may be time for us to leave and to let nature get on with its business."

"I'll be completely honest with you Ollie; I was just lost in the sheer beauty of nature. I really don't want to leave. I desperately don't want to leave. It's like I'm having a dream about the world that once existed, a world that we took for granted, and I don't want to wake up and lose it. *Please*, another 5 minutes?"

"I know exactly how you feel, I was like that when I first started coming here, and even now I sometimes find it hard to pull myself away. You just wait 'till I show you some of the other secret ecosystems we have.

"I know I'm very privileged. It's like I have a different world to visit every day, and I can choose them to suit my mood."

"I would very much like to see those other worlds," she said.

"Well, perhaps I may just have to ask you out on another date. And hopefully we won't have to talk so much business next time."

"I'm going to hold you to that. I shall hold you to everything you have said," she said with a smile.

They sat there on a damp log listening to and watching this tiny world. A beetle crawled over Jan's shoe, and then continued about its business, oblivious to who or what these god-like creatures were.

Jan got her extra 5 minutes, then by torchlight Ollie led her to the exit. After another long service tunnel, they re-emerged into the back of a huge laundry room. The workers were busily feeding the noisy machines that tumbled and dried the habitat's clothes. No one saw them enter, and no one saw them leave.

By the end of the 'date', Jan had agreed to go on the mission to Oak Ridge. However, this was only after getting very strong reassurances from Ollie regarding how Mazie and Sally would be looked after while she was gone.

Now she would have to break the news

to the girls. She was sure that they wouldn't like that she would be gone, however, they were always excited by her adventures, and always encouraged her to do new things. And anyway, they were both strong and independent for their ages. She knew they would be fine. Probably, they would deal with the separation better than herself.

CHAPTER 18

The dock-side warehouses had been converted into an enormous igloo on the edge of the ice sheet that now covered Sydney Harbour. A series of tunnels beneath the city linked the submarine docks to the habitats, allowing the transfer of crew and materiel between boats and habitats without exposure to the surface.

The MHEVs had been driven across the surface from KI-44 and were now parked in the igloo ready to be loaded into their submarine capsules. These were streamline shaped, with buoyancy and steering controlled remotely from the submarines that towed them.

Mazie and Sally stood with Jan as she checked her bag one last time. Although the girls were sad that she was leaving, they were also excited that she had been chosen for such an important mission. They knew that she was going stir-crazy in the habitat and was the type of person who always needed a challenge and a new adventure.

Jan had gone to lengths to explain the mission, and the technology they were using, so that the girls had a rational appreciation of both the safety, and the risks.

The girls were also pleased that Ollie was going with her, and constantly teased her about the two of them being locked up together in a submarine. She would tell them to shush, and then change the subject.

Ollie arrived with Danny and Roy. The latter was not going on the mission, but instead would fulfill a caretaker role during Ollie's absence. He was left with detailed instructions, plans, and responses, should certain scenarios occur while Ollie was out of contact over the next few months.

Ollie did not believe that there would be any technological problems, however, he was not so sure about human problems, and specifically, political problems. There was always someone who wanted power for power's sake, and he feared that someone may exploit the vacuum brought about by his absence. There were many potential candidates.

It is always easy to sell a dream, even the empty ones, to oppressed or depressed people, despite, as it was in their case, that everyone was in the same boat. This was part of the reason it was important to give the people a new dream and the belief that it could be achieved. This mission was a crucial step toward a bigger dream.

Ollie gave a rousing speech to all

those assembled at the dock, emphasizing the importance of the mission, and how every precaution had been, and would be, taken to insure everyone's safety.

He said, "We are embarking upon this mission to expand our horizons. We need to not only get humanity back to the level of technology we were at before the Emergency, but to push our knowledge and abilities far beyond where they were. We must imagine, and then strive for, a better future. If we are to ever break free from the frozen confines of Earth, then this must be our goal."

Mission commanders, and key personnel, boarded the Nevada. The remainder of the mission crew were to transit on the De Grasse. This meant that Jan and Ollie would be traveling together, and like other key personnel, would be able to fine tune the strategies while enroute.

The submarine crews were very efficient at loading the MHEVs and stowing all the equipment and luggage.

It then came time to climb down into the belly of the submarines. Mazie and Sally gave Jan a big hug, and there were a few tears, before she filed across the gangway with the others, and disappeared down the hatch.

Ollie was a little embarrassed that his quarters were located with the other naval officers, affording him privacy and a small office.

The rest of the Oak Ridge Team were bunked in yeoman's quarters. It was an experience that proved to be more confined and spartan than most had experienced, even during the early days of the habitat. However, they took it all in their stride with professionalism and good cheer.

The naval crews enjoyed the new faces and the change in routine. Given that there were no longer any enemies to spy on, or ships to hunt, and no more drills for launching torpedoes and missiles, the submarines were now, for all intents and purposes, just a ferry for transporting people and goods between Australian habitats and Pacific outposts.

In short time they were underway. There were no waves, currents, or sea creatures. There were no more massive whales, for they could not be saved, just like many marine mammals. All that remained, in small numbers and in relative confinement, were various species of dolphins, orcas and seals, all being rescued from marine parks and zoos.

They were kept in aquariums and heated pools, but the practice was sub-optimal. Their long-term viability was unknown, especially with their genetic pool being so small, but still humanity was making every effort to save them from extinction. Thus, in a cold, still and empty ocean, the journey was silent and uneventful.

It was as if they were traveling through the

nothingness of space. It was frightening to be in a submarine at the best of times, knowing that you are surrounded by a vast ocean in every direction, filled with all manner of strange sea creatures. And with the only protection being a thin metal hull doing its best to resist the crushing weight of water. But, it was even more disconcerting to be in that same ocean when it was pitch-black and devoid of life, as if one was drifting through the bleakness of death.

Sonar allowed them to follow the contours of the ocean floor, it having been mapped over the previous decades. Above them was sea ice with an average depth less than 1 meter. It was likely, that with time, it would become thicker, but that could take thousands of years. It was not accumulating mass from the surface, such as snow, and the waters below were insulated by it, hence the freeze was very slow.

After ten days underwater the captain announced they had rounded the bottom of South America and were beginning their journey North into the Atlantic. This meant they had passed the halfway point of the underwater part of the mission.

Ollie had been busier than he thought. There was a stream of people visiting his cramped office to discuss the mission, or to discuss the politics that comes with living in such close quarters.

Regarding the latter, he would refer the matter to the captain, given he had years of experience managing confined people with confined egos. When Ollie needed to meet with more than two people, he was given access to the wardroom. It could accommodate up to 10 people in relative comfort.

He had spent many late-night hours listening to Danny discuss his theories. Tonight was one of those nights.

Ollie asked, "So how does such a spacecraft propel itself if there is no conventional propulsion system?"

"Ah well, there is a micro propulsion system for manoeuvring. This can be ion or other kinetic thrusters. But, you must remember, anything you are expelling from the craft to make it move will be a loss in total mass. Hence, it must be restocked at some point, or you will have nothing to push out into space. So, we can think of this as fuel, regardless of its make-up.

"Now at high enough speed, traveling through what I would call 'dirty space', then we could perhaps collect fuel in the form of atoms and dust. Think of it like a stellar scram jet. We scoop it up in the engine's intake, and then thrust it out the back at a higher rate, compensating for the inertial lost due to the collision of particles that are entering the engine."

"OK, but that is just the manoeuvring

engines, not the primary drive."

"Ah, yes, correct. Now, the beauty of the primary drive is it utilises the inherent mass of the universe, expressed as the gravity soup, if you recall the analogy of the universe being like soup, and that when we turn on the drive, we start to repel that watery soup.

"Well, then think of this submarine. If we could create a void around the submarine, an ocean-repellent void, and we could stretch that void into a cone out the front and the back, then all we would need to do is regulate the difference between it and the universe trying to fill that void.

"If it tries to fill it from the back, then we are pushed forward, and if it tries to fill it from the front then we are pushed backward. What we need to control is the balance between the universe and the void. This then determines speed, and between the front and the back, determines direction. The manoeuvring engines don't work in the void because they will have nothing to, um, it's not the right word, but nothing to push against because there is no ocean of gravity, or no reality."

"And what is in this void? I mean, is it like the ocean that surrounds us in this submarine?"

"To be honest, I really don't know. I can only speculate. My first though is to say that it is absolute nothingness, at least as far as our perceptions of our current universe goes. There is no light, no energy, no matter, no time. In short, it is the opposite of everything we know and experience.

"Perhaps you could call it anti-matter or anti-gravity. But that does not mean there is nothing there. It is just that we may not be able to perceive it. We would basically be entering a different dimension with its own realities."

Just then there was a knock at the door. Danny, who by this stage was pacing around the tiny room, reached over and opened the door.

"Hello, Jan. Don't tell me you can't sleep as well. I was just here explaining my theories to Ollie. You know, the theory about alternative reality propulsion. Oh, hang on, I don't think I've told you about it. I was just explaining the difference between manoeuvring thrusters and primary drive propulsion theory in a void..."

Ollie said, "Danny, I'm thinking Jan didn't come here for a lecture in astrophysics, and I'm also feeling like I've had enough for one day. Let me digest what you have told me and then we can pick this up again tomorrow."

"Yes, of course. I do ramble on sometimes. Sorry about that," said Danny.

"No, don't be sorry. Keep rambling. It allows you to organize your thoughts, and it allows me to imagine what we could do with your visions. So, keep it coming, but that is enough for tonight. Oh, and by the way, you may want to cut back on the coffee, you're in a confined space, in case you didn't realize."

They all laughed as Danny excused himself and closed the door.

Jan sat down and fiddled with a nautical trinket on the desk, turning it over and over in her hand.

She said, "He was right, I couldn't sleep. I went for a walk. Not that you can go very far in a submarine. Then I heard Danny talking, and saw your light on, so I thought I would knock. You would think that after ten days into the mission, I'd be used to life onboard. But I've got to admit, its driving me crazy."

"You are not the only one who can't sleep or is going crazy. It takes a special kind of person to work in these conditions. Even though we have gotten used to the tunnels, this is another order of discomfort and confinement.

However, I am also sensing that we all have some concerns about the mission. For me it's all the unknows, and for others it's the heavy burden that falls upon the individual. There are only 60 of us, with a huge task ahead of us, and each person has a crucial role to play."

"Yes, very true, and I am responsible for getting all of us to Oak Ridge safely," said Jan.

"You'll do fine. Just remember how you got Mazie, Sally, and the others, halfway across the country during the Emergency. That took a lot of skill and courage. This will be a walk in the park compared to that."

"Thank you, but right now, all I want is to sit in that mountain meadow, like we did, and enjoy a glass of wine while the sun sets. It was one of the best experiences I have had in so many years."

"Don't you mean, since the Emergency?"

"Ha, you would think so, but no. It was the best time I have had in years. Many, many years. So, will you take me somewhere else when we get back? Like the desert, or this beach you described?"

"Of course, I will, I promise. And if I am completely honest, it was also the best time I have had in many years. It is amazing how much extra pleasure an experience brings when it is shared.

"Maybe next time we can go to a reproduction of the Sonoran Desert. It is really hot and dry in there. And it has those tall thin cactuses, the Saguaro, and all kinds of animals, including bobcats, rattle snakes, road runners, scorpions, you name it."

"Is it safe? It doesn't sound very safe," said Jan.

"Yeah, it's safe, but just be sure to shake out your sleeping bag," laughed Ollie.

"Have you slept in there?"

"A few times, actually. The nights are cool

and clear. We have it in an igloo with a clear glass roof. So, you can lay out in the desert and look up at the stars. Yes, it really is kind of magical. Especially because most of the creatures come out at night."

"Oh, wow, I'd love to do that."

The conversation with Ollie had taken her mind completely off of the mission and all of the concerns that she had. Her imagination was now filled with the stories and pictures that he had so creatively placed into her mind. He was good at doing that. At giving her hope and dangling serenity in front of her, but always just in front of her and out of reach. One day, maybe she would grab hold of it.

CHAPTER 19

The Nevada's captain navigated the submarine along the deep offshore channel carved by the Cooper River during repeated glacial periods when the sea level was much lower. However, this time when the Earth froze, the sea level barely changed. This was because there was no snow building up on the land, no advancing glaciers, just a forever snapshot of the 21st Century.

It allowed them travel right into, and under, Charleston Harbor. They then proceeded upriver as far as Waterfront Park Pier, near the French Quarter. Beyond that point, the distance between the bottom of the ice and the riverbed was too shallow to be navigated safely.

The overlaying ice was about half a meter thick, but due to the shallow water, they were unable to pitch-up the bow to break through the ice. Neither could they get enough vertical momentum through buoyancy to break the ice. At first attempt they appeared to be stuck. It would be a disaster if they had come so far, and put in so much effort, just be thwarted by the sheet of ice that covered the harbor.

Ollie sat silently in the submarine's command-and-control center as the captain and officers discussed options for breaching. It was being suggested that they move to deeper water where they could get the speed and angle to breach. Maybe they would have to do it several times to smash up the ice so that that the MHEV pods could also surface. However, such a repositioning would put them well outside of the harbor.

Another problem was that it would be tricky to reverse the submarines because of the towed pods, and they were not sure if they had enough width or depth to turn the submarine around. The last thing they wanted was to disconnect the pods in order to turn around. That would involve divers operating in the cold, dark bay.

Like Alexander the Great in Gordion, Ollie's suggestion was unexpected, direct, and simple.

"Captain, if I may?"

"Yes, Mr Truss, please feel free to speak up."

"You have torpedoes, which I presume can be detonated remotely. I suggest that you just blow a couple of huge holes in the ice. That ought to solve the problem, then we can get straight to unloading."

The captain pushed back his cap and wiped his forehead, through for a moment and then said, "You know, that may just work."

Then he said, "TDC Operator, can you give me a firing solution?"

"Aye, Captain. We can launch from tubes one and two in 20 and in 40 seconds. Range set for detonation 300 meters for tube 1, and 400 meters for tube 2"

"AO, confirm solution. Are we green?"

"Aye, Captain. TDC, you are confirmed. We are green."

"FC, you are clear to fire."

"Aye, Captain. Firing torpedo tube 1, on my mark. Mark. Torpedo 1 away and counting Captain."

"AO confirms torpedo away."

"FC firing torpedo tube 2, on my mark. Mark. Torpedo 2 away and counting Captain."

"AO confirms torpedo away."

"Brace, all hands, brace."

For the first time in over 20 days there was a sound from outside the steel cocoon. Two dull explosions were heard and felt.

"Helmsman, all ahead one-third, maintain 3 knots. All stop 375m."

"Aye Captain, all ahead, one-third."

Soundings confirmed that the ice was broken, and the submarines could surface side by side.

Once on the surface they pushed forward, lengthening the hole in the fractured ice so the cargo pods could also surface. A thin crust of ice quickly re-formed around the vessels, strong enough for the MHEVs to drive upon, but not enough to get the submarines stuck and stop them from diving.

Four people were required to suit up and transfer to the MHEVs, this being the driver and co-pilot for each. This meant that Jan would be the first out onto the surface. Missile launch tubes had been modified with airlocks specifically for this purpose.

After going through dehydration and decompression, she climbed out onto the long bulbus vessel. Its spotlights illuminated the matte black hull and the cargo pods in the distance. The space between them, although snap frozen, was ice-boulder strewn and uneven from the explosions and breaching. However, off to the sides it was as flat as a skating rink.

Because of their distance from the city, and the absolute black of the sky, all she could see was perfectly flat and clear ice to every illumination horizon. She climbed down from the vessel and stepped onto the ice. Everything was extremely slippery. She was the first living thing to walk on the Americas in nearly 2 years. The other crew made their way down to the ice, and in their respective pairs, headed to the pods.

Each suit had lights, and when they looked down, they could see that the ice was like a sheet of clear glass. There was no powdered layer of snow, no dust or air bubbles, it was completely transparent. Hard, brittle, and perfectly transparent as if they floated above the surface. It added to the danger because one could not tell if there was any ice under foot at all. It was only the cold that guaranteed it.

The pod doors were opened remotely, actuated by electric motors. This was in anticipation of the doors being snap frozen shut upon surfacing. The ice shattered as they began to lower, revealing the MHEVs with their TMs in tow. With their reactors and systems kept on standby throughout the journey, they were brought up to operational condition in short time.

Jan sat in the driver's seat, turned on the lights and began to exit the pod. The recently broken ice was already like concrete, probably 100mm thick, and resting directly on the water below. It was unnerving to advance due to its transparency. It was like she was diving directly out onto black water. Under any other circumstances this could prove extremely dangerous, that is, not being able to differentiate between water and ice, but she knew that nothing on the surface could remain liquid at -260°C.

The MHEV spread its weight across its 8 wheels and silently crunched forward. The tracks that it left were as visible, and as permanent, as those left by the NASA Lunar Rover over 50 years earlier. The MHEV's were driven up next to the submarines, and the slow clumsy process of transferring crew and luggage commenced.

Ollie had only worn a spacesuit on a couple of occasions, and that was for only short durations during preparation for this mission. Some people found it very claustrophobic and inhibiting, like an old-fashion diving suit, the type with the brass spherical helmet. He was one of those people. Wearing it raised his anxiety levels and dulled his coordination.

He moved very slowly and awkwardly as he made his way from the airlock onto the hull. The surface was slippery, and he was having trouble staying on his feet. As he made his way toward the ladder, the curvature of the hull made the problem worse. Fortunately, each person making the transfer was tethered by an alloy cable to the submarine, thus stopping them from falling hard onto the ice if they slid off the submarine.

As he approached the ladder, he felt his feet slide out beneath him and, after a bump and tumble, found himself unceremoniously dangling by the cable a couple of meters above the ice. He could feel something cold on his back and noticed his suit deflating. Immediately, he knew that he had torn the fabric and was leaking. Across the intercom he sounded the alert.

The decision was made to lower him to the ice so that the tear could be assessed. Upon inspection it was deemed that it was sufficiently small that he had about 10 minutes of safe operating time. He headed for the MHEV and immediately entered the airlock. It was going to be a close race between running out of oxygen, getting a cold burn, and recompressing without incident.

As he sat in the chamber, Jan anxiously watched through the window, one eye on Ollie, and the other on the rising temperature and pressure. The acclimatization had to happen at a set rate to avoid medical, and mechanical, complications.

At the very moment the minimum requirements were met, Jan cracked open the inner airlock door. There was still a slight imbalance, and as the air rushed into the chamber, it immediately fogged up. She groped around in the mist until she found Ollie's arm and dragged him out into the cabin. Then without hesitation, she unlocked his fogged-up helmet, only to see Ollie's calm, smiling face beaming at her. She punched him in the arm, twice.

"What are you smiling about? You ass. I was so worried. How could you be so clumsy? Are you OK? Does anything hurt?"

"Nice to see you too," he said. "I knew there was a reason I chose you to head up the land party."

"You realize you could have been seriously injured. Or worse," said Jan.

"Yes, I do realize how dangerous it is every time we go to the surface. I will be more careful next time. Do you forgive me?"

"You know I do. Just don't pull a stunt like that again or I'll... I'll restrict you to the MHEV for the rest of the journey."

After several hours, the Oak Ridge team had transferred, along with equipment and personal effects. The small convoy farewelled the submarines and headed across the frozen river toward the city.

The vehicle's bright lights began to reflect off the buildings and structures that lined the riverbank. When they were close enough, they drove along the edge until they found a point of egress. There was a slight bump and climb, which the MHEVs negotiated with little effort, and within a few minutes they found themselves downtown and surrounded by tall buildings.

It looked similar to their sojourns through Sydney, with its tall, dark, and lifeless structures. Yet, unlike Sydney, there were still cars on the roads. Many were abandoned, some with their doors still open, and a few had dark shapes inside of them.

As they passed close to one car, the side lights shone directly inside revealing a body. It was slumped over the steering wheel, but otherwise fully intact. It was almost as if the person was only resting or sleeping. Further along they saw a body lying on the side of the road, in the foetal position, as if doubled over in pain. The empty vessel would stay where it lay for millions of years, silently drifting on the North American plate until one day it may get buried through continental subduction. Everything now happened at a tectonic pace.

The co-pilot was scanning the navigation system. It had been loaded with city maps from before the Emergency.

He said, "Continue on Cumberland Street, then in 200 meters turn right, onto E Bay Street. We can follow that all the way to Route 26, which will eventually get us to Asheville. Then we take Route 40 through to Oak Ridge. Easy peasy."

Jan replied, "I hope so, but it almost sounds too good to be true."

Jan handled the cumbersome centipede as if it were a B-double truck, weaving around abandoned vehicles, and sometimes slowing to a crawl and carefully squeezing past. On occasion, she had no choice but to clip or push cars out of the way. The ice that gripped them would shatter and then they would slide with ease.

She could clearly see the street signs and noticed that even the leaves and trash were snap frozen in the gutters and piled along the fences. They passed a billboard for 'Mr Frosty, The Crunchy Ice Maker'. Everyone recognized the irony, but no one said anything.

It took them four hours to cover the 180km to Colombia, South Carolina, the first city beyond Charleston. They stayed on the highway, bypassing the city proper, because there were less abandoned vehicles to negotiate and there was more room to get past any that they came across.

From what they could see of the landscape, it had been farming country. The crops still stood in the fields. In many cases they weren't even withered. A few hours later they crossed the border into North Carolina, on their way to Asheville, and then onto Knoxville, Tennessee.

They passed through the forests of the Great Smokey Mountains, and with each corner, the headlights pierced deep into the woods. The light was scattered by the crystals on the branches and leaves as if it were a forest of chandeliers.

Finally, they arrived at the Oak Ridge National Laboratory, around 45km West of Knoxville, Tennessee. It had taken them twelve hours to travel the 620km from the submarines. The MHEV had served them well, and they arrived feeling relatively fresh and rested, except for perhaps Jan and the co-pilot, who had concentrated on the road for the whole journey.

They knew that if they damaged the MHEVs, or even just slid off the road and became bogged, it would not only be the end of the mission, but possibly the end of their lives. This would have also meant that humanity would have lost many of its top scientists, and that it would have lost Ollie, the person who had saved it and was now planning its future.

CHAPTER 20

When the convoy reached Oak Ridge, people were transferred. Then the second MHEV, with a smaller crew, continued for a further 70km to the Watts Bar Nuclear Power Station. As they proceeded, they deployed communication transmitters so that both teams could keep in touch.

The power station was located on the banks of the Tennessee River, adjacent the Watts Bar Reservoir and Hydroelectric Plant. The facility housed two Gen-II fission reactors with pressurised steam turbines, all semi-buried and capped with a concrete containment dome.

High voltage power lines ran directly from the power station to Oak Ridge. Provided the power lines were still intact, then if they got the reactors back online, they would have more than enough power to run all the advanced equipment at Oak Ridge.

Fortunately, the transmission system had been upgraded before the Emergency to cope with solar flares and extreme weather, but it was unknown if these had proven sufficient to survive the Emergency, and thereafter the extreme cold.

However, one advantage of the extreme cold, was that the transmission lines became superconducting, therefore, they were working at optimum efficiency. Something that could never have been achieved before the Emergency.

It was still unknown if they could access liquid water from below the ice sheet to run the cooling system. If that was not feasible, then they would have to do some creative engineering and utilize the outside temperature to condense the steam.

Back at Oak Ridge, Jan drove the overcrowded Team 1 MHEV onto the National Laboratory campus. The co-pilot located the Spallation Neutron Source (SNS) Building, whereupon most of the team disembarked. Jan and Ollie remained in the MHEV to monitor the situation, and to facilitate airlock transfers.

Surface crews entered the building and immediately headed for 'Neutrino Alley', part of the elaborate basement complex that housed high energy experimentation equipment. The basement would become their primary habitat, and reanimating the equipment was their primary mission.

When they reached the basement, they found the temperature was around 100°C warmer than the surface, but still a frigid -160°C. However, at this temperature, oxygen and nitrogen remained gasses, thus they had an atmosphere. It had thinned by about 50% due to leakage, but an atmosphere all the same. Yet, at this temperature it was still lethal. It would flash-freeze the lungs if inhaled, indeed in some ways it was more dangerous than no atmosphere, because now there was a pathway for heat to escape and cold to enter.

As the narrow beams of light flashed down the long dark hallways, and into the recesses, they began to discover bodies. Young, fit, and once active people. Many were wrapped in blankets and huddled together. It was a poignant scene of so many brilliant minds, with so much potential, poised in their last minutes of life.

It was reminiscent of scenes from Pompeii and Herculaneum. It was a great loss to humanity, and to science. It was also a very real reminder of their own potential fate, should they ignore safety protocols, or in some way fail in their mission.

They immediately began to pressure seal the basement, as well as parts of the surface building. When sufficiently sealed, they activated several mobile micro-nuclear-powered atmosphere and heat generators. These were fed chunks of frozen atmosphere brought down from the surface. It was like putting leaves and branches into a garden mulcher. The devices also managed the oxygen to nitrogen ratio.

Slowly the atmospheric pressure, and temperature, in the nascent habitat began rising. It was closely regulated to manage thawing and expansion of the building, and of the delicate equipment.

As that process was underway, which was expected to take a few days, work began on iglooing critical surface structures, reconnaissance of the campus, including the High Flux Isotope Reactor, and scavenging any food and resources.

Once they had a basic habitat established, an HMEV could travel the 45km back to Knoxville on a scavenging run, probably getting enough food and resources for several months or longer.

The team that continued to Watts Bar Nuclear Power Station encountered a welcome surprise. The thick concrete containment dome housing the reactor had remained sealed. It already had airlocks in place, and most conveniently, had maintained a temperature just above zero degrees. This was by virtue of being insulated, sealed, and the heat radiating from nuclear fuel rods. Thus, apart from various shutdown protocols that had been implemented, now needing to be reversed, they essentially had two stable and operating fission reactors.

This meant that they could focus their attention on producing steam for the turbines, which were capable of up to 1,150 megawatts each. Enough to power a city. They put in place atmosphere and temperature generators to warm the facility and to scrub CO_2, and then commenced the start-up procedures.

The piping for the cooling system ran underground to the cooling towers. It went without question that any liquids exposed to the surface would be frozen, although fortunately, the plumbing had been designed to compensate for expansion, hence, they did not have to deal with burst pipes.

As the reactor gained heat, steam formed, and the cooling system slowly started to liquify. If they did a slow and controlled start up, and applied heat to surface pipes in the form of active thermal wraps, then it was hoped the cooling system would eventually melt and be self-sustaining.

It took about 3 days for the Watts Bar Nuclear Power Station to thaw enough to become operational, at least at a rudimental level. The next challenge was to see if the transmission lines could deliver power to Oak Ridge.

Potential weak links included ice-covered insulators, frozen switching gear, and frozen transformers. Almost all this infrastructure was on the surface and fully exposed to cold and deposition.

With superconducting transmission lines, there would be little to no heat generated through electrical resistance, hence they would not thaw with use. Conversely though, due to superconducting, there was less chance of electrical shorts.

Given their situation, the only way to test the network would be to turn it on and see what happens. They switched off all transmission lines except for those that went directly to Oak Ridge. At the Oak Ridge end, they shut down lines that continued past the facility, such that when the connection was energised, the only live lines were the ones that went directly into Oak Ridge.

The Oak Ridge basements were now up to pressure and the ambient air temperature was creeping past 5°C. It was still mostly dark, being only illuminated by strategically placed battery lanterns.

The bodies of the former researchers, and workers, had been moved, while still frozen, and placed in a building on the surface. It was intended that some ceremony would be performed once the habitat had been stabilized.

Ollie was on the telephone to the team at Watts Bar.

"Hello, Watts Bar. All switching gear and breakers have been set to 'Off' at this end. We should be able to do a staged powering-up once you energize the lines."

They said, "Ok, Oak Ridge. We are ready to energize the line. Standby in three, two, one, contacts closed."

Ollie then said, "Main switching operator for Oak Ridge, close the contacts on the lighting circuit."

With that simple command the lights came on all over the campus, even some on the surface that were photoactivated. In succession, other circuits were made live, which then brought various pieces of equipment on to standby mode.

So far, the mission had been successful. They had created a habitat, and they had brought the facility up to operational readiness. The MHEV returned from Watts Bar, leaving behind just a skeleton crew to manage the power plant. This MHEV then did a run back to Knoxville for a quick scavenge bringing back a respectable haul of food and supplies.

Over the coming days, other buildings were sealed and brought up to habitat standard. In some cases, surface tunnels were created to allow pressurized access between buildings. Once they had iglooed the Computational Science and Engineering Technology building, they were able to access supercomputing technology and advanced engineering equipment.

At the commencement of their second week on campus, Ollie called a meeting. Everyone was present or patched in via mobile phone.

He said, "We have been more successful than any of us could have imagined. I just hope our run of good luck continues. Tomorrow, some of you will start to work with the equipment, and hopefully we can begin some of the experiments that are crucial to Danny's theories. So, well done everyone."

There was a congratulatory cheer and clapping from the crowd, then he continued.

"Given the pace and degree of our success, and some of the materials and resources we have acquired, including from the Engineering labs, I am going to make a suggestion. We are presented with an opportunity. But firstly, I will say that I am acutely aware of mission creep, but hear me out, and then we can take a vote.

"We are approximately 360km from Fort Knox, Kentucky, which currently houses 150 million ounces of gold. We will probably never find a more concentrated store of pure gold on earth. For us, it has enormous industrial value.

"Now, given the equipment we have recently acquired, we should be able to, dare I say, break into the vault and take as much gold as we can carry. So, here is what I am proposing. Tomorrow MHEV 1, with a TM, heads out for Fort Knox, while MHEV 2 does more scavenge runs into Knoxville for food and resources.

"After MHEV 1 returns with a load of gold, then both vehicles head back to Fort Knox repeatedly until we have a decent supply of gold here at Oak Ridge. Of course, we know that the gold at Fort Knox isn't going anywhere. It's not like anyone is going to steal it. But, while we have the two MHEVs on site, we may as well make the most of their utility. I am thinking we put 5 people in each MHEV for their respective missions, leaving 50 people to continue work here at Oak Ridge."

A vote by show of hands was taken and the proposition passed unanimously. They all ate a hearty meal together, digging deep into their remaining food stocks, and then each person, exhausted from the week's work, and stresses, retired.

Almost everyone had a small office, or lab, they could use as personal sleeping and living space. It was a luxury compared with the cramped conditions on the MHEVs, and the submarines before that. Indeed, in many cases people had more room, and luxury, then they did in the habitats back in Australia. Each person personalized their new apartment as best they could, rearranging furniture and helping themselves to the possessions once owned by the previous occupants.

Jan had an office diagonal from Ollie's. Based on its pictures and decoration, it must have belonged to a woman with a family. She felt sad that it had all been wiped away in an instant. Jan left the photograph of a young and happy family on the desk out of respect.

She opened the door to one of the cupboards and there were a couple of packets of unopened crackers. Then she opened the cupboard below and saw an unopened bottle of spirits. She picked it up and noticed it had a bow and a note on it. It was a gift to someone named Cherry, and it thanked her for all her support.

The label on the bottle read 'Lincoln Straight Bourbon Whiskey, Boundary Oak Distillery, Radcliff, Kentucky'. She found a glass and poured a shot of the 96-proof mahogany elixir. The aroma was honey and vanilla, and the drinking was sweet, smooth and all pleasure. She reached in the cupboard for a second glass, picked up the bottle, and walked across to Ollie's new digs.

His office was larger than hers, with an olde world opulence. She thought that perhaps it was the former director's office. Off to the side of a grand desk were two deep burgundy high-back chesterfield chairs. Nestled into one, Ollie sat, deep in thought. A graceful low table separated the chairs, as if placed purposefully to receive a bottle of Kentucky bourbon and two glasses.

"Would you like some company?" she asked.

He looked up and smiled. "I cannot think of anything I'd like better."

"Look what I found."

Jiggling the bottle, she entered the

room with theatrical swank. "Kentucky bourbon whiskey. I tried some, its smooth and warm." Then she reached into her pocked and pulled out a packet of crackers, saying, "And I have these."

"Dinner and a drink. So, is this our second date? I did say I'd take you somewhere. Well, here we are on the other side of the world. Was that far enough?"

"Yes, you can call it that, but I wasn't expecting to be the one driving," she said with a laugh.

They stayed up for several hours making a dent in the bottle and eating crackers, yet being mindful and restrained because they had a big day tomorrow.

For the first time she began to get an insight into Ollie and his past. She had never pried, but tonight he began to open up. Either it was due to increased familiarity, or maybe it was just the warming and loosening qualities of alcohol.

The lights had been dimmed throughout the basements to simulate night. This resulted in long dim hallways, dark rooms and recesses. It was important to keep everyone's circadian rhythms synchronized, and to have a standardized habitat-wide clock.

Ollie finished his drink and said, "It's probably time to sleep. Tomorrow we've got a long drive. I mean, you have got a long drive, and then we have a lot of heavy work to do. That gold won't move itself."

"Yes, I suppose you are right." Then after a long silence Jan said, "I've been in some pretty dodgy and dangerous places in the past. I've slept out in the bush all alone, and I've seen a lot of strange things. But this place? This place really gives me the creeps.

"There were all those bodies, and there are probably many more that we haven't found yet. All those poor people, and some of the messages that they left, they were so personal and heartbreaking. I feel like their spirits are trapped in here. Maybe they will stay trapped until we give them a burial or some kind of dignified send off.

"It's not that I'm a religious person, well I never thought I was, but it just feels like it's something that shouldn't be left undone.

"Then there are all the noises down here in the basements. I know it's just the building, and the pipes, and the equipment, expanding and dripping from being thawed, but as it echoes through the dark corridors, it's just so creepy."

Ollie reached over and put his hand on top of Jan's.

"It's OK to be scared. I'm often scared. Especially when I'm in that damn space suit."

Jan laughed and Ollie pulled a funny face, acting like a puppet dangling from a string.

Then he continued, "I'm sure everyone is

operating on the ragged edge of courage and sanity. We are really pushing technology, and our luck, as hard as we can.

"I often think of what it would have been like as a caveman living in a small tribe, facing the cold, and hunger, and the dangers of the ice age. I really don't think our current existence is much different, although I suppose we don't have to worry about sabre tooth tigers and cave bears anymore.

"Still, it's as if the clock has been turned back 20,000 years and we are trying to kickstart civilization all over again. I'm sure back then every noise in the night was scary and there was a very real chance of danger. So, we are all hardwired through evolution to fear noises in the dark and to seek protection and comfort with others."

There was a long silence that was interrupted by a creaking noise from somewhere down the dark corridor. It was probably a doorframe expanding, but it still made Jan flinch and let out a soft gasp.

Ollie looked at her and said, "I have an idea. How about you stay in here tonight? I've made a bed over there on that sumptuous rug. I'll go with you to get your mattress, and then we can put it on the far side of mine against the bookcase. That way the boogie man will get me first."

She smiled and then said, "I feel so

embarrassed. I'm acting like a scared little girl. It's just that I'm so sick of the constant dark, and the danger, and death around every corner. I just want a break. I just want to let go of all the struggle, anxiety, and ugliness.

"That's why I was so happy in the simulated mountain meadow. I knew it wasn't real, but the dream, and the feelings it generated, were good enough to give me happiness and hope.

"It was also because you were there to look after me, Mr Caveman, and I could just let go of all that fear and pain and just be myself once again. My old self. To be happy and carefree like I was when I was younger, so much younger."

He stood up and said, "OK, then its settled. Let's get your gear and set up a camp in here. We'll put a lamp in the middle as if it were our campfire and pretend we're under the stars in that safe and peaceful meadow."

After a few trips they collected all of her stuff, as if she was moving in permanently. They set up the beds, closed the door, and dimmed the light. Under a stack of blankets, and cradled in Ollie's arms, Jan fell asleep the moment her head hit the pillow. It had been a long time since she had slept so quickly or so deeply.

CHAPTER 21

Over the past week a building was iglooed to house the MHEVs, thus allowing people and equipment to be transferred without exposure to the surface. This saved a great amount of time and reduced the risks associated with the transfer between the inner and outer worlds.

They loaded the Fort Knox MHEV with laser and plasma cutters salvaged from Engineering. It was high powered equipment capable of getting through whatever security they may come across. The MHEV was able to generate enough electricity to run the equipment, for it was of itself a mobile power station.

Jan, Ollie, and three others shut themselves in the MHEV, went through the building's airlock and then headed for Route 40. That would take them North to Kentucky. While Jan drove, Ollie sat in the co-pilot's seat and provided navigation.

Beyond the town of Monterey, Tennessee, about 100km North of Oak Ridge, they began to climb into the Mountains. It was a place of significance for the Cherokee and Shawnee Nations, as well as for Civil War history, and was only about 100km East of Nashville, Tennessee. It was a spiritual, hearth and heart land for the many cultures of North America, but it now lay as a silent memorial to what once was.

Jan turned to Ollie and said, "When you designed this contraption, did you think to put in anything to play music on? I know a radio would be no good, obviously, but is there anything we can use to play tunes on?"

"Have you got any music?" he asked.

"Yes, I have, actually. I found an SD card in my room, and it is loaded with music, country music, which is kind of fitting for this region. I admit I felt kind of nosey looking through her stuff, the former resident, but then again, are we not now post-Emergency archaeologists? Should we be showing restraint, humility, and apologize for surviving, or should we be getting on with our lives?

"I believe we must move forward. As survivors, and heirs to human civilization, we have the right, and indeed the obligation, to sift through the ashes, as to put it, and to build something new. I believe we actually honour their memories by discovering, and using, some of the things they loved and cherished and pass them on to future generations."

Jan pulled the SD card out of her pocket and handed it to Ollie. He inserted it into a slot and fiddled around on the control panel. Throughout the MHEV country music began to play. It was nostalgic. They knew the words to some of the songs, and to others they just tapped their feet. It was a welcome link to the past, and a reminder of the subtleties of human interaction and emotion. The trucks, guitars, and cornfields, were all just props for the real stories of love, belonging, and loss.

They continued their lonely journey through the dark mountains that may as well have been made of obsidian, climbing and cresting, to magnificent vistas that their headlights were not powerful enough to illuminate. They just shone out toward an indeterminant horizon, photons being scatted and lost into the empty black.

How odd it would have been to see lights coming toward them from the other side of the valley, another traveller, but there were none.

A few kilometres short of Fort Knox they passed a sign that read 'Boundary Oak Distillery'.

Ollie said, "Would you look at that!"

Jan looked out the side window and said, "Oh yeah, what a coincidence! That was a pretty good drop last night. Just what I needed. It got me sleeping like a baby."

"Yeah, a baby that snores," teased Ollie.

"I don't snore, you bastard," Jan said with indignation.

She tried to hit his arm, but he was too

quick and moved it out of the way.

The Ollie said, "Maybe next trip we can stop and scavenge a few cases. Hopefully, they'd survive the trip back to Oak Ridge."

"Maybe we ought to get a barrel, just in case the bottles break," Jan said with a cheeky grin.

She drove the MHEV slowly up the entrance road to Fort Knox. There was a razor wire perimeter fence. She nudged up against it and the poles just snapped as if they were glass. She then proceeded to an iron-bar gate that spanned the roadway. Once again, she nudged up against it, and again the brittle metal just shattered.

When they arrived out in front of the building, Ollie stayed in the MHEV. It was protocol that someone stayed at the controls while the other four donned their space suits and went through the airlocks. Most of their equipment had been stored on the outside of the vehicle, including a specially forged, and weighted, aluminium-magnesium alloy sledgehammer. It was specially forged and crafted to resist the extreme cold.

By the lights of the MHEV they walked up the stone steps to the 22-ton front doors. As they stood there looking, one of the crew pushed against a door, but it did not budge.

Jan said, "We should be so lucky."

Ollie came over the intercom, "Swing the sledgehammer at one of the doors. Do it at the bottom in the center."

The sledgehammer was swung with great force, and although there was no sound, they could feel the vibration through their feet. Spider-cracking appeared in the lower corner where the blow struck, as if it were a car windshield that had been hit by a stone. As they continued to hit the same spot, pieces of brittle metal flew like shrapnel, and the impacts ate deeper into the steel.

Jan said, "At this rate we will be here for hours, also there is the risk of puncturing a spacesuit with sharp flying fragments."

Ollie replied, "Yes, you are right. I suggest we go to plan B."

"What is plan B?" asked Jan.

"Use the laser and plasma cutters to bore several holes. Then we will set some charges and blow the doors."

Jan said with surprise, "What charges? I didn't know we had any charges. What is it dynamite, or something? Would that even work in cryogenic conditions, and with no oxygen?"

"No, not dynamite. I've got some special charges I had the chemists make up just in case we needed them. It's explosives packed into insulated containers with electrical detonators. They called it C5," he said with a laugh.

They set up the cutting equipment at the foot of the doors and then ran the power cables back to the MHEV. With surprisingly little effort they bored several holes in the doors, then collected the charges from the airlock and plugged them into the holes. After setting the charges, and removing their equipment, they sheltered themselves and the MHEV on the right side of the reinforced concrete and granite building.

There was no noise when the explosion went off, although they could feel a shudder and saw fragments pepper the ground at the front of the building. There was no cloud of smoke or debris as everything just fell parabolically to the ground under the force of gravity.

When they returned to the front, there was a gaping hole where the doors had once blocked their access. The sledgehammer then made short work of the doors that remained between themselves and the main vault, a 20-ton cylindrical behemoth.

This time they went straight to using the laser cutter and setting charges. Given that they were working in a confined area, they placed fewer charges, not wanting to cause structural damage to the building. When the charges had been set and the fusing wires run through to the outside of the building, the MHEV was moved to a safe distance, and they took shelter behind it.

The detonation was performed, but there was no sign that anything had happened.

Nothing emanated from the building. However, when they returned to the vault room, they found the vault door had shattered into millions of pieces. Inside they saw a couple of pallets of gold, but it wasn't until they broke into the many adjoining rooms that they found them were stacked to the ceiling with gold ingots.

None of them had ever seen so much gold. It glowed warm in the torch light as if the cold had no effect upon it. Indeed, the gold remained ductile even in extreme cold. Gold was gold no matter the circumstances, hence its value. Even Ollie was lost for words as he viewed the live stream from Jan's suit camera.

There were trollies for moving the gold, and once they had cleared the debris from the explosion, they began to move the ingots out to the MHEV, which was now parked in a rear loading dock which had been opened from inside the building. With 4,850 metric tons of gold at the facility, and each ingot weighing 12.5kg, it was going to take a lot of hefting and many trips to make even the smallest dent in the stockpile. Based on the price of gold before the Emergency, they would be digging into a plie valued at around US $290.9 billion.

Ollie thought to himself, *not bad for a day's work.*

Gold is abundant in the oceans, probably in the Earth's core, and no doubt scattered throughout the solar system, but the problem was finding it concentrated. But now they had hit the motherload. Still, they had to keep reminding themselves that its only value to them was for its industrial applications. In a merit-based society that did not rely on money gold was merely a heavy yellow brick.

The crew returned to the MHEV to replace their air tanks. Jan stayed inside so she could have a sleep after the long drive. She wore a vibrating bracelet that would alert her if the others got into trouble. Ollie took over her shift to help with the transfer of the gold.

About half the gold they removed was stacked on the outside of the vehicle, with the rest being loaded in through the airlocks. With gold being so dense, it really didn't look like much when they reached their weight limit of 6 tons, being split 40/60 between the MHEV and the TM, respectively.

After loading, they searched through other vaults and came across an enormous supply of morphine. They were surprised to see the stash, and realizing its value to humanity, took several crates, formally worth millions of dollars, to be distributed among the habitats.

It had been 12 hours since leaving Oak Ridge, and they had spent half of that time extracting and transferring the gold. Everyone was exhausted from the heavy work, especially because it was performed in bulky space suits. Jan had reclined her seat and was still asleep when they emerged from the airlock. They decided to leave her sleeping and everyone followed her example and took a nap.

Later, Ollie was awakened by Jan speaking in a low voice, "Ollie, wake up. I've got some food and drink for you."

She had risen while the others slept, and quietly busied herself preparing dinner for the crew, drawing on stocks of canned food they had brought with them. He sat up slowly and rubbed his eyes. The air in the spacesuit irritated his eyes. It made them feel dry. No one else had reported this problem, so it must have been something particular to himself.

The meal was good. It always tastes better when someone else makes it, especially someone you are fond of. Perhaps she put in some extra effort for him, or maybe that was just how she always did things.

Jan said, "I'm rested and ready for the drive home. I was thinking of leaving the others sleeping. They can eat when they wake up. But as you know, protocol dictates that I can't drive without a co-pilot, so are you up for it?"

Ollie replied, "Ooh, this coffee is good, and strong. After I drink this, I'll be alert for the next 12 days, so yes, we may as well hit the road."

Jan said, "I'm figuring that given we've got

extra weight onboard, and that we have to go back over those mountains, then this is likely to be a long slow trip."

She drove the MHEV slowly and carefully, beginning the journey back to Oak Ridge. While they were still at low speed, Ollie used the bathroom in the back of the cabin. It was not unlike what would be found on an aircraft.

While in there he felt the vehicle come to a halt. When he came out, Jan was looking through the window at a sign on the side of the road. It was the one they had seen earlier for Boundary Oak Distillery.

She said, "Do you realize it's only two or three minutes down this side road?"

"What, the distillery?" ask Ollie.

"Yes. What do you think, do you want to go and have a look, and maybe do a scavenge?"

Ollie looked around. The crew was still sleeping.

"I suppose it wouldn't hurt. It's not like we have a deadline to meet. And as they say, it's the simple things in life that give the greatest pleasure. Perhaps, if we got enough to share around, then we could rationalize the detour by saying we are spreading the joy."

Jan cheerfully said, "That's the spirit, pardon the pun." And she proceeded in the direction indicated by the sign.

As they crawled down the narrow road,

Ollie put on his spacesuit and went into the airlock. He was becoming more confident with his surface abilities since working most of the day in his spacesuit.

Upon arrival they expected to see an old wooden building, perhaps a barn, and some wagon wheels. Instead, it was a modern steel and glass structure that fronted extensive distilling and storage sheds. Instead of a backyard operation, it had operated at a commercial scale.

As Ollie disembarked, he said over the intercom, "I won't be long. Do you have any preferences?"

Jan replied, "Be sure to get some of what we had last night and, I don't know, whatever looks interesting and is easy to scavenge. Don't go to too much effort, and for god's sake don't take any risks! Remember you are on your own out there."

As Ollie approached the large glass door, his light shone inside. He could see people, frozen people, slumped over at tables and lying on the floor next to overturned chairs. He pushed the door, and it opened. No one had bothered to lock it.

Upon surveying the scene, it became apparent that the gathering, a dozen people, had decided to drink away their final hours. Perhaps they were a family, or a group of friends, telling the stories of their lives, confessing sins, asking for forgiveness, and saying their last goodbyes.

It was like still-life art, or a poem, a moment captured in time. He was glad Jan was not doing the scavenging; she would have found this diorama upsetting. It was something that could burn into a person's subconscious and infiltrate their dreams.

Behind the counter were stacks of wooden cases emblazoned with the company's name and containing selections of the distillery's produce. Nearby was a hand trolly, no doubt for loading cases into customer's cars. He stacked up a selection and wheeled them out to the MHEV waiting in the carpark. It was a surreal shopping experience. He had never done scavenging before. He had always been too busy with the big picture jobs.

Jan came through on the intercom, "Looks like you have done well. That is probably enough, given how much weight we already have onboard."

He left the loaded trolly by the ladder and said, "I'll be back in a minute."

And with that, he disappeared into the building. He must have gone through a doorway, and into another room, because Jan could no longer see his light.

It had been nearly 5 minutes, and her nerves were getting the better of her. She called him on the intercom,

"Are you OK? I can't see your light."

There was silence, she waited 20 seconds and then called again, this time more panicked.

"Ollie, are you OK? Please answer me!"

A panting breathless voice came back over the intercom.

"Yes, I'm OK. I'm almost back into the reception area. You should see my light shortly."

It took another 2 minutes before his light was visible through the distillery's front windows.

When Ollie came out the main door, he was rolling a large oak barrel.

He said, "I remembered what you said about getting a barrel as back-up. So anyway, happy birthday, Merry Christmas and whatever else you celebrate. This is my gift to you. Just don't drink it all at once."

Jan laughed and said, "How are you planning on getting that onto the MHEV."

"Oh, don't you worry, I've got it all figured out. I've got some cable, and I'll hoist it up onto the back of the TM, and then tie it in place," he said as he was panting.

"Oh great, we'll be going down the road looking like Okies, or Steinbeck's Joads in a jalopy with all our worldly positions poking out the back.

"Just imagine if we got stopped by the police. Let's see, what have we got here? $400 million in stolen gold, enough morphine to put a drug cartel out of business, and now it looks like we just come back from Copperhead Road with a load of moonshine," she said while laughing.

"I'm trying to make your life interesting. Is it working?" said Ollie.

"Oh, you've certainly done that. You are a very strange, but somehow endearing Caveman. Oh and master thief," she said.

The remainder of the journey was slow and uneventful. At an average speed of 40kph, it took them nearly 8 hours before the lights of Oak Ridge came into view. They stopped outside the airlock to unload the drugs and booze so it could be placed in slow thaw.

Once they were inside, a crowd gathered to gaze upon their haul of gold. Even though it was no longer worth money, the memory of gold as currency still held enormous magical power.

Perhaps because humans had lusted over it for thousands, or tens of thousands of years, it had altered the very structure of our DNA. Maybe it triggers something in the human brain like no other natural element.

MHEV 2 had already completed several scavenging missions into Knoxville and had collected enough food and supplies to last well over a year.

Ollie and Jan retired early. Jan was scheduled to do a return trip to Fort Knox in the morning, while Ollie would remain at Oak Ridge, conferring with Danny and the other scientists.

In the same fashion as the previous night, they sat, they sipped, they talked, they laughed, and they slept on the rug by the bookcase. It was almost like one of those "What happens in Vegas, stays in Vegas" types of situations. She wondered if that was how it was going to be.

CHAPTER 22

Danny was in his office writing emails. Who would have thought, in a post-apocalyptic world, office emails would have survived? He was corresponding with his colleagues in the Computing and Computational Sciences Directorate (CCSD) building.

They had enormous resources and potential at their disposal, including Artificial Intelligence programs, Quantum Computing prototypes, CRISPR genome sequencing projects, and Frontier, the world's most powerful supercomputer. They worked tirelessly to understand the technologies and how they may be applied to their current changes. They needed to stand on the shoulders of lost giants, and then to reach further than anyone had ever dared to dream.

For Danny's theories to ever work, he would need to harness fusion energy. His theories called for something more powerful than a hydrogen bomb but miniaturized and controlled. He wasn't hoping for much- it was only the holy grail of limitless energy production. No wonder people thought he was mad.

The ITER Tokamak prototype fusion reactor was partially constructed on campus, and although it would be years before survivors had the resources to make it operational, they could, however, reverse engineer it. They could also take the design in new directions that better aligned with the "reality drive" concept.

Once they had harnessed vast amounts of energy, they would need Artificial Intelligence, running on quantum computers, to manage energy production and the propulsion system. This would require a thorough understanding of quantum physics, and then unlocking the mystery of how to create a void-field beyond reality. Therefore, outside of the perceivable universe. Crazy upon crazy, but if one wanted to reach the stars within a human lifetime, then this was the only way to do it.

What haunted him was that it was all theoretically possible yet had always been so far out of reach. It was amazing that it had taken the Emergency to bring him closer to his dream than at any other time during his career. He rationalized, that as one door closes, another one opens. But it was such a shame that so much was lost in the process.

Ollie tapped on the door and Danny beckoned him to enter.

Ollie asked, "How are things progressing?"

"Oh well, you know, we must first get a handle on what it is that we have here. These guys really have some cool equipment and were working on some far-out projects. We could spend years here, even decades, continuing their work, refining it, and publishing papers."

"But you won't, will you?"

"No, no, no, I get it, we are here for a purpose. I haven't lost sight of that. Anyway, who is left to read any papers that we may publish? Instead of putting our results in international journals, now we just put them in emails and shoot them off to each other."

Ollie said, "Still, I hear you, and I believe that this site will make for a viable long-term habitat. Hopefully, there will be people working here for many years to come and the population can grow as we expand the habitat."

"I'm pretty sure that most of the people here would like to stay, especially if they could have their families with them. They are like kids in a candy shop. It's a shame we can't just put a dome over the whole campus, that way we could utilize everything, and even walk around outside," said Danny.

"I don't see why that couldn't be done. Domed cities? I can image it now. Perhaps we can get someone working on some designs," already the cogs were turning in Ollies mind.

"That aside, I suspect you are here for a

progress report," said Danny.

"Yes, we have been on site for nearly one month and are now expected to rendezvous back with the submarines at Charleston in a day or so. It is our hope to depart tomorrow morning. We will be leaving most of the crew here, and one of the MHEVs and its TM. You will be responsible for the stack of gold, as well as some drugs and booze, so use them wisely," Ollie said, and they both laughed.

"When do you think the next supply submarine will come?" asked Danny.

"I'm hoping within a couple of months, but that depends on a few factors, including conditions back in Australia, and the submarine's schedules."

Danny then asked, "And when do you think you will be back?"

"Possibly in 6 – 12 months. I suppose that depends on many factors also, but especially on your rate of progress. Build me a spaceship and I'll be back as soon as I get the call."

"Well at least we know the weather won't be a factor. Haha."

Danny then provided Ollie with a detailed update of progress before he left to do the rounds of the campus and to say his goodbyes.

That evening Ollie and Jan were nestled in the two large leather chairs in his Oak Ridge apartment.

Jan wistfully said, "I think I'm going to miss all of this. Even though I miss Mazie and Sally terribly, I'm also going to miss the new life, and friends, I have made here. I think I've even gotten used to this creepy basement."

"Ah ha, now you tell me. So, you've been sharing my apartment under false pretences. I feel like I've been used. Violated even," joked Ollie.

"Oh God, you talk rubbish. It's been me looking after you all this time. Who do you think watches over you, in the middle of the night, when you are asleep? Or sends people away when they turn up at all hours trying to disturb you?

"I'm sure you don't even realize half the things I do for you. You are always fed and have a hot coffee; the proverbial path is always cleared for you. And what do I ask for in return? I'll tell you. Simply to not be left alone in this dungeon during these scary and uncertain times," she said.

"You are right, perhaps I take you for granted. And the truth of the matter is that I don't want to be left alone either. I do want you here, and there, and everywhere," Ollie said as he made silly hand gestures around the room.

Jan laughed and said, "There you go again funny man."

The journey back to Charleston was slow and uneventful. Apart from Ollie and Jan, four others of the crew returned with them. They drove through the city and then out onto the ice. Using bright searchlights, they scanned the glassy surface, but they could not see the dark towers of the submarines protruding through the ice.

Ollie got on the radio and tried to contact them, but there was no reply. Not so much as a crackle through the speakers. It was anticipated that this may be a problem, so they had a back-up plan.

One of the crew had to disembark the MHEV and, using a hand auger, drill down through the ice until they reached liquid water. They then lowered a transmitter and hydrophone into the water in the hope the submarines would hear them and respond. It took about 5 minutes of transmitting before they got a reply. They were given instructions via Morse Code to retreat back toward the shore while the Nebraska surfaced.

The submarines had been resting just below the surface, but regularly rising and falling a meter at a time to keep the ice sheet from getting too thick.

The submarine crew assisted in stowing the MHEV and TM into the pod, and also transferring them and their equipment. When climbing back onto the hull, Ollie was careful not to repeat his former mistake. But just to be sure, Jan followed closely and held his arm. She joked that he was, "The Old Man of the Sea."

The captain and crew were pleased to

see them, and especially pleased with the scavenged food, including smoked hams, cheese, and Kentucky bourbon rations they brough with them.

"Captain, how did the reconnaissance go while we were gone?" asked Ollie.

The captain responded as if Ollie were his CO, which in reality, if not in letter, he was.

"Good news, Mr Truss. We came across another two Ohio-Class submarines sheltering together at Naval Submarine Base Kings Bay, Georgia. It's about 150 nautical miles Southwest of our current position. They were the USS Maine and the USS Alabama. They were both crewed, although the men were in very bad shape from malnutrition. They are now stationed just out from Charleston Harbor.

"We have now had them on food rations for three weeks, and although some are in worse shape than others, they will be able to sail their boat back to Sydney with us. I'm sure they will be very thankful to get onto solid ground and stretch their legs. Nearly two years in a submarine must have been hell, especially not knowing if a rescue was ever going to come.

"There were another two nuclear submarines there, a Los Angeles-Class, and a Virginia-Class, and although the crews were unfortunately lost, we believe the boats can be salvaged. It is our intention that on our return trip we crew them and bring them back to Australia. So, to summarize, the results are better than I expected, and that is despite the tragic loss of life."

Ollie responded, "Yes, captain, that is very good news, but I also sympathize with you over the inordinate loss of life, and also under such horrific circumstances."

The convoy of four submarines, including the De Grasse, were underway within the day, heading South for The Strait of Magellan, then across the Pacific Ocean directly to Sydney. Now, with more submarines, they could increase the frequency of visits to outposts, but for this return voyage, it was agreed to beeline for the primary habitat in Sydney for some well-earned rest.

When they arrived back at the igloo dock, the same one from where they had departed three months ago, all the submarines were able fit inside, although it was tight. The rescued crews were given medical, and psychiatric support, comfortable accommodation, and food, lots of food, so they could put on weight and convalesce. They were overwhelmed just to be able to walk around the dock and to see new faces and sights. Ollie suggested that they be taken to the mountain meadow and other expansive ecosystems, for a few hours each day, to help them regain their sanity.

When Ollie and Jan walked the gangway

and finally stepped onto solid ground, Roy was there to greet them. In his typical cheerful manner he said, "Welcome back Ollie. Jan. Hmm, so you two seem to have become rather friendly. Didn't go to Vegas, did we?"

Ollie got flustered, and Jan blushed and looked away.

Ollie then said, "I'm sure I don't know what you are talking about. It was a very professional, successful mission. We achieved everything we had hoped for and so much more."

"Everything, hey?", said Roy with a heavy dose of double entendre. Then he added, "It's OK, I'm just playing with you. Look, I'll let you unpack and unwind, and then we need to have a meeting. There are some pressing issues we need to discuss."

"Yes, good idea, but I don't want to hear about anything right now, unless you believe it can't wait. So, if it can wait, then how about we set a time for later?" said Ollie.

"Sure, it can wait. Let's catch up at 9am tomorrow."

The submarines had arrived unannounced; therefore, Mazie and Sally did not know that Jan was back home. As she stood dockside, there was no one to meet her, unlike Ollie, who had many officials welcoming him home. They had been alerted when the first submarine surfaced and had stopped their work and rushed down to the dock.

She thought that perhaps now that they were home, he would be too busy for her trivial needs. Too important and crucial to the survival of humanity. Always working, always in demand. Who was she to interfere, and demand attention, being just a glorified truck driver?

Then she thought to herself, *I know what this feeling is, it's just the end of mission blues. That lost feeling you get after a long and arduous ordeal. The body doesn't know what to do with the adrenaline and stress hormones anymore now that the journey and the dangers are done.* She recalled this from her army days and had often heard people from Special Forces talking about it.

She went to pick up her duffel bag, and as she reached down, there was a hand already holding the straps.

Ollie then said, "Where to madam?"

"I'll be fine, I'm sure you have people to see. I'm just going to head home and see my girls," said Jan.

"To hell with all the administrators and officials, I'm off the clock till tomorrow morning. Did you really think I was going to let you walk off without me? Besides, you're the one who is supposed to be looking after me. I probably need your protection now more than ever."

Jan's blues faded and were replaced with a warm glow. They walked through the busy tunnels toward her apartment. Despite the confinement and the crowds, it still felt spacious, warm, and safe, especially compared to the 25 days they had just spent in the submarine. It felt like they had returned to normality. Sure, it was crowded, loud, and smelly, but it was home.

When they arrived at the apartment, Jan burst in and surprised Mazie and Sally. They were both ecstatic and ran over to hug her. Ollie was left holding the bags in the doorway. The girls had so many questions for Jan that she couldn't answer one before the next one was asked.

Ollie walked in by himself and put the bags down against the wall. Sally came over and gave him a hug.

She said, "I'm glad you have come back home as well, Mr Ollie."

Ollie said, "Hello Sally, hello Mazie. I am glad to be home also. Were you well looked after while Jan was gone?"

"Oh, yes. We can look after ourselves, but someone came by every day to check on us. But, as you know, it's all just one big family here, especially in our home tunnel."

Cheekily Mazie asked, "Did you look after Jan?"

"Well, actually it was her who looked after me. I'm sure she will tell you stories, especially about the time I fell off the submarine. But don't believe everything she says. I'm not as clumsy, or hopeless, as she may make me out to be."

He stayed for a short time having a cup of tea and some biscuits the girls brought out for them on a tray.

After he had finished he said, "Well, I suppose I ought to be going. You girls must have a lot of catching up to do."

"Aww, really, so soon?" said a despondent Jan.

He stood up and walked over to the door. Jan went over and gave him a hug and then whispered into his ear, "Thank you. Thank you for everything, you interesting, funny, gothic Caveman."

With that he smiled and walked away, but only after a lingering touch of their hands. As he walked back to his apartment, the one next to the C&C Center, he noticed a slight skip in his step. He hadn't recalled walking or feeling like that for many years. Perhaps he was developing a normal life? Maybe this is how other people felt?

Unlike in the hectic early days, there was now only a few people in the C&C control room. Much had been automated, but still those that worked there expeditiously relayed messages and monitored movements. He walked through virtually unnoticed and made his way down the corridor to his room. The walls were still the colour of dull cement-grey, and there was still that lonely picture of a Greek Island on the wall to torment him.

Within 30 minutes he had collapsed onto his bed. It felt odd to be alone, like a part of his life was missing. A large and important part. He had spent such a long time in constant company with others, especially with Jan. Perhaps it was post-mission blues or perhaps he was just missing Jan.

His mind wandered, then it occurred to him, how would she know how to get in touch with him? Would his minders patch through her calls or relay a message to him? Would the security guards turn her away if she tried to see him? He drifted off to sleep with a small lamp casting a soft light over the room, just as another lamp had done during the heady yet wonderful nights back at Oak Ridge.

CHAPTER 23

They sat across from each other in the C&C meeting room.

Ollie said, "Give me the update Roy, what's been going on while I was away?"

"The technical aspects of the habitats are all good. Food and energy production are exceeding expectations, as is industrial production. We have two new MHEVs that successfully made sea-ice surface journeys and were delivered to Melbourne and Brisbane, respectively."

"Each with a TM?"

"Yes, each with a trailer module."

Ollie leaned back in his chair, looking relaxed and satisfied.

"Sounds like you handled everything just fine. So why the urgent meeting?"

"As I said, the technology and habitat operations are fine, but I can't say the same about the political and societal aspects," said Roy.

"That's always the tricky bit. The fifth column you never see coming."

Roy said, "We have a low-level politician

trying to stage a power grab, or maybe even a coup, down in Melbourne. We also have what seems to be a religious cult staring up in Sydney, but I'm not sure how far it has spread, or how devout the followers are, but we are monitoring it."

Ollie leaned forward. His expression had become serious.

"Let's deal with the Melbourne issue first. What can you tell me?"

"There is a guy called Allan McLeod. From what I understand he was a local councillor, minor official, and political aspirant, before the Emergency. There is also a cloud hanging over his past financial dealings and integrity, so he may have been a bit crooked.

"Anyway, since the Emergency he has worked his way into the political system, developed a popularist following, and he has a gang of thugs he uses to intimidate people, not unlike Hitler's brown shirts. The current bunch of elected politicians, and senior officials, seem to be appeasing him for fear of losing their positions, or worse."

"I was hoping that by removing money from the equation, there would be less incentive for this kind of behaviour, and ambition. Do you know what he wants, or at least what he tells people he wants?" asked Ollie.

"I'm of the opinion that he just wants

power for the sake of power. It's not clear if he has a moral, or rational, agenda. I suppose he can make one up at any time to suit the circumstances. However, what he tells people is that he is fighting to get them more rights and better conditions, and he has suggested the reintroduction of money."

"That figures. It's one of the quickest ways to consolidate power. Just create a wealth hierarchy with yourself at the top," mused Ollie.

"He is also telling people that there is a habitat elite that are hoarding, and living the good life, while the common people have it hard. It's just classic catch-all popularism that doesn't rely on facts or evidence. Instead, it exploits people's struggles, fears, and imagination.

"He's doing the classic 'us versus them' ploy, with 'them' being C&C, and unfortunately, that means you are portrayed as the head of the snake. And it doesn't help that you have remained, for all intents and purposes, anonymous," said Roy.

"Hmm, this is an unfortunate development, but not unexpected. In fact, I am surprised it has taken so long, and I'm sure it won't be the last time it happens. As sure as breathing and breeding, power struggles are part of human nature and civil society."

Roy's demeanour was serious and devoid of his usual jokes.

Ollie continued, "Unfortunately, we cannot deal with this simply by presenting the facts and appealing to reason, at least not with this Allan character, or his party of followers. This is something that Plato and Aristotle warned us about over two thousand years ago, and yet in all that time since, no immune and rational polis has existed.

"Ironically, we are tempted to think, or even delude ourselves, that under our tutelage, maybe the next generation will be different if we just teach them the 'right' facts and values. Do you recognize the slippery slope here?" questioned Ollie. "The curtailing of freedom of expression, self-determination, and creativity? The allure of imposing one's morality, our morality, as in you and me, over another's, and of our own resistance to change and evolution? Is just so easy to give into this way of thinking."

"Yes, I do. Vexing, isn't it?" said Roy.

"If this Allan uses neither truth nor facts, then we are at a disadvantage if we remain honourable, despite what almost every proverb says on the subject. This situation is Machiavellian and requires a more cunning and strategic response. So, tell me Roy, at present, is he just one person surrounded by a small group of enablers?"

"My intelligence suggests that apart from the leader, there is a core group of 5 people. Apart from that, the thug army is just a collection of young wannabe gangsters. They could probably be distracted, or redirected, into other pursuits.

"And as for the general population, they are just desperate people clinging to hollow promises. Give them something shiny and pleasant, and a belief in better things to come, and they are likely to settle down again."

Ollie laughed, "Maybe you fail to see the irony. We have a population in need of an opioid, and then we also have an unwanted religion in our midst. They go together like peas in a pod."

"You're not quoting Marx are you? Wash your mouth out Mr Truss," said Roy.

They both chuckled, but it was peppered with a dose of introspection and contemplation.

"We must deal with this Melbourne situation immediately, thoroughly, and conclusively. The habitats, and the societies within, are too fragile to handle political intrigue, social division, and the distractions that may ensue. But we must also handle this discretely. We cannot create a martyr, a movement, or the perception of a malevolent controlling power. Thus, we must also protect our own reputation.

"However, having said that, that is exactly what we are in the eyes of our opponents, an evil overlord. And unfortunately, we must use the force of the State, in our case C&C, to commit coercion, and potentially violence, to dismember and bury all that this Allan has, or intends, to create.

"I will admit that I am uncomfortable with this, but as I see it, we are still under Emergency conditions, and as such, bullies, fools, and thugs cannot be tolerated."

Ollie paused and then said, "I'm sure every tyrant and dictator throughout history has uttered these same words."

"So, how do we put this into effect?" asked Roy.

"The first step is to neutralize Allan and his inner circle. I am presuming they suspect nothing of our hostility toward them?"

"I do not think so, but it is difficult to tell. I believe they are riding high and feel untouchable because of the appeasement thus far. But on the other hand, I do not know how paranoid they are. He has been proactive and successful so far, so he may already have plans in advance. Indeed, plans for us," said Roy.

"Understood, but I believe we need to make a move. Get Allan and the group of 5 up here under the pretext of official business. Be sure to make them feel important so they are motivated into our web by force of their own egos.

"Then, through some unforeseen event, split them up so they arrive separately. Once they are here, have them kept in comfortable isolation, I don't want them to think they are incarcerated, just waylaid and inconvenienced."

"I'm sure we can do that easily enough, things break, plans get changed. I understand what you are getting at," said Roy.

"Good. Now as for the thug army, I have a special treat for them. I want them press-ganged into the Submarine Corps. Split them up between the submarines or the Navy's ancillary services, such as in the Pacific Islands. Basically, give them new lives, and make them good lives in the service of humanity. Let's turn them into loyal seamen and guardian angels before they go too far over to the dark side.

"I want them to lose contact with their former ruffian affiliates and thereafter to organically form allegiance with what they perceive as a new gang, being the Submarine Navy. Actually, the timing works out well. We have two new submarines that require relief crews to be trained.

"Perhaps, you may consider fabricating an incident, the news of which is circulated only in Melbourne, and thus steer them toward a reality whereby they are almost willingly conscripted. I'll leave the details up to you. If in doubt, just review the history of war, and conscription, in the 20th century. You're an ex-military person, I'm sure you'll know what to do."

"I have some ideas and also a network of agents in place, so we should be able to make this happen quickly," said Roy.

"As for the general population, I have a different strategy. Just like here in Sydney, we have some secret ecosystems in Melbourne that were cultivated to preserve natural wildlife. Those ecosystems are probably stable enough to be opened to the public, but only under controlled conditions.

"This should work as a short-term distraction and a boost to moral. We will also announce, and begin construction on, better living conditions, better transport between the city habitats of the East Coast, and a program to construct surface domes to be enjoyed by the public. In effect we will do some good old fashion pork barrelling," said Ollie.

"That sounds like an achievable, and sustainable strategy. Now what are we going to do about the cult?" asked Roy.

"Can you give me some more background?" said Ollie.

"Yes. I have a couple of agents that have infiltrated the cult, so we have gotten some first-hand knowledge.

"As you are aware, there was a lot of soul searching immediately after the Emergency, although it was less than we had expected. Probably this was due to only 10-20% of the population being actively religious prior to the Emergency. And even then, that figure was split across several different religions.

"This new group is essentially a rapture cult. They preach that we, the survivors, are in a state of purgatory. The righteous have already gone to heaven and the wicked have already gone to hell."

Ollie had a confused look and said, "But already that doesn't make sense. People were spared, or survived, by virtue of their location and good fortune, not their religiosity or behaviour, how righteous or sinful they were."

"I'm not saying that it's rational, but then again are any cults rational? Heck is any religion rational? No, of course not. That's why they require faith," said Roy.

"So very true, please continue."

"To cleanse the soul and advance to heaven, devotees must adhere to certain practices and rituals. These may include how they dress, what they eat, what they can touch, and there are rules about how they gather and worship. Which, on the surface, are pretty much the fundamentals for any religion or secret society.

"Where I start to get worried, though, is that just one person is the divine interpreter and messenger. He has basically set himself up as a post-Emergency Jesus, Mohammad, Budda, Pope, Dali Lama, John Smith, whatever higher voice you may want to insert."

Ollie stood up and started to pace the room.

He said, "This one is going to be tricky to deal with, not unlike other non-state-sponsored religions that have existed in the past. The typical State response to an unwanted religion has been banishment, oppression, or genocide. However, these tactics never seem to have much success, and usually lead to civil unrest through to sectarian wars.

"If we crush this cult, then how can we, in good conscience, tolerate any other religions? It would be better to let it exist, but keep it constrained. Therefore, do not let it grow in power and therefore exert a disproportionate influence over society.

"I suppose, however, my greatest concern is the self-appointed leader. How long will it be before he starts to amass power and privilege, or how long before he becomes evangelical, or perceives himself, or themselves, as persecuted, or if they were to become suicidal?

"One of the beauties in the relationship between the State and sanctioned religions, is that they have agreed upon rules that respect secular society, placing boundaries on social influence. The general population knows the drill, and can either engage with a religion, or ignore it without guilt or fear of reprisal.

"But we are now in post-apocalyptic times. Perhaps those long-established rules, where the Church and State exist side by side, no longer apply."

"But won't it just fade away if we ignore it? If we don't give it support or attention, or at the very least, wouldn't it just remain a small splinter group?" asked Roy.

"It emerged from nothing, and so you suggest it may dissolve again to nothing? Yes, it may self-implode, but I doubt that it will, given our current circumstances.

"There is no arguing with the statistics, being that the more stable, safe, and educated a population is, the less it relies upon religion for answers and hope.

"Before the Emergency, religions were fading away. But then we lost our stability and safety, so it is to be expected that they should be on the rise again. I think all we can do is work on education and hope. Indeed that is part of the reason for advancing science and the mission to reach the stars.

"We must get this cult leader to meet with us, but without ceremony, so as not to legitimize him. Then we will lay down some ground rules for their existence. If he is smart, he will take the deal and behave within a secularized State. Our State. But if he is deranged, as may prove to be the case, then we will be forced to deal with it in a more repressive way."

That afternoon Ollie visited Production & Manufacturing (P&M), to discuss scavenging glass to construct domes. His plan was to build surface domes in each city, and for them to be as accessible to the population as a public park would be. It would allow people to see the sky, to see the remains of the cities, which could be artistically illuminated, and for the population to experience greater freedom. For them to believe that progress was being made.

The experts at P&M concurred that such structures could be built relatively quickly, and efficiently, using office-tower laminated glass and other resources readily available from the cities.

Ollie was walking back through a crowded tunnel lined with living quarters, then turned into a narrow cross-tunnel. The latter was long, dark, and deserted. As he reached the halfway point, three men stepped out of a recess and blocked his way.

He looked behind him and there were another two men entering the tunnel from where he had just come. He did not know if it was merely a coincidence, or if it was a plan to jump him. One of the three men blocking his way spoke.

"Where are *you* going man?"

Ollie didn't answer, but instead slowed his walk and looked behind a second time. The man spoke again.

"That's right, you better turn around and go back where you came from."

Ollie stopped. He knew it was no good

yelling for help. The crowds at either end of the tunnel were so loud that his voice would have been drowned out.

Finally, he said, "What do you want?"

"Nah, we don't want anything man. We were just told to give you a warning. Was told to tell you that you aren't such a big man, and you ought to keep your nose out of other people's business."

The other two men were now right behind him. One of them pushed him in the back and he stumbled forward, coming into striking range of the man doing the talking.

Ollie received a blow on the face, and another in the back, knocking the wind out of him and sending him to his knees. There were several more punches and kicks before he heard a distant shout. This caused his attackers to run off.

Two C&C agents helped him to his feet, blood was dripping from his nose and a gash above his eye. They wiped him down and took him to a nearby office where they patched him up. He had not been hurt badly but was roughed up sufficiently to look worse for wear. They also had delivered their message loud and clear.

However, that didn't mean he was intimidated or would heed it. Indeed, it was quite the opposite. It would make him more determined to follow through with his plans. If this is what things were coming to, then the situations in the tunnels, in the society, were more perilous than he had previously imagined.

Ollie said to the C&C agents, "I'm certainly lucky you guys came along when you did."

One of the men replied, "Sir, we are very sorry that we were not there sooner. This could have all been prevented."

"What were you doing in that sector?" asked Ollie.

"Sir, we were instructed to keep you under surveillance from a distance, and to make sure you did not come to any harm."

"Who placed that order?" asked Ollie.

"We receive our orders directly from Colonel Bright at C&C. We are part of your security detail."

"Ollie looked closer at the agent.

"Oh yes, I've seen you before. Sometimes you are standing guard at the entrance to the communications center. Does Roy Sandalwood know about this?"

"I believe so, sir. It was the Major who made the recommendation to Colonel Bright upon your return. It was on account of the deteriorating political, and social conditions. We were instructed to monitor you from a distance, but to not interfere unless you were in danger."

So, it seemed the military had formed a coven in his absence. He supposed that this was a natural response to their situation. It's what they had been trained to do all their careers. They were now police, security, and spies, all wrapped into one. And furthermore, it seemed that the 'force' was his own personal 'Swiss Guard'.

As handy as this was, especially saving him today, he would still need to keep a close eye on it. It could be as dangerous, or worse, than a rogue politician, or an unsanctioned religion.

"Did you manage to identify, or catch, the assailants?" asked Ollie.

"Not yet, sir, but I am sure they would have passed one or more surveillance cameras. The footage will be reviewed, and we will hopefully pick them up in a day or so. There are not too many places they can hide."

Ollie said, "You may want to consider keeping an eye on submarine boardings, I have a suspicion they may try to return to Melbourne. Also, when you do pick them up, do not mistreat them. Instead hold them in individual cells and notify me."

"Yes, sir. Sir, we have a trolly waiting to take you back to the C&C communications center."

They helped him onto the trolley and as he travelled through the crowded streets with his armed escort, he obscured his face with a bloodied cloth. He was helped to his room, as the busing began to hurt. Especially on his back and ribs.

Later a guard knocked on the door of his

apartment.

"Yes, ah, he squinted as he read the name badge, Agent Sanchez?"

"Sir, you have a visitor at the main door, shall I let her through? She says her name is Jan and she is a friend of yours."

"Yes, please, bring her through," mumbled Ollie. He had taken a significant dosage of painkillers and was feeling drowsy. Then he thought to himself, 'How did she know where to find me, and why is she turning up straight after his incident?'

Jan came through the door almost running. She went to hug him and then stopped, fearing she may cause pain, so she just grabbed his arm.

"Are you OK? Are you hurt?"

She looked him over and turned his face to better see the cut above his eye.

"I'm OK, just a bit bruised and a few scrapes."

She led him over to the bed and made him sit down.

"Who did this? Have they caught them? Why did they do this? You haven't hurt anyone have you?" Then in a sterner tone she repeated, "Have you?"

"We don't know who is responsible yet, but C&C will pick them up soon. We are not sure of the reason, but there are some political undercurrents, and I suspect it is related to them," he said.

Ollie continued, "As for if I have done anything wrong, well, I suppose that depends on who you ask. If you ask me, then no. At least not deliberately. But we have all had to endure some crazy things since the Emergency, so who can say. There will always be someone with a grudge, or ambition. I suppose in this game you must get them before they get you."

"So, does this mean you're not safe anymore? I suppose it does. Heck, is anyone safe anymore if there are gangs roaming the tunnels!" said Jan.

Ollie then asked, "How did you know what had happened, and where to find me?"

"Roy called at the apartment and told me what happened, and where I could find you," she said.

Ollie said, "That was nice of him."

"Roy said that he had put a security detail on you since you returned yesterday. He was worried something like this might happen. Oh my God, I had no idea that things had changed so much in the time we were away."

"I'm not sure if they have changed. Trouble was always brewing below the surface. It was probably more a case that they made the best of an opportunity. That is, me being alone in a secluded tunnel," he said.

Jan smiled and said, "See, you need me. I'm away from you for one day and look what happens."

Ollie laughed, and then winced and said, "Ouch," as he held his jaw.

"I don't care what you say, I'm staying here tonight. You need someone to watch over you," said Jan in a defiant voice.

"I'm in the second most heavily guarded part of the habitat, after the submarine base, and they have nuclear missiles."

"I don't care, I'm staying," she said.

Two meals were delivered to his room. Ollie opened the small cupboard under his desk and retrieved a bottle of whiskey. It was one that he had scavenged from the distillery. He couldn't drink much due to his medication, but he knew Jan would appreciate a shot.

As Jan took her glass, she looked around his room and noticed the picture.

She gestured to it and said, "I've been there. I caught a ferry across to Mykonos in the Cyclades. That's in Greece, if you didn't know."

"I thought it was somewhere around there, maybe Santorini?"

"No, it's definitely Mykonos," she said.

She walked over and looked closely at the picture, and then pointed a finger.

"See that windmill in the corner? I stood right there and took a picture. It's a shame I don't have it. Well, actually, it's probably still at my parents' house, along with everything else from my early years. You don't suppose we could go and get our stuff back one day?"

"I imagine that one day we will, that is provided someone else doesn't get there first. They won't know if they are survivor's possessions or not, so you can't blame them. Anyway, how was your trip to Greece?" he asked.

"It was fantastic. I went with a girlfriend of mine, but she hooked up with a guy, another tourist, so we parted ways. I basically toured the island by myself.

"I would have loved to take you there. You would have really enjoyed it. And oh my God, the food, and the sunsets. A calamari dinner at sunset with the Aegean lapping at your feet. It is something I will treasure forever," she looked into the distance as she said it.

"I'm kind of jealous. I don't have any memories like that. When I first saw the picture, I thought of how much I would have liked to have gone there. But I didn't, and now it's too late."

"Well, Mr Oliver Truss, we are all relying on you to find us another planet with a bright warm sun. So, as soon as you do that, we can create another Mykonos, or what have you, and then we can make you some memories. Happy memories."

They enjoyed a desert of chocolate cake. It seemed better than the normal packet mix that had been the standard ration since the Emergency. Perhaps Roy had a word with the cooks and asked them to whip something up especially for him, given his sorry condition.

This time it was Jan who held Ollie while he slept. He was out cold on account of the drugs. She lay there looking at the picture and thinking that surely it was going to get better than this. Better than living in an underground bunker and looking at a picture from the past. Maybe not for her generation, but perhaps for those to come.

Maybe Mazie or Sally would once again experience the sun on their faces, and the wind in their hair. If anyone was going to make that happen it would be Ollie. She vowed to look after him, to do whatever it took to never let anything like this happen to him again. She would talk to Roy and see if she could get included in the security briefs, as they related to Ollie, and if possible, accompany him when he would otherwise think that he was unguarded.

CHAPTER 24

Through rapid development and intensive use of technology, the conditions of life and security in the habitats improved for the survivors. After his return from Oak Ridge, Ollie commissioned work to build a magnetic levitation train that ran to Brisbane, Sydney, and Melbourne.

Many of the difficulties that had plagued designs in the past no longer existed. The surface was now so cold that super-conducting and super-magnetism were achieved with little effort. And because there was no atmosphere, there was no air resistance. Thus, they could achieve extremely high speeds without friction and energy loss. Also, due to the frozen ocean, they could lay down perfectly level tracks on the ice that, for most of their distance, curved as gentle arcs spanning 1000's of kilometres.

It was a monorail design, so just a single track laid on the ice. No bridges, cuttings, or tunnels. The single rail did not even need to be one continuous piece in the straight high-speed sections. Strong magnetic fields spanned gaps between rails and the 250m carriages spanned multiple gaps. The train had been tested up to 5,000kph, but was limited to 3,000kph until long term studies had been completed. The travel time between the Australian habitats was now around 30 minutes for both passengers and freight.

Construction had also begun on a line that ran from Sydney to Charleston. The route would run Sydney to Wellington, New Zealand, (2,250km), to Tierra del Fuego, at the Southern tip of South America (8,000km), to Recife, on the Eastern tip of Brazil (6000km), and then finally to Charleston, United States (6,500km).

It was a total length of 22,750km with only 3 bends, the rest being perfectly straight and flat. At 3,000kph the train would take less than 8 hours from Sydney to Charleston, not including stops at outposts, as opposed to the 20+ days in the cramped submarines. Outposts had been established at each of the bends in the track, thus expanding the footprint of the post-Emergency civilization.

Four telecommunication satellites of the Starlink type were uncovered at Oak Ridge. They were modified to run on nuclear batteries and launched from a disarmed, multiple warhead, intercontinental ballistic missile from a submarine. Although they only provided moderate bandwidth, it was now possible to have a 24-hour link between all habitats, including the Pacific Islands, Oak Ridge, as well as submarines when they surfaced.

Each settlement constructed surface domes of varying sizes. Oak Ridge got a dome that completely covered the campus. The construction utilized a frame of salvaged materials and argon filled triple glazed glass panel sections. The domes did not have to contend with sun or weather, only gravity, which was partly offset by the atmospheric pressure inside the dome.

However, they did risk being punctured by micro-meteors due to the loss of Earth's protective atmosphere. Ironically though, with the Earth now effectively being in 'clearer' interstellar space, there were far fewer meteors.

The domes were predominately used as native plant and animal ecosystems. They had simulated day and night, as well as weather conditions commensurate with the appropriate season for the location. People could wander throughout the ecosystems under the domes enjoying nature and the freedom that comes with open spaces.

Within the habitats, the secret ecosystems were also opened to the public, but under controlled conditions, so not to cause damage or disrupt breeding programs.

Through the combination of structural and social engineering, the political and social problems that were beginning to fester quickly dissipated. Allan McLeod was interrogated and charged with initiating the assault on Ollie, as well as various other offenses. He was relocated to Hawaii under a relatively comfortable house arrest. His five co-conspirators were given lesser, but similar, punishments.

The thug army, including the thugs that attacked Ollie, were absorbed into the submarine services. Within a short time they were transformed into respectable sailors and productive members of the community.

Jan was meeting Ollie for lunch. Since his assault, Jan had become known to the guards, so they waved her through whenever she came to see him. She entered the command center and found him at his desk reading a report.

"Did you remember we were going out for lunch?" she asked.

He looked up and said, "Yes, but I'm sorry, I can't make it. I've got some issues that need immediate attention."

In a frustrated tone she said, "Why didn't you let me know? I didn't come all this way just to be turned away."

He sounded apologetic as he said, "I tried to call you, but Sally answered your phone. She said that you had already left."

"Yes, I left early because I had some things to do. And Sally had my phone because she misplaced hers. Again! But still, this is the second time this week you have cancelled on me," she said in a defiant voice.

"I'm really, really sorry, but I do have a plan to make it up to you. How would you like to go away for the weekend? And I'm thinking all of us. You, Mazie, Sally and myself, and no business, I promise," he smiled and made big eyes at her.

"Where would we be going and what would we be doing?" was her sulking response.

"I'm going to keep that a secret. All I can say is bring clothes for warm weather and something to swim in."

This lifted her mood, "Ooh, I am intrigued. And I'm sure the girls will love it," she said with a smile.

The train route between Sydney and Brisbane had already begun operating but was not officially opened to the public. The railway station was located next to the submarine dock on the edge of the Pacific Ocean. The train looked very futuristic, as if it were something from science fiction.

Ollie, Jan, and the girls entered the bright, long, cabin. It was cylindrical, with the lower half being metal covered in generic public transport carpet, whereas the upper section was composite windows. When one sat in the seats, again salvaged from public transport, there was an uninterrupted view from above waist height that included the dark landscape and the full sky.

There were other people on the train, all of them dressed in work clothes and carrying supplies and equipment. No doubt they were commuting to work from Sydney to Brisbane. The train moved forward smoothly and silently into the long thin airlock. It was an igloo that stretched out onto the ice. After depressurization the door opened, and they headed out into the cold and dark.

It was the first time that Sally had been on the surface since the Emergency, and she looked in wonder at the vast open space and the stars above. To their left and behind them were the lights of the habitat's surface structures. Spotlights had also been strategically placed around the city to illuminate features of cultural significance like the Harbour Bridge and Opera House.

The train rapidly gathered speed, all the while remaining perfectly smooth and balanced, as it rode a cushion of magnetic repulsion. They were able to go to the front of the cabin and view the rail ahead. The interior lights had dimmed, and the bright headlight pushed deep into the black. In the cabin it was like traveling on a jetliner at night with each person having their own small light on a retractable stalk.

There was a digital readout that showed their speed. Within five minutes they had passed 2,000kph, yet they only experienced a slight, but persistent, sensation of acceleration. The vast featureless plain of ice gave the impression they were not moving at all. It was only when one focused on the rail, or the beacon lights that flashed past every five kilometres, that one could appreciate the incredible speed.

Within thirty minutes they could see the habitat lights of Brisbane on the horizon and began to feel a gentle deceleration. It was ironic that it was not until after the Emergency that such a method of transport could be built for public use.

The train curved to the left and entered the Brisbane River. They passed the former Port of Brisbane, and then continued upriver until the city rose around them. Ahead was another igloo airlock, the outer doors open and ready to receive. Once they had repressurized, they alighted onto what was once the Riverside Walkway.

The panorama in front, and above them, was a portion of the city that had come back to life, protected under a massive clear dome. Former office and residential apartments reached high into the enclosed sky. The streets had restaurants and cafes', and there was the Brisbane River, with clear water lapping the walkway and the opposite bank. The temperature was warm, probably 28°C, and the air was slightly humid. This was a change from Sydney that usually sat around 24°C midday in the tunnels, and was less humid.

Jan gasped and said, "Oh my God, how did you do this? How far back does it extend? It's just how I remember it from before the Emergency."

Ollie responded with pride, "The dome extends just past the first line of high-rise buildings, then across the river and just beyond the civic buildings. It includes the art gallery, library, museum and performing arts center. We managed to cover several square kilometres of city and, as you can see, included a portion of the river.

"We re-established the recreation precinct, the parklands, and the botanical gardens. Then we sealed off and thawed a section of river, filtered the water, and warmed it to its natural temperature. This dome is warmer than you are used to in Sydney, and it is the river that gives it the humidity."

"Can we swim, maybe in the river?" Sally excitedly asked.

"You can, but perhaps not in the river. It's a bit deep, there is a current, and there is aquatic life that we are trying to re-establish, including bull sharks and sting rays. However, if you look over in the distance, you will see that there is a large swimming pool which is part of the South Bank recreation precinct. It is safe, and lovely for swimming, and then afterward we can go for a ride on the Ferris wheel."

The protected surface was a hive of activity, with people working on re-opening cafes, re-furbishing apartment buildings, and re-establishing plants. There were many dead trees devoid of leaves, however, these were getting vines and ferns draped over them until newly planted trees became established.

The light above was that of midday, but there was no sensation of heat from a sun. Rather, it was the air that was warm, and it carried a breeze. In places the breeze was stronger as it wound its way around buildings and down alleyways, allowing leaves to rustle and flowers to sway. They crossed a footbridge, the Goodwill Bridge, and stopped at a café to get a drink and cake. It was just like old times, except without so much sugar, and with no money changing hands.

After the girls had used the change rooms, they jumped into the clear blue water of the pool. Jan and Ollie sat on the newly established lawn and watched them.

Jan said, "Oh look, there's a bee," then continued, "Did they manage to save much in the art gallery and museum?"

"Yes, everything was almost perfectly preserved. It was quite amazing. And during the Emergency many species of invertebrate that were being studied at the Museum were taken underground and saved."

"So does that mean we still have funnel

web spiders?" Jan said, contorting her body with disgust.

Ollie laughed and said, "Yes, unfortunately it does. Along with fruit bats and box jelly fish. But hey, everything in its place, right?"

"Which leads me to my next question, where will we be staying tonight?" she enquired.

"Pretty much anywhere we want."

Then Ollie pointed to a tall building on the CBD side of the river, and said, "How about the Queen's Wharf Tower over there? I think it's now ready to take guests."

"OK, that sounds nice. So, is the plan to turn Brisbane into a tourist and entertainment precinct?" Jan asked.

"Yes. Well, this part at least. They still have normal habitat below, just like we do down in Sydney. Eventually we want to create similar surface environments in every place we create a habitat, be that in Australia or Pacific Islands and eventually, across the world."

"Wow, across the world. That's really exciting. So that means that one day we actually *could* go to Mykonos!" Jan asked with excitement.

"Sure, why not. I suppose we are now only limited by our imaginations and our population," said Ollie.

The girls got out of the pool and dried off on the grass and then asked if they could all go on the Ferris wheel.

There was no line to stand and wait in. Perhaps in a few weeks it would be busy, but for now they had it all to themselves. The carriage took them high above the river and almost level with the tops of the buildings. They could almost touch the dome, and they could see beyond its lights and into the night sky above.

It was getting late in the afternoon and the dome was starting to dim and turn orange.

Mazie said, "I wish I could see and feel the sun again."

"You will." Ollie said, "Someday in some way, I'm sure you will."

When they came down from the ride, they went to a Mexican cantina style restaurant. The cook did his best to recreate tacos using the supplies he had on hand. They all agreed that they tasted good, and that it felt authentic.

After their meal they walked along the banks of the river as the faux sun was setting. Sprinkles of fairy-lights lit the trees, and fish jumped in the water trying to grab insects. It was just like a pre-Emergency family outing. It was exactly what Ollie had wanted to create for the general population, and also for Jan and the girls.

Their apartment was opulent, spacious, and had a fantastic view of the river and entertainment district. It was such a novel experience compared to what they had endured for the past few years.

There were enough bedrooms for each person to have their own, however, Jan sneaked into Ollie's room after the girls had gone to sleep.

"This has been such a perfect day," she said.

"Was it as perfect as the mountain meadow?" asked Ollie.

"No, that was different. That was the first time experiencing absolute and overwhelming happiness. Perhaps it was because I had been scared and sad for so long." And then she said coyly, "That was more a romantic fantasy, whereas this is more real."

When they woke up in the morning, it was as if they were still dreaming. Being able to open the curtains and have a view was such a novel luxury. They went down an elevator to the dining area and had a buffet style breakfast.

It was busy, filled with workers having their breakfasts. They, too, had been staying in the apartments. Scrambled eggs, beans, and sausages were a treat, but the best part was tropical fruit. There was mango, pineapple, pawpaw, and other fruits they had never seen before but tasted great.

These had been grown underground in orchards, most of the varieties being fast growing, but in other cases mature trees must have somehow been rescued or protected during the Emergency.

They spent the day enjoying the warm

weather, swimming, and exploring the streets. They came across a bookshop that was filled with paper books. This fascinated them, especially Sally, and they spent hours inspecting the shelves and leafing through pages.

Paper had all but been eliminated from the habitats, with the exception of toilet paper. This was because it was so resource intensive to make, especially with all of the necessary trees being in plantations far from their underground settlements.

Where possible paper was replaced with digital formats, so there were very few books to be found anymore. And during the emergency, no one was worried about preserving books or magazines, so they were either left behind or burned for warmth. People were more concerned about clothes and food than literature and lifestyle.

They returned to the dockside station for the evening maglev back to Sydney. It had been a wonderful experience, and it lifted their spirts like nothing else could.

In the past this may have been just a normal weekend in a city, but now it was savoured as a rare treat. All of them realized how much they had taken for granted in the past. Like people who had lived in paradise and yet complained about the monotony of perfect weather.

The return journey was only 30 minutes before they were back in Sydney. When they entered the habitat proper, they noticed that the smell was different. So, it was true. Every place has its own smell and, no doubt, subtle cultural differences.

They wondered how long it would be before there were sporting rivalries between the cities, like a revival of State of Origin rugby matches, Test Cricket, or Super Bowl. Would that be a sign that finally the Emergency was over? It was worth pondering.

CHAPTER 25

The train had just repressurized in Wellington, (Te Whanganui-a-Tara), New Zealand. The trip from Syndey had taken around one hour. This was as far as the Intercontinental railway had progressed. The Wellington outpost was still under construction, with its worker population reliant on imports of food and supplies.

Apart from the site's convenience as a rest-stop along the railway line, there were also plans to develop it further. Although its seismic history had to be taken into consideration. Regardless, there was great enthusiasm by New Zealanders to revive and preserve Aotearoa and Māori culture. Ollie stepped off the train and headed to the nearby submarine port to catch the USS Nebraska to Charleston.

Compared to the train, the submarine trip was long and cramped, and it made him feel like he was wasting valuable days of his life in transit. It was so under-appreciated how much speed had changed the world, and it is only when the pace is restricted that its drudgery becomes apparent. Of course, people used to say that the pace of the world was too fast in the past, but that was only true if you were in a rush to get nowhere and engage in pointless tasks.

Upon arrival at Charleston, the Nebraska surfaced inside an igloo out on the river. Ollie recalled his first trip, when he had fallen off the edge of the submarine and torn his suit. Oh, how that seemed so long ago. Now they had a safe and comfortable gangway for the passengers and goods being transferred.

The igloo was a long tunnel that ran all the way to shore where there was a small outpost acting as a transit hub. In time they would establish a train through to Oak Ridge, but for now he would have to travel by MHEV. It was waiting for him at the transit hub. He climbed into the familiar vehicle and made the dark 8-hour journey.

He laughed as they passed the sign for Oak Boundary distillery. Apparently, scavengers from Oak Ridge had removed most of the stock, and it was slowly being sipped away between hard days in the lab.

Danny was there to meet him when they repressurized. The two had maintained contact via email since the satellites were launched, but now that he was seeing him face to face, he realized that Danny's hair had grown long, and he was sporting a beard. He really did look like a mad scientist now. He still looked ratty, but if there was such a thing as a woolly rat, like a woolly mammoth or rhino, then that was what he reminded Ollie of.

Ollie extended his hand and said, "Danny, hello, good to see you. It's been a long time. It looks like you've gone native. Are you going for the grizzly bear look?"

"Ah yes, the hair and beard. No, no, I've just been too busy to worry about things like that. You wait. You wait 'till you see how far we have come. Ooh, you are going to like this," Danny said in his fast exited way.

"I was hoping to unpack first, and maybe grab a meal, and then some sleep. That submarine trip really takes it out of you. Would it be OK if we got into the heavy stuff tomorrow?"

"Yeah, yeah, sure, I'll walk with you. I suppose I should eat something too. I can't remember when I last ate. Not that I'm hungry. I mean I am hungry, I could eat, but I'm not always hungry. We have good food here. There is still a lot coming from Knoxville, and when that gets depleted, there are plenty of other cities that can be scavenged. They are not very far, so it's OK."

"How much coffee have you had today?" enquired Ollie.

"I'm not sure, about the same as usual. Yeah, probably had too much coffee, but then again, there is so much to do. But you just wait, I'll show you tomorrow."

Danny accompanied Ollie, all the time engaging in his distracted rambles that regularly spat out incredibly interesting facts. They walked across the surface of the campus under its dome. Some enterprising scientists had converted carparks to vegetable gardens and orchards of fruit, including peaches and cherries.

Ollie was accommodated in his old office, the one he had shared with Jan in the past. After Danny left him for the night, he reclined in the large leather chair. It wasn't the same without Jan, as the nostalgia of those heady dangerous days came flooding back. He sent Jan a text message but received no reply by the time he had fallen asleep. In the middle of the night, he checked his phone again and she had replied while he had been sleeping. He smiled but thought it too late to begin a conversation. It could wait till morning. At least she knew he had arrived safely.

The following morning Danny took Ollie to a lab that was abnormally secure.

"I just can't have anyone wandering in here. It's not that I have secrets, it's just that what I am doing may be too dangerous or unpredictable. So, I put a lock on the door. I don't lock anything else, just this door," Danny said as he rummaged through his pockets for the key.

The lab was full of equipment that had been cobbled together. Although it was a large room, maybe two thirds of the floor space was taken up by apparatus connected to high voltage power cables and cooling tubes. As they walked through the room, they had to step over all manner of items, including cables and pipes running in every direction.

Danny went over to a large console and pushed some buttons. Lights blinked, pump motors began to whirl, while other equipment started to hum. A small metal sphere, about the size of a walnut, levitated and then remained hovering between what appeared to be two large magnets. Danny handed Ollie a hard hat and some tinted goggles.

He said, "Just pays to be safe, but don't worry, if I thought you were in any danger, we'd be standing outside and looking through the viewing window."

"I trust you," said Ollie. "So, Danny, tell me what I am supposed to be looking at?"

"Yes, OK, OK. Now, all you have to do is watch the metal sphere. The light will brighten a bit, but it won't get too bright, so you shouldn't have a problem seeing if you keep the glasses on. OK, just keep watching."

Danny pushed some more buttons, and the humming became louder. A bright blue plasma glowed and shimmered around the metal sphere, then there was a slight dimming of the lights in the lab.

Ollie looked over at him and said, "How much power are you using?"

"Ah, I'm not sure. Maybe most of it," said Danny in a carefree manner.

"What, you mean most of the output from a nuclear power station?" ask Ollie.

"Yeah, probably. Do you want the exact numbers in megawatts?"

"No, that's OK, I'm sure you know what you're doing," said Ollie.

Danny shrugged and continued his work at the consol. Then, as Ollie watched, the sphere faded out of existence. It just disappeared. Danny then pushed another button, and the sphere reappeared about five seconds later.

Ollie was confused and said, "Did what I think happened, just happen? Did the sphere disappear and then reappear?"

"Yes, your eyes were not deceiving you. It completely vanished and then reappeared, but that's not the coolest part. Now watch it again."

Ollie concentrated on the sphere, and again the equipment got louder, the glow brightened, and then the sphere disappeared. About five seconds later there was the sound of something metal dropping on the concrete floor at the other side of the room. Immediately, he turned his attention to where he heard the noise, and there was an identical metal sphere rolling to a stop on the floor. Surely, it wasn't the same sphere, was it?

Danny began talking before Ollie could get a word out.

"So how cool is that? It's the same sphere. The first time it disappeared, it entered the void, you know, from the theory I have discussed with you on numerous occasions. All this equipment you can see generated the void around the sphere, which allowed it to enter it. Then when I turned off the void generator, it reappeared.

Then the second time I turned it on, I ever-so-slightly nudged the balance between the two poles of the void field generator, and this caused the sphere to move through the void relative to our perception of space. I then turned off the void generator and the sphere fell back into reality at a different location. I just nudged it a tiny bit. If I nudge it more, then it can move much further."

"How much further?" asked Ollie.

"Well, I did some experimenting. I've dropped spheres in the neighbouring building, out on the campus grounds, and there are a few that I never found. I believe they may be in orbit around Jupiter. The distance is a function of the intensity of polar imbalance, and of duration. Yeah, so it is somewhere in the orbital plane of Jupiter, if Jupiter is still there, or at least at that distance from Earth."

"So, you are you saying, the longer the duration, and the greater the imbalance, then the faster, and therefore further, it moves?"

questioned Ollie.

"Correct. To give you a rudimentary explanation, to move it to the other side of this room is a nano second. To send it to another lab is 1.25 nano seconds, and then to the other side of the campus is a 1.5 nano second. According to my calculations, when I did the imbalance for 10 seconds, the sphere should have travelled 744 million kilometres.

"That's the beauty of exponential functions. You know the story about folding a piece of paper and reaching the moon? Well, same thing. However, there are also other variables such as the length of the void field projection, but I am yet to get data on that. I really need to build a different shaped vehicle, and re-design the generators to understand the full potential," he said.

"And the sphere, or a future vehicle, will not be affected by any structures, like walls, or the dome, or anything?" asked Ollie.

"As far as I can tell, no. The trajectory, if I can call it that, is a perfectly linear vector from the point of origin. So, if I send it to the next lab, it will traverse the dialled-in distance, but not interact with the wall between the labs. Then it will re-emerge at the same height as the sphere originally was in this lab if the vector is level. Then, under gravity, it will fall to the floor. If my point of origin is below ground level then, if I sent it outside, it would emerge below ground level, and we would have to dig it up to retrieve it. The object will only interact with the realities of this universe once it comes out of the void."

"I am a bit confused. If the field generator is here, then how does it fall out of the void somewhere else?" asked Ollie.

"That is a good question. It is because we give the sphere imbued energy. Let's call it dark energy. And that energy dissipates. So, I will give it enough energy, and a vector, to reach a certain point in the void, and then it will fall out of the void when the energy has dissipated. However, if the sphere has its own field generator on board, then it could manipulate the dark energy however it wished, such as remaining in the void, speeding up or slowing down, or even changing direction, all within the void."

Ollie was excited and said, "I must say, this is an amazing achievement, congratulations, extremely well done."

"Thank you. I am rather proud of myself, and so happy that my theory has been proven to work."

"So, Danny, where do we go from here?" he asked.

"I was thinking that my next step would be to send a larger object into the void and then have it return, perhaps something the size of a basketball. But to do that I would have to build a larger void generator."

"And how long would that take?"

"About as long as it took to build this one, but obviously using more resources," said Danny.

"But isn't the ultimate goal to have the field generator inside the object being transferred, and for that to be a spaceship?" said Ollie.

"Yes, you are right. Technically it is not difficult to incorporate the generator into a large ship and focus the void field into beams that project out either end of the craft. The problem is having the portable power required to run the void field generator," said Danny.

"And I suppose that is what the nuclear fusion research is for?" said Ollie.

"Correct. It is the only way we can achieve the sustained power density. And the size of the fusion unit will determine the size of the spaceship. Currently it's too big. We need to miniaturize it. And on top of that, we need an energy source to kick start the fusion reactor. So, we will need a small fission rector, or similar, to generate the plasma and magnetic containment fields for the fusion process. Once the fusion side of things gets running, then it can be self-sustaining."

Ollie thought about it and then said, "Here is my advice Danny. Put all your teams' efforts into building the power source and void generator for a spacecraft. It's all very well to do incremental experiments, and I know that as scientist it is what you are trained to do, but in this instance, I just want you to have faith and start to build the inner workings of the spaceship."

"So, you are saying, just do it?" asked Danny with youthful enthusiasm.

"That is exactly what I am saying. You develop the power supply, the void generator, and figure out the propulsion strength and vectoring issues. I will set up another team to work on constructing the hull, life support, and other particulars. I will send you as many people as you need.

"I want this fast tracked, just like everything else we have been doing. This is our real future. To explore the stars and colonise new worlds, not to live like moles beneath the permafrost."

Danny rubbed his hands together and said, "I've got some ideas, but I hope I don't blow anything up while testing them."

Ollie calmly responded, "As they say, 'eggs get broken'. If you need to do something a bit dangerous, then get an MHEV and go out into the wilderness and do it. For God's sake, don't blow up the habitat."

They both knew that the slightest breach of the dome, or destruction of key life support systems, would be disastrous and could result in the loss of many lives. They had been methodical in the construction and operation of the habitats, and so far, there had not been any catastrophic failures. Yet still, there was always a risk. They lived so close to the conditions of outer space it was as if they resided in a very fragile space station.

CHAPTER 26

It had been 3 years since the Emergency and the expansion of human colonies was now only limited by insufficient population and skills. There needed to be a minimum of both, to maintain a civic habitat. There was a heavy focus on training and re-skilling. So many of the jobs that existed before the Emergency were no longer of any use. As people graduated into new and relevant fields, they would be put to work. Some locally, but most out in the growing colonies, formerly known as the outposts.

Three fully fledged habitats existed in Australia, two in New Zealand, one on Guam and two on Hawaii. Two new outpost habitats were created along the International Train route, one at Tierra Del Fuego, Chile, and the other at Recife, on the East coast of Brazil. In North America there were two sites, being the rail terminus and transfer station at Charleston, and the domed campus city at Oak Ridge.

Submarines had explored coastlines around the globe, but the results had always been the same. Apart from the already discovered survivors, the world was dead. Two more serviceable nuclear submarines had been found on the East Coast of the United States and were reactivated, but they were presumed to be the last.

High levels of radiation had been found along the Chinese coast, as well as in the Bay of Biscay West of France. It was presumed that nuclear power plants had gone critical after the Emergency and exploded. Their radiation had not spread very far, due to a shut-down in global winds, not long after the loss of the sun.

There had been a submarine mission to the Svalbard Global Seed Vault in Norway to retrieve seeds for reestablishment. Many of the seeds were viable, but not all. Once habitat space for populations had been satisfied, most newly reclaimed areas, that is domed areas, were dedicated to creating natural ecosystems. And although humans could visit them, they could not settle in them or conduct agriculture or industry within them. They were the equivalent of yesteryear's national parks, and some even contained bears, wolves, tigers, and other apex predators.

Work was also fast-tracked in genetic engineering, including cloning and de-extinction. There had been moderate success in re-establishing various animals and marine species.

There was also a concerted effort to increase the human birth rate, and to also broaden the population's genetic diversity. Various social programs were implemented to encourage interaction between people of differing genetic heritage, and thereafter, breeding was incentivized. The idea was to create the strongest stock of humans before they once again diversified through isolation.

Mazie was almost 18 years old and had graduated from Knowledge in biology. She had already been approached by several suiters, but as yet had not found anyone she wanted to partner with. She was focussed on her studies and wanted to achieve a doctorate before having a baby.

Social structures and rituals were no longer how they had been before the Emergency. It was no longer fashionable to get married anymore, but some people still did. Yet, married or not, people were encouraged to have large families, and these would be supported by the community and by the State. While the habitats had the capacity to expand, repopulating the Earth was seen as a civic duty. It was like the old saying, 'Lay back and think of England.' Although unlike in times past, there were no arranged or forced marriages. It was a more nuanced approach.

Jan was regularly propositioned by men, and in social circles she was often nagged about why she was neither married nor had children. She would always say that she had Mazie and Sally, but that was just her making excuses. Most of her free time was spent either with the girls or, when he was available, with Ollie.

Ollie had relocated to a grand residence on the surface after the Sydney dome had been completed. Whether it was fair or not, he had been awarded the privileged to live up there, whereas most people remained in tunnel apartments. Some had argued that he should take the residence because he was constantly entertaining officials from other habitats, and that it was appropriate for someone regarded as the Head of State to live in a place befitting the title.

It was only a short trolley ride for Jan. She enjoyed being on the surface and walking through the Royal Botanical Parklands to visit him at Government House. The view of the Sydney Opera House reminded her of a time when monuments were symbols of National pride. The Opera House had reopened, and performances had begun. Some of them were rather amateur, but then again, the pool of virtuosos had shrunk dramatically after the Emergency, so any excuse for a night out was welcomed.

On more than one occasion she had been tempted to put Ollie on the spot and ask him where their relationship was going. She found, surprisingly, that she was old fashion in that way. Maybe it was just that time on her biological clock. She did want to get married and have children rather than just be someone's mistress.

She knew she had options. Some of the men that propositioned her were attractive, and pleasant to be with. But unfortunately, they were not Ollie, and they did not make her feel the way he had made her feel at crucial times in her life. Ollie and she were good together. It was always fun and exciting, either when they were doing mundane things, or dangerous things. He knew just what to do, or say, to keep her thinking of him, and always coming back.

She also knew that he was faithful. He literally had no time to be anything else. He was always pleased to see her, and he never wanted her to leave, yet he never obligated her to stay, and that was frustrating. Why couldn't he just lose his cool, his temper, and demand that she stay? Put a damn ring on her finger or something. This free to come and go as she wished was convenient and pragmatic, yet infuriating.

She passed the guards and entered the building, no longer needing to knock or announce herself. Ollie was in the kitchen cooking,

"I thought you had someone to do that for you?" she said.

"I do, but I sent them home. When I have

the time, I actually enjoy cooking." He wiped his hands and then said, "I hope you are hungry, because I made something special."

"I honestly didn't know that you could cook. I suppose the subject never came up. It smells really good, what is it?" asked Jan.

"It's grilled salmon and steamed vegetables with hollandaise sauce," he said proudly.

Jan exclaimed, "Oh my God, yum! But where on earth did you get salmon?"

"We have been working on a breeding program for a while now, and this is from the first harvest. Soon they will be rationed across the habitats, but for now they are very rare. I was presented with this one for my appraisal, so here we are, and you are going to be the official taster," he said as he put the plate on the kitchen bench.

"Well, aren't I lucky," said Jan. "I suppose it's true that it's not what you know, but who you know."

"And, I have a bottle of Pinot Grigio to complement it. I hope you like white wine."

"It has been so long since I had a glass of white wine. Probably not since well before the Emergency. Yes, I love it, as long as it's chilled. Everything you do is perfect. What makes you so clever? Aww, and look, you even set the patio table, put the wine on ice, and there are fresh flowers in a vase. It looks more like a fancy restaurant, than dinner at home," she said as she walked through the French doors outside to the patio. He followed her outside with the plates of food, then ran back inside to fetch some freshly baked bread rolls.

They sat on the patio looking at the expanse of thawed harbor under the dome. There was a small boat sailing upon the water, pushed by a light breeze. It was a simulated summer's evening, and if one were short-sighted, then the scene would be thoroughly believable.

Ollie put on some music and poured Jan a glass of wine.

"Cheers. I hope you enjoy it," he said.

Jan tasted the fish, then the vegetables and sauce, and then the wine. She closed her eyes and savoured everything. Then she broke open a bread roll, put butter on it and took a bite. It made her pull a face as if she was swooning, and then started all over again with the fish.

"It is so delicious I feel I could cry. And I feel so sorry for all those people who died. This is the reason for living, moments like this," she said philosophically.

"So, you like the fish then?" Ollie said with a laugh.

"You are such an oaf sometimes. Couldn't you see I was having a moment? Yes, I love the fish. Yes, you are an excellent cook, Mr Big Head. I love everything. Why do you do this to me? Oh, and I love the music. Sometimes all I want to listen to is instrumental, chill music, and your choice is perfect, of course!" she said while putting on theatrics.

After they finished the meal, Ollie took away the plates, and then called out from the kitchen, "I hope you feel like desert."

"Yes, please. I know it will be something that I can't resist, so I'll just give in now," she said as she looked down at her already bulging stomach.

Ollie came back holding a giant banana sundae with two spoons poking out. As he put it on the table between them, he said, "I assumed you wouldn't mind sharing."

Jan just looked at him and said, "I could kiss you. How in the hell did you get bananas and ice-cream? I understand the other ingredients like the chocolate, maraschino cherries, and nuts. They can all be scavenged. But the bananas and fresh ice-cream?" And then she looked closer and said, "Oh, and whipped cream! What the hell?"

"You probably didn't know, but we have a dairy. After the Emergency we relied on scavenged powdered milk. But then as production at the dairy increased, we also powdered that milk to supplement our scavenged stock. However, we have now come to the point where we produce enough to ration out fresh milk and cream. So, voilà, fresh ice-cream, and whipped cream, for you. This is the first batch.

As for the bananas, same thing. We have been growing them for three years and finally they were ready to pick. I was given a bunch from the first harvest, and as you know, what is mine is yours."

She smiled and said, "There you go again, oozing with charm and completely disarming me. And, by the way, this is delicious," she said as she wiped chocolate syrup from her chin and giggled with embarrassment.

"Are you able to stay tonight?" he enquired.

"So, is that what you have been buttering me up for? I knew there must be a reason for the romantic setting, and why you keep topping up my glass with wine."

Ollie laughed. He knew she would stay, but he asked anyway out of respect, then changed the subject.

"I need to go to Oak Ridge in a couple of days, I was wondering if you would like to come with me."

"I'm not sure. I would need to get someone to fill my work shifts, unless it is on the weekend, and I would need to talk to Sally."

Ollie said, "I was thinking we take Mazie and Sally with us, like we did when we went to Brisbane."

"I'm sure the girls would love that. Are we going by train? I would hate to do the submarine crossing again, and I wouldn't like the idea of

Mazie being crammed into a submarine with all those young fit sailors."

"Yes, we would go by train. It would give the girls a chance to see the colonies along the way, and then to visit Oak Ridge. It has changed a lot since you were last there," he said.

Jan enquired, "What's the reason for the trip? I hope you won't be just working all the time, meaning the girls and I would have to stand in the background getting bored."

"Well, it is kind of work, but it's something that you will be a part of. A bit like this dinner, let's call it 'pleasant work'," he said.

"If it's anything like this dinner, then yes, we are in."

"I'm so glad you said that. I wouldn't want to make this trip without you," he said with a cheeky smile.

"Oh, now I really am intrigued. Will we need to bring anything special for this secret mission you have planned?"

He thought and then said, "No, just an open mind and a spirit of adventure."

They stayed up late on the couch watching a movie. They also slept in late before a wonderful breakfast of eggs and bacon. Jan hadn't had real bacon for three years and was beside herself with food lust.

At the end of the week, they all boarded the Intercontinental Train. It was more luxurious than the East Coast Train they had taken to Brisbane, and it included sleeper births. As it exited the airlock and travelled out upon the ice, they could see behind them the Sydney dome shining brightly as it simulated daytime.

The train accelerated quicky. It was not long before the dome disappeared over the horizon, and because there was no atmosphere or clouds, there was no afterglow. One minute it was there, and then next it was gone. The speed indicator climbed to 3000kph as they approached the midway point, and then began to drop as Wellington's dome came into view.

The population of Wellington had increased substantially since Ollie was last there. In the station there were lots of Māori cultural items on display. They sampled some unique foods and then were treated to a haka and traditional singing. The stopover was approximately one hour before they were back in transit.

The next leg to Tierra Del Fuego took nearly three hours, and so far, no dome had been constructed at the site. Few people lived full-time at the outpost, but for travellers, there was indigenous art and an information board. The only available food was snacks scavenged from Ushuaia, Argentina, or imported items. The stop was brief while goods were transferred, and then the announcement came to board the train.

Recife, Brazil was another two and a half ^{hours} along the route, and proved to be bright and lively. Part of the old Portuguese section of the town had been domed, and there were vibrant coloured stone buildings radiating under the faux blue sky. There was a substantial and still growing population, mainly of expats, with café's serving a wide variety of exotic and spicy foods.

Ollie and Jan shared a Cachaça Caipirinha cocktail. It was fresh but, oh so strong. Apparently, there were stocks of the rum left over from before the Emergency. But even so, they had started growing sugarcane for fermentation so they could keep the national drink alive.

They stopped there for one hour and did some eating and exploring. The weather under the dome was tropical and monsoonal, allowing many of the indigenous plant and animal species to be reintroduced. Many had to go through a de-extinction program, using Australian zoo specimens as hosts.

Recife was a significantly different visual, and cultural, experience from what they were used to in Sydney, thus it would make a good holiday destination. They did not have enough time to take it all in and they were disappointed to leave, promising themselves that they would come back for a holiday.

They departed for the final leg of their train journey, two and a half hours to Charleston.

There had not been much development at the terminus and transfer station, with most of the construction, and population growth, occurring at Oak Ridge instead.

Therefore, like everyone else, they just passed through Charleston, transferring from the Intercontinental Train to a much slower land train. It was basically an MHEV that had been adapted to run on a rail. Its maximum speed was 150kph, but it would often slow down to negotiate the many curves and mountains along the route. Jan nudged Ollie as they passed the distillery sign, suggesting they should illuminate it because it was a cultural heritage site. They both laughed.

It took six hours from Charleston before they were under the Oak Ridge dome. Jan was amazed at the transformation since she was last there. The girls and she walked through the campus, and she explained to them what it was like when she first arrived. She described how they had travelled there in the MHEVs, and what it was like in the creepy basements. But then she added that Ollie had looked after her. Or was it the other way around?

This time their accommodations were on the surface in a modern and spacious apartment. Later in the evening, Jan and Ollie went for a wander by themselves down to his old office in the basement. They sat in the chairs and reminisced. They even had a sip of the whiskey, the bottle still half full in the cupboard where it had been left.

Although the creepy noises had gone, and the basement hallways and recesses were properly lit, Jan still found it uncomfortable and disturbing. Perhaps it was the memory of all those frozen people, and that even after they had moved them, they still lived among their possessions and memories.

Mazie and Sally had gotten used to finding Jan in Ollie's room in the mornings. Tomorrow would be as expected.

CHAPTER 27

Danny was knocking on their apartment door. It was 7:30 in the morning and they were just finishing breakfast. The food was an excellent combination of scavenged items from Knoxville and fresh produce from the campus, including asparagus and scrambled eggs. Another luxury was the freshly squeezed orange juice from the Oak Ridge orchard. Something that was a rarity back in Sydney.

They filed out onto the campus grounds wearing warm jackets. It was considerably cooler than in Recife, because at Oak Ridge they were simulating the Tennessee winter. In predictable fashion, Danny was very excited and constantly talking, but as per Ollie's instructions, he didn't let on to Jan and the girls what was in store.

They were led to a very large building that had been newly constructed under the dome.

They stopped at the door and Danny said excitedly, "Are you ready for this?"

"I'm very ready," said Ollie.

Even the girls were getting excited by all the intrigue.

They entered what appeared to be a very large aircraft hangar. In the middle was a long cylinder that reduced to a ridiculously sharp point at each end. It floated about one meter above the ground, and in the middle, steps led up to a doorway. It was of a type where the door and the steps were one unit, so as the door opened downward, the steps were presented on its inner side.

The outer surface of the craft was gloss black. So dark, and yet so reflective, that it was hard to focus one's eyes upon it to determine its depth. It was like looking into the absolute dark of a cave. Several circular porthole windows were on each side of craft, but other than that it was completely smooth and featureless. Danny walked over to the craft and ran his hand over the hull.

He said, "It's perfectly smooth down to the atom, and the points at each end are equally sharp. It slips perfectly in and out of the void. And as you can see, we have it levitating. We managed to solve the gravity buffer issue, so now we are able to displace enough gravity to support the craft, but not too much as to open the void. It's a very elegant solution because now we can also use the gravity buffer technology for non-void manoeuvring and propulsion, or what I like to call 'reality propulsion'.

"However, in that mode our speed is

limited by hull integrity. If we run too fast in reality mode, then we get too much friction and abrasion from atoms, dust, and other stellar particles. It's probably cleaner interstellar, but then why would you use reality propulsion if you can go full void mode? I'm expecting the reality mode limit will be around 0.1 to 0.2 the speed of light, but as you know, in void mode there are probably limits, but we haven't reached them yet."

Jan was holding on to Ollie's arm as if she herself was holding on to reality. She whispered in his ear, "Is that what I think it is?"

"What do you think it is?" he said.

"A spaceship. Like the one you have talked about building for the last couple of years. Is this it?"

"That's exactly what it is. This is the vehicle to humanity's future," he said proudly.

She squeezed his arm and said, "Well, don't that just beat grilled salmon and hollandaise sauce. Aren't you a smarty pants, Mr Truss!"

He laughed and said, "I'm not the clever one. The credit goes to Danny and all the other scientists. I'm just the dreamer, motivator, and facilitator."

Danny walked up the steps and said, "Come, come, have a look inside."

He began pointing and gesturing, then said, "We've got the fission reactor back there to kick start the fusion reactor, then at each end, inside the cones, we have the void generators. They develop a beam at each end of the craft that opens the void more efficiently than we did before with the sphere. Oh, and there is also a field around the main hull. So, when running the void generators at low intensity, therefore still in reality mode, they deflect cosmic radiation, hence, we won't get fried. It's as if we are wearing sunscreen. Pretty cool hey!"

Ollie addressed Danny for the first time since seeing the craft,

"How far have you travelled during testing?"

Danny rattled off the figures as if they were written down in front of him.

"We went as far as the orbit of Venus one hundred twenty times, but as you suggested, we couldn't find it. So, unless we were extremely unlucky, it's just not there. Then we went out as far as Mars one hundred fifty times, but again nothing, it has also disappeared. Yet, we could see Saturn from several locations, so we know that it is still there."

Ollie conjectured, "It seems that during the Emergency, when the solar system was scattered, Earth and Saturn were on the same angular trajectory before being liberated from the sun's gravity. Hence, we are now traveling parallel through space.

However, we are probably moving at different speeds, therefore, we will eventually lose each other. So, Danny, you are telling me that you have tested this spacecraft two hundred seventy times in stellar, or formally stellar, space?"

"Well, actually it's been about three hundred times. We did some journeys around the Earth and to the moon. Yes, the moon is still there," he said.

"And each time you returned to this same location?" enquired Ollie.

Danny wiggled his hand and said, "Well, yes and no. We also tried different locations, so not all of the trips were just out and back. Some had several waypoints, but we always found our way back here to the hangar."

Ollie beckoned Jan and the girls to walk up the steps and enter the spaceship. They were in awe and very careful not to touch anything. The inside of the craft had very clean lines. It was minimalist, and ergonomic. There was seating for 10 people, with two of those people being at control consoles. There were facilities the same as would be found on an MHEV including a bathroom and kitchenette.

Danny sat at one of the consoles and said, "Watch this."

He pushed a button, and the walls of the cabin seemed to disappear. Jan put her hand out and touched the wall. It was still solid. Transparent, but solid. The area immediately near where her hand touched turned to opaque, and then slowly back to invisible as she removed her hand.

Danny said, "The walls are covered with curved monitors linked to external cameras and sensors. This means we can duplicate what is outside. That can be at any wavelength on the electromagnetic or gravity spectrum, and then onto the inside walls making them appear transparent. Also, those portholes that you saw on the outside, they can be completely shuttered if necessary, so from the outside they disappear and all you see is solid hull."

Ollie was impressed and said, "That's a pretty neat trick."

Danny replied with excitement, "Oh, you wait. That's not the best trick, but I would need to show you either out in space, or on the Earth's unprotected surface. How about I take us all for a spin and show you what this baby can do?"

Ollie looked at Jan and then at the girls. He smiled and asked, "Who wants to go for a ride in a spaceship?"

After Mazie and Sally enthusiastically said, 'Yes please', Jan asked, "Are you sure this is safe? The girls aren't likely to get sick or anything are they?"

Danny replied, "In over three hundred

trips, we have had no mishaps, and no one has experienced any ill, or unpleasant, effects. I assure you that where we are going, and what we will do, has been tested and is safe."

"OK then, we are game," said Jan.

Two technicians joined them to assist with operating the craft. Ollie sat next to Danny, as the latter started to explain what he was doing on the console. The automatic door closed silently, and then there was a clinking sound as its bolts locked it into place.

There was an almost imperceptible hum throughout the ship, then the porthole windows went black as if someone had turned off the hanger lights. Then, within a moment, the view through the windows was of the stars. That was it. No launch countdown, loud noises, acceleration, no fanfare. Just blink like a genie, and you go form one spot to another in a span of time imperceptible to the human mind. They had not travelled far, just around 100km above the Earth. Were they to travel light years, then that could take hours, at least that was what the calculations suggested, but that was yet to be tested.

Danny flicked the switch to make the walls invisible, and the girls went 'ooh' as the darkness appeared around them. They could see the Milky Way spanning above them, and below, a dark ominous globe. It was barely perceptible against the black of space. It was, of course, the dark Earth. Danny pointed out a small light on the surface and explained that it was the illuminated dome at Oak Ridge.

He then changed the view settings to thermal radiation and the Earth brightened slightly. Now there was some texture as certain parts glowed brighter than others, representing volcanic activity.

Again, he switched the view, this time to gravity, and the Earth appeared bright and solid. Across, on the other side of the craft, the moon appeared from the dark of space. He changed the walls back to solid, pushed a button, and the stars disappeared from the windows. In an instant they re-emerged back in the hangar exactly where they had started.

Ollie congratulated him and said, "That was absolutely amazing. It was just like going through a portal."

Danny said with a big grin, "Yes, we can basically 'portal' to anywhere, providing we have the coordinates. But, of course, there are limitations, with the greatest being that everything is moving through space, and relative to everything else. This is why we need the Quantum Artificial Intelligence. It needs to know our starting point relative to every other move we make, so it can triangulate how to get home. The problem is made more difficult because we no longer have the sun as a reference point. Apart from its gravity signature, which is imperceptibly small in the vastness of space, the Earth is a mere atom in the ocean. So, the further we travel away from it, and the longer the time we are gone, the harder it becomes to find our way home.

"We basically have to use the local stars, which are all moving themselves, to find Earth's approximate position, and then once we get in the general region of home, which may still be millions of kilometres out, we need to switch to gravity search and find it by identifying its signature, that being the gravity well the planet and moon create. Once we have found the Earth, then it's not so difficult because we can use the surface terrain to geolocate our position relative to any other point on the Earth.

"One of the other problems is if we re-emerge from the void inside of something solid like a star. That could get a bit messy. While we are in the void, we effectively travel right through any object along our vector, but once we emerge back into reality, we are subject to all of the laws of physics in our universe."

Ollie responded, "So the computer is plotting our position all the time? It would tell us if we were about to drop out of the void into a star, and it can always tell us how to get home?"

"Yes, all that and more. The computer is monitoring every move, every button I push, even every breath each person takes, and then collating and learning from that. So, the more we use the spaceship, the better it becomes at everything it does. It will even learn an individual's idiosyncrasies and tailor responses to their preferences. Now, remember I said I was going to show you something awesome. I'll take you out again, a bit further this time, but don't worry, we've done this many times now."

Once again, the windows darkened, but this time it was a perceptibly longer duration before the stars appeared. Danny activated the view, and one side of the craft had stars, and the other side was black. Then he switched to gravity view and next to them appeared a bright object. It soon became apparent, due to the texture of its surface, that it was Luna, the Earth's moon.

He engaged reality drive, and they began a shallow dive toward its surface. It was like being in an open cockpit aeroplane doing acrobatics, but with no sensation of g-force. As they got closer, they slowed down until they were just above the surface, and then went into a hover about one meter off the grey powdery ground.

Danny got up and walked over to the door, the same one through which they had entered the spaceship. When he touched it, it reverted to solid, and then it opened with its steps leading to the surface. The others watched in amazement as he walked to the bottom of the stairs.

They came over and peered at him, either through the doorway, or through the transparent hull. He put on a glove, and then slowly poked his finger out in front of him. There was a slight shimmer in the air that radiated from the spot he poked, and it occurred each time he moved his finger.

Finally, he said, "This is a gravity curtain, it is based on the same principle, and generator, we use to make the spaceship hover. When activated, it forms a gravity distortion field that is strong enough to contain the atmosphere and heat within the spaceship. If I push on it beyond three atmospheres of pressure, I can put my hand right through it.

"The field strength is adjustable, as is also how far we project it from the ship, but only up to a certain limit. And, because the AI is constantly monitoring my moves and the environment, if I take a step forward, it will extend the field to keep me protected. See, watch."

And with that Danny took the final step off the bottom of the stairs and was standing on the surface of the moon. He bent over and using his gloved hand, picked up a small rock, then stepped back onto the stairs.

He turned to Ollie and made the rhetorical statement, "How handy do you think this is going to be!"

Ollie walked down the steps to have a

closer look, and then said, "Once again you have totally amazed me. With this technology, and no doubt more to come, we could colonize the galaxy. Am I also able to step out onto the surface of the moon?"

"Sure, be my guest," said Danny.

Ollie took a slow step forward and could see the shimmer from the gravity field below him as it expanded. His foot touched the surface and sank a few millimetres into the dust. He stood there and looked around him, then up at Jan and reached out his hand to her.

He said to her, "Would you like to join me?"

Jan, followed by the girls, made their way down the steps, and then carefully took the final step down onto the surface. They looked about themselves in absolute awe.

Jan said to Ollie, "When you said to have an open mind and a sense of adventure, this is not what I was expecting. Now I can truly say you have taken me to the moon and back."

They returned to the spacecraft and the door closed.

Danny said, "There is somewhere we were planning to go for our next mission. I suppose we could do it now if you are in agreement?"

"And where might that be?" asked Ollie.

"We were going to take a closer look at Saturn, given it seems to be the only member of our solar family left," said Danny.

"Hell yeah, sure, let's do it," said Ollie, and the others agreed.

Danny pushed some more buttons and typed instructions onto a keyboard. He said that they would soon be upgrading to voice activation, which would make it quicker and easier to interact with the ship's computer. He joked that it would be just like Star Trek. The hull turned solid, and the windows blackened. It was about 30 seconds before the stars appeared once again.

This time instead of a black blanked out area of sky where the Earth or Moon may be, there was a soft luminescent sphere in misty shades of blue, green and gold. Across the surface were constant flashes of what appeared to be lightening, and by the faint glow of the planet, the massive ring structure could just be made out.

It was nowhere near as bright as it would have been if the sun still shone upon it, but it was visible all the same. Danny enhanced the scene being projected onto the inner walls with the use of a visual gravity overlay. Then the computer was instructed to do all manner of data manipulation such that the planet and the rings became clear to see.

He opted for its natural colours and optimised them for human eyes. The landscape, or planetary scape, was absolutely stunning. Then by using reality drive, he swept down toward the rings and nestled the spaceship gently within the thickest part. They could now look out either side of the spaceship and see the absolute vastness of the rings, stretching as if to infinity in both directions. The ring particles appeared as tiny sparkling crystals of sapphire, emerald and garnet, slowly revolving and reflecting the plant's luminescence. It was cold and lonely, yet breathtaking. Truly breathtakingly beautiful.

Its vastness was inconceivable. The only scale humans had ever had in the past was that of the Earth and its features. Saturn's rings had about the same span as the distance between the Earth and the Moon, yet they were only about 1km thick at their deepest. It played tricks with the mind and made one question their own perception.

Danny put on a glove, opened the door, and went outside. He reached down and picked out a handful of crystals. When he brought them back inside, he put them down on a small bench protruding from the wall so that everyone could come over and wonder at them. They were of course dangerously cold at -260°C, so it would be a while before they could be touched. They spent about an hour flying around Saturn and diving into the outer layers of its atmosphere. They were like a dolphin surfing the gas ocean of the giant blue, red planet.

Finally, Danny set the coordinates to return to Oak Ridge, and again, the outside went dark.

Then around thirty seconds later, the familiar surroundings of the hangar appeared through the portholes. When they had exited the ship, Ollie again commended Danny and his team on the exceptional work that they had done. He then addressed those who had gathered with an impromptu speech.

"This technology will forever change the destiny of humanity. No longer will we be marooned on a frozen planet and limited to making the best of an unfortunate circumstance.

"No longer will we be living in the past and lamenting the loss of treasured moments. Instead, we will discover new worlds and create new civilizations. We have great moments to look forward to, and life experiences that will be beyond our wildest dreams."

They spent one more day on the campus. Jan allowed Ollie to meet with scientists working in fields other than aerospace, even though he had promised that the trip was not going to include work. He kept those meetings short, and for the most part, he was briefed on breakthroughs in computing, genetics, and biotechnology. Mazie accompanied him and engaged the biological scientist with great enthusiasm. It was clear that she would become an astrobiologist, and maybe be the first person to catalogue the galaxy's flora and fauna. She had been bitten by the space bug and couldn't wait to go on an adventure to an alien world full of exotic life.

Danny offered to take them back to the Sydney habitat in the spaceship, thus they could be home in an instant as opposed to the long train journey. Of course, they jumped at the chance, and Ollie now realized that he could go anywhere on the planet in an instant.

It was clear that this new technology was going to change the whole experience of living on Earth, be that with travel, or even creating habitats and ecosystems. The potential now existed to engineer the surface of the Earth far beyond anything they had be capable of doing in the past.

Yet still, for all its potential, human technology could not replace the sun, the thing that was most missed. However, would they really want to replace the sun? If the Earth was to get warmed by a star again, all of the dead life would end up in the oceans and be broken down into poisonous gasses. These would escape into the atmosphere and make the planet toxic for millions of years. Hence, even with a sun, the surface would not be habitable outside of a dome. They had to accept that the old Earth had been lost. If they wanted sunlight on their faces and backs, it would have to be from standing on an alien planet that orbited a distant star.

They said goodbye to the Oak Ridge staff

and returned to the spacecraft with their luggage. Within a second, the door reopened, and they were in the botanical gardens that surrounded Ollie's house. They stepped out into the faux warm day and looked back in wonder at the craft.

People who were walking and relaxing in the garden came over to marvel at the spaceship. The population had known about the project, but they were not aware of how far it had advanced, or that a spaceship had already been built.

Ollie said, "You know Danny, we really need to give this ship a name instead of just 'Spaceship'."

All of them bandied around ideas until Jan said, "Prima Luce. It means 'first light' in Italian."

They agreed that it was an appropriate name. The ES (Earth Ship) Prima Luce represented the first glimmer of hope for humanity to find a new Goldilocks world orbiting a K-type main sequence, iron rich star.

CHAPTER 28

That night the girls and Jan stayed over at Ollie's residence. After a fine dinner that had been prepared for them, they went for a walk over to the Sydney Opera House. Although the girls had seen it from a distance, they had never walked up the steps or explored inside of it.

It was all lit-up, both outside and inside. There was no longer any need for it to be night, and people could enter and use it at will. There were many people walking around the outside, and also admiring the interior. You could even take a ride on a small boat and view it from out on the harbor.

Ollie asked the Jan and the girls to take a seat in the audience, front and center. He then left them and disappeared somewhere backstage. The house lights dimmed, and when a spotlight came onto the stage, Ollie was sitting at the Steinway & Sons Model D-274 concert grand piano. Other people who were walking around the auditorium took seats in anticipation of an impromptu performance.

He began to play Erik Satie's Gymnopédie

No.1. The music filled the hall, and it was soft and relaxing. So much so, that it could transport you to a place with no fear or pain. Jan and the girls had no idea that Ollie could play the piano, let alone at a concert level. He had kept it secret even though there was a piano in his residence. They were absolutely floored by the performance, and by the emotion telegraphed through his fingers.

He had been taking piano lessons since a young age, and when he wasn't on the computer, playing was another form of escape. On nights when he was alone and couldn't sleep, he would slip into the Opera House and sometimes play for hours. Every now and then someone would walk in and listen, but for most of the time he was undisturbed and alone with his thoughts and the music of long-gone masters.

It reminded him of humanities beautiful creations. Pieces of art that had been penned hundreds of years ago during times of war, famine, or plague, yet they had survived. It reminded him of why humanity needed to survive.

It wasn't just because of the innate drive for self-preservation, but it was because humanity had something to offer the universe. A species that could produce things so beautiful and pure, despite all its vices and flaws, did deserve to live. They did have a right to exist, and they did have a right to colonize new planets.

He played a few more classical pieces before departing the stage and joining Jan and the girls. There was lots of clapping coming from the audience that had grown substantially since he had begun playing.

When he met back up with them, Jan said, "That was so lovely I started to cry."

"Me too," said Mazie.

Sally said, "I didn't cry because I'm tough. But I did like it, Mr Ollie. Do you think you could teach me how to play like that?"

Ollie said, "Sure. It would be my pleasure to teach you, even if you are tough," and they all laughed.

They walked back out into the night. The gardens were lit with lamps, and couple walked arm in arm. They sat on the porch and talked late into the evening about where they had gone and what they had seen today. The girls then went to bed while Ollie and Jan lounged on a couch.

"You are a very impressive man, Mr Truss," said Jan as she leaned up against him and ran her fingers through his hair."

"Aww, wasn't noth'n missus," he said with a thick Southern drawl.

"No, I'm serious," she said. "If it wasn't for you, we'd all be dead. If it wasn't for you, we'd all be at each other's throats. And if it wasn't for you, we wouldn't be about to head for the stars."

He said, "I know there is good in people.

Good in everyone, even if they do bad things from time to time. So, what I try to do is to steer them toward the good and to resource them to achieve their best."

"But, I don't know where you get all of these ideas from How can you plan things out so that we get ourselves out of danger, or out of the mire, each time?" asked Jan.

"I don't know. I just see or imagine bad things and then think about where I would rather be. Then I work out a plan of how to get there, like leaving Earth for somewhere better."

Jan then asked, "So, when are we going to do that?"

"Soon, very soon," he said.

"And will you take me with you?" she asked.

Ollie replied, "I would never dream of leaving this Earth without you."

The End

ABOUT THE AUTHOR

About the Author Mike graduated in Environmental and Political Science, then worked for government and industry writing on climate change, food, and energy security. His background is reflected in the 'hard' science of 'Deep Sahara' and the 'Dark Earth' Sci-Fi novel series. Even in the darkest of times Mike's stories offer humanity a glimmer of hope by exploring alternative societies and futures.